Raging Blue

By:

Renee Daniel Flagler

Raging Blue
Copyright July 2012, Flagler, Renee Daniel
Printed in the United States of America
Published by Sitting Bull Publications, LLC

Raging Blue

Blue Holiday has decided to call foul and leave her destructive marriage. But her cheating husband, Jaylin, decides he needs her money to survive and insists on a rematch. Usually, Blue would be game, but after discovering the depths of his depravity, she drops him from her roster of eligibles. Unaccustomed to rejection, especially from his wife, Jaylin decides to take what he feels is rightfully his. Problem is, he forgot a woman in love will put up with a lot. But a woman enraged, she'll let you think you're winning, just before she snatches it all. *Raging Blue* a contemporary romance by author, Renee Daniel Flagler.

****

"Raging Blue" by Renee Daniel Flagler is a gripping fast paced tale. Renee Daniel Flagler brings these characters and their stories together like a veteran story teller that she is. "Raging Blue" is the real **Basketball Wives...** **Alicia Evans, President of Sugar & Spice Book Club**

CHAPTER 1

Blue

He slapped her so hard that her sight blurred for a minute. After a few moments, Blue Holiday focused on her husband's towering frame as it loomed over her. Jaylin Mack's rich, dark complexion appeared even darker. His French-cuffed shirt was half buttoned and sloped lazily off his shoulders. His slacks hung low around his slim waist, and his belt was only partially looped.

"See what you made me do!" he screamed, applying pressure to his temples with the fingers of both hands.

Shocked into silence, Blue stood still, absorbing the verbal assault. Tears had yet to find their way down her cheek. In the five years they'd been married, Jay had never put his hands on her. However, she'd grown accustomed to his crassness, initially intrigued by what she'd perceived as confidence.

The slap still sent a pulsing sensation across her cheek. The tears finally appeared, welling up in her eyes. Her unresponsiveness fell away in clumps. She stared at his moving lips and began to hear him clearly. His words carried as much sting as the slap.

"See what you made me do," he repeated. The liquor made his tongue lazy, causing each word to slide into the next.

Blue looked into his wild eyes and blinked. Tears trickled down her cheeks, making dark circles wherever they landed on her champagne-colored cocktail dress. She swatted them away. Her eyes were fixed on Jay. He was obviously hopped up on something more potent than scotch.

Blue's eyes darted around the living room of their lavish

penthouse, taking in the massive floor-to-ceiling windows that framed the dazzling Manhattan skyline. A pair of handsome floor vases sprouting dried flora caused Blue to pause, but they were too heavy to pick up. Her sight then rested on his set of prized golf clubs. Blue took slow steps in the direction of the irons as Jay continued rambling.

"Don't walk away from me. You're supposed to be my wife! A woman! Act. Like. One!" he yelled as Blue continued to walk towards the clubs. "I saw you whispering to that man," he said, his voice growing louder. "I saw him kiss you!"

Blue shook her head. Jay's words lashed at her back. She swatted at them in her mind and imagined the cold steel of the golf club in her hands—as protection. With a few short steps, Jay was right behind her just as she reached for a club. He grabbed at her, pulling her from the pit of her thoughts.

"Get off of me!" Blue jerked away from him. Her voice returned, rising to a shaky screech. "Don't. Touch. Me." Her eyes narrowed to slits. "Don't ever touch me again."

Jay stared at her, seeming to sober up for just a moment. Blue stared back for a beat before turning to walk away.

"Don't walk away from me," he said, reaching for her again.

"I said don't touch me! I can't believe you put your hands on me!" she screamed. Her heart felt like it was filled with air. She gasped before her voice came back full force. "I've put up with enough from you. But this…," Blue pointed at the spot on her face that still tingled from the slap, "…I won't put up with."

His jealousy was toxic and intensified under the influence of cocaine. No matter how much he denied using it, Blue could always tell when he'd been sniffing. Glassy eyes, dilated pupils and runny nose confirmed words that never passed his lips. Despite his infidelities, it was apparent he couldn't cope with the idea of Blue being with another man. It sickened her how he always accused her, yet she was never unfaithful. She'd sensed his lies but didn't have proof to act on any of them. So, she held what little she gleaned for herself.

"You embarrassed me in front of the people I work with and your teammates. I saw you with that woman on the balcony before you disappeared. And you have the nerve to accuse me?"

"I don't give a damn about those people. No man should be that close to you! This is your fault," he huffed. "Nobody touches my woman!" he screamed, stabbing the air with his finger.

"Only you, right?" Blue snapped, and walked away. She stopped mid-step and turned back to him. "Maybe I should have just disappeared with him like you did with that woman tonight," she added, flicking her wrist.

Jay's eyes filled with surprise and then rage. His breathing became ragged. "What woman?"

Blue refused to buy into the beliefs and acceptance of the other basketball wives. She could care less if all athletes cheated or not. She had her own life to live, and chasing down his infidelities wasn't in her plan. She'd deal with a problem if it arose, but she wasn't going to seek it out just to do nothing about it like the others.

"I should have done it!" she taunted while watching Jay's eyes grow a shade darker. "But that's not what you're really concerned about. Is it, Jay?" she asked and sauntered back in his direction. Jay's jaw clenched.

"You knew he wasn't flirting?" she asked, calming her tone.

Jay's jaw twitched again and his hands folded into fists.

"You know what he said to me, don't you?"

Now it was Jay's turn to be speechless.

"Why did I have to find out from someone else that you were cut from the team?" Blue screamed. "They warned you over and over again. You claimed the coach was out to get you, but it's time for you to take a look in the mirror and realize this world does not revolve around you. I'm done!" she said, then waved him off with a hard downward fling of her arm.

Jay finally broke his silence. "I'll kill his ass!" He stomped the floorboards beneath him. "That was none of his business. Those bastards are the problem, not me. And what do you mean you're done?"

Blue threw her hands up. Jay was playing the victim again, just like his mother had always taught him.

"No, you're the problem." Blue pulled off her five-carat princess-cut engagement ring and matching wedding band, then threw them at him. "I'm finished with you," she said before walking away.

Jay grabbed her by the arm.

"Get off of me!"

"I'm still the man of this house!"

"You're no man!" she yelled. "You're a…"

Before she could complete her sentence, Jay grabbed her head with his large hand, swallowing the side of it the same way he cupped the basketball on the court. He pushed her with so much force, she went crashing to the floor along with the expensive golf clubs. While trying to shake off the sense of disorientation, Blue attempted to scramble to her feet. She reached for a golf club, but couldn't grab hold. Jay ripped across the room like lightning, tossed the club, and grabbed her arms.

"I *am* a man," he said in staccato, pinning her against the floor.

Blue searched the emptiness of his eyes for mercy, and then summoned every bit of energy she could muster and drew him back to reality with a swift kick between his legs.

Jay released her and grabbed his groin as he howled.

She scuttled out of his reach. This time, she made it to her feet, leapt over Jay, who was curled in a fetal position, and ran towards the door. Jay reached out and caught her by the leg, and she fell. The side of Blue's head met the floor with force.

Jay cursed, still declaring his manliness. As the room grew blurry, he let her know he was indeed a man. His ranting grew distant, until everything subsided and fell mute.

CHAPTER 2

Gavin

Lisa smiled at him with a dreaminess that Gavin Gray could appreciate from a woman of her caliber. She wasn't caught up by the possible connections she could garner through his association with star athletes. That smile was all for him. Unlike other women, her eyeballs didn't slowly morph into sparkling dollar signs as he explained his job to her. Lisa listened intently as he shared a recent encounter with a green, starry-eyed college basketball player.

"This kid was so excited he couldn't even sit still during the meeting," Gavin said, driving his fist into the opposite palm. "And his dad…" He paused and took a sip of wine. "That man is a hell of a negotiator. I really want to close this deal. His game is amazing, and he's so humble." Gavin stressed his point by pressing his finger against the table, appreciative of the kid's humility. "I'd love to sign him. I would personally mentor him. Try to keep him from getting a big head and ruining his character."

"I'll keep my fingers crossed for you," Lisa said, and curled the corners of her lips into a delicate smile.

He liked it so much that he purposely tried to be charming just to coax her grin to the surface. Even when they spoke over the phone, he could tell when her smile escorted her speech, making her voice flutter just a little.

"Keep me posted. When you close the deal, we should celebrate."

Gavin could have sworn he spotted a slight glimmer in her eyes when she said 'celebrate.' He found himself wondering exactly what she had in mind. Chuckling inwardly, he reeled his thoughts back to less provocative notions.

Lisa didn't have a soft and frilly persona, but her petite yet curvy frame, full pouty lips, and large brown doe eyes defied her no-nonsense demeanor. The contrast intrigued Gavin.

"Are you finished working on these?" the young waitress asked. She carried a pleasant voice that seemed to fluctuate with every other word, like she was trying hard to be polite.

"We're all done. Thank you," Gavin replied, answering for both. "I'll take the check now."

"Sure. I'll be right back, sir," the waitress said, then bounced off towards the exposed kitchen of the famed soul food gem of East Harlem.

LaBelle's was one of Gavin's favorite restaurants for a variety of reasons, including its Southern-Caribbean fusion cuisine, quiet dining, and cozy atmosphere. His frequent visits and hefty tips garnered him special treatment and the occasional complimentary cocktail. The eatery provided the perfect setting for his second date with Lisa. He didn't share this place with many of the women he dated because he dined there so often. The last thing he wanted was to run into an ex while trying to enjoy a solo meal or the company of another woman.

"So what's next?" Lisa asked, with her eyes on Gavin while sipping the last of her drink.

"Whatever you want to do," he said with a smile as he mentally swatted the mischievous thoughts racing through his mind. "Tonight is your night."

She smiled also. "Wow! I must be a lucky girl! But, I can't stay out too late. I've got to get up early tomorrow, and it's going to be a long day."

"What's on the agenda?" Gavin inquired. He was intrigued about her photography career because she seemed so passionate. Many of the women who ran in the athletic circles only seemed to have a passion for the athlete's money.

"I have a magazine shoot in Central Park at first light, and then I'm shooting a black-tie benefit tomorrow night," Lisa said.

"Expecting anyone interesting?" Gavin asked as he took the bill from the returning waitress, smiled, and thanked her.

"It'll be mostly supermodels, designers, and possibly a few local politicians. People you probably wouldn't know. However, I did hear Lady Gaga is supposed to make an appearance at the benefit. Apparently, she's a huge supporter of the organization."

"That sounds cool. When are you going to take some pictures of me?" Gavin teased, his voice lowered by a husky quality.

Lisa flashed a demure smile. "We'll have to see about that. Can I expect you to behave?"

"Now that depends," he responded, staring directly into her eyes.

"On what?" She asked, meeting his gaze without wavering.

Gavin threw his head back and laughed. If he said the words that came to mind, Lisa would probably slap him. He'd save that discussion for a date further down the line.

"Ready to go?" he asked, signing the check while avoiding her question. Like a true gentleman, he stood and gently helped her out of her seat. "How about we take a walk?" he suggested, not wanting the night to end. "I promise I won't keep you out too late."

"I think I can manage that."

Gavin suspected she wanted the date to last longer, just like him. Holding hands, they walked to his SUV. He drove a few miles before pulling into the garage near his home alongside Central Park. The evening was alive with bikers, joggers, the whiz of passing taxis, and couples walking hand-in-hand in the park. They walked and chatted until they reached the entrance near the carriages.

"Have you ever been on a carriage ride?" Gavin asked, nodding toward the buggies.

"Actually, no! Can you believe that? I've been in New York all my life, and I've never been on a carriage ride."

Gavin smiled. He was happy he could be her first—in that way. He led her in the direction of the horses, paid for a ride, and helped her into the carriage. Her smile reappeared, and Gavin wished he could rewind the last few moments just to see it again. He hadn't fallen for her completely, but he was happy with what he'd experienced thus far.

Lisa rested her head on his shoulder as the horse trotted around the park. Afterwards, they had a few more cocktails at a hotel bar overlooking the park. Gavin saw Lisa home, arriving later than they had planned.

***

Gavin walked in and dropped his keys on the console next to his apartment's elevator entry. He sang and stepped in tune as he moseyed through his Zen-inspired penthouse toward the bedroom in the back. As he passed the double glass doors leading to the rooftop deck, he checked out his reflection, winked, and smiled. His second date with Lisa had gone well, which was refreshing after his long dry spell of dateless nights.

Gavin discarded the suit he'd worn to dinner, slipped into a pair of comfortable cotton lounge pants, and walked barefoot onto the patio. A sated smile lifted the corner of his lips as he dialed Lisa's number. Happy she answered right away, his smile spread wider.

"You made it home safely," she said, her raspy voice reminding him of old blues songs.

"I did. Are you in bed yet?"

"Yes. I'm exhausted. I had a wonderful time—again! Thanks."

Once again, Gavin could hear the smile in her tone.

"Shall we do it again sometime?" Gavin asked coolly.

"I'd love to. How about we make plans at a more reasonable hour. I'm much more coherent when I'm not sleepy."

She smiled. He could tell.

"Call you tomorrow?"

"Sounds like a plan. Goodnight." It sounded like she sang the last word.

"Sleep well,"

Gavin hit the end button and sat in the darkness, taking in the stars. He felt like sleeping outside but thought better of it. He didn't want to wake up to hot bird droppings on his head.

Gavin knew what he wanted in a girlfriend, and Lisa was close to that. The standard he compared everyone against was his best friend's wife, Blue. She represented everything he desired, but she was off limits. However, Lisa had potential and was the closest he'd ever come to what he truly longed for.

CHAPTER 3

Mia

The doorbell chimed, reminding Mia Reynolds that she was expecting company. She rose from her scented bath water, not bothering to towel off, and planted a trail of moist footprints down the carpeted stairs and across the hardwood floors to the front door. Her body was wet and flower petals clung to her skin.

"Coming," she crooned while reaching for the doorknob.

"Hmmm!" Trent Harvey moaned at the sight of her glistening nakedness.

Trent stepped in to the spacious living room with its creamy white walls, sleek white furniture and zebra print accents. Her landlord and best friend, Blue, chose the crisp set up.

Trent lifted her into his muscular arms. "And you smell good, too," he said, caressing her back.

Mia wrapped her bare legs around him, nestled her face into his beefy neck, and took a long whiff. He always smelled magnificent. Then Mia slid down his taut body, slowing near his groin. When her feet touched down, she took him in one hand, and with the other hand, motioned her finger in a "come hither" gesture. Trent followed like an obedient puppy.

He's going to be perfect, Mia thought as she led him up to the master bath.

"Your body is so beautiful," he said in his deep Southern drawl.

He looked up at her nude portrait hanging in the bathroom and smiled.

This man doesn't own a single ounce of body fat. She watched him disrobe as she examined the crevices of his toned physique. Trent was as black as night, with skin as supple as butter. He came fully equipped with an athletic build, a handsome baby face, and plump, inviting lips. He was also the youngest, least experienced of her suitors—and freshly married. His inexperience was just what Mia liked about him. He'd been in the NFL for only a few years, but it was the fact that he had just gotten married and was new to Atlanta that made him appealing to her.

Trent was a country boy from Mississippi. His sultry voice seemed to be swathed in a syrupy slur. When he entered a room, all eyes were on him. That's how Mia had noticed him, but she'd laid low until the right time. She knew one day she'd have him, but the timing and setup had to be perfect. Mia seduced him from afar with sexy smiles, her killer gait, and flirtatious gazes. To lay her foundation, she had done just enough to invite his curiosity until it was time to make her move, and Trent had fallen right into her provocative clutches.

When they reached the bath, Mia stepped in the large Jacuzzi tub and invited him in with a hand gesture and sly smile. Trent stepped in one leg at a time, sinking into the sweet-smelling, foamy water. Once he was completely submerged, Mia positioned herself between his thick, firm legs. She felt his main muscle against her back. Trent dipped his hands underwater and caressed her wet skin. A soft moan caught in Mia's throat. The sounds Mia emitted gave Trent license to go further.

"You like that, baby?" Trent teased, dipping his fingers into her center. "I can't get enough of you," he whispered into her ear between nibbles.

Mia arched her back and rolled her hips. She felt Trent's swollen member grow even more rigid, jabbing her from behind. He toyed with her center until she swelled and purred like a kitten.

"Stand up," he said, and lifted her from behind. Trent stood, pressing his chest against her back. He reached around her and tweaked her nipples then gently guided her forward. Mia obliged placing her hands on the edge of the tub offering Trent greater access to her heated center. Mia winced as he slid his expansive manhood into her from behind. This was the best kind of pain.

Mia wanted to scream, but gnawed her bottom lip instead. Her eyes rolled back into her head. Groans resonated from her core and escaped without her permission. A flicker of heat rose in her belly, and she couldn't hold back anymore. Her knees grew weak and gave out, forcing Trent to support her fully. Muscle spasms erupted randomly along her legs. Mia shook her head from side to side, clamped her teeth, and screamed before collapsing into his arms.

Their excursion began in the bathroom, journeyed through the master bedroom, and ended on the back deck. Trent, looking sated, licked his lips and smiled at Mia. The coolness of the night caressed her skin, causing her nipples to harden again. Still naked, Mia sat on Trent's bare lap and kissed him. She wanted to tell him how amazing he was as a lover, but instead, she held her tongue.

"What if I told you I was pregnant?" Mia asked in a near whisper.

Trent's content smile crumbled. Unable to tell where his thoughts were taking him, she remained quiet, allowing the silence to absorb the moment.

"I'm married," Trent said with a look of confusion, as if he was confessing this news to her for the first time.

"I know that. I didn't ask you about your marriage," Mia stated calmly. She wanted to calculate his response by his facial expression, but all she could read was uncertainty. This wasn't the reaction she wanted to see. She wasn't interested in wrecking his home. As far as she was concerned, his wife never had to know about the baby. All he had to do was set her and the baby up financially, and she would be fine.

Trent looked perplexed. He opened his mouth several times though no words came out. "I thought you were on the pill or . . . something," he finally said. "How far along are you?"

"I'm not completely sure, but I think I'm around two months. When I go to my doctor's appointment, I'll find out for sure." She paused to gauge his reaction. However, his face hadn't changed. "I was on the pill, but you know that stuff isn't guaranteed."

"But I always wear protection," he said, looking down at the shriveled plastic lying beside the chair. "It can't be me." His brows creased.

Mia stood, removing herself from his lap. She followed his gaze to her belly and turned her back to him.

"Trent, the first time we had sex, everything happened so fast that I don't think we used protection, remember?" she huffed. "Do you think I want this? I'm not trying to break up your *happy* home," she said, curling her fingers to make air quotes when she stressed the word 'happy.' "These things happen. So what are we going to do?"

Trent stood and stared at Mia while pacing the deck. "I can't believe this. I just got married," he said, appearing deflated.

Mia watched him from the corner of her eyes.

"I'll go to the doctor with you. How soon can we get a DNA test?" he asked.

Mia walked back into the house, retrieved his clothes, and threw them at him. In silence, Trent dressed quickly, shaking his head a time or two.

Even though she'd stashed nearly a half million dollars in her accounts over the years, she needed more to secure her financial future for the long haul. A baby was the key—at least for the next eighteen years. She would have to find someone else to take the fall because the real father would have to remain a secret.

Once Mia was alone, the depth of her situation settled on her chest like dead weight. Still wearing her robe, she hadn't bothered to get dressed after throwing Trent out. She'd been pacing for the better part of an hour. Her plan wasn't coming together like she intended. *One of these men is going to accept my baby,* she thought to herself. Someone easygoing, who wouldn't question the possibility that it belonged to him or push her for too many details.

Mia picked up the phone to call Kendrick King. She held it in her hand, but never dialed the number. Even though she was a petite woman, his wife, Peyton, was a force—a true match for Mia's antics. She couldn't stand Peyton, and getting Kendrick to accept the baby would mean she'd have to deal with Peyton head on. Plopping down on the couch, Mia tossed the phone to the side, squeezed her eyes shut, and huffed. Her grumble filled the room.

The real father of her unborn child could never be revealed. There would be too much fallout even though he had the right credentials, an athlete with a lucrative contract who could set her up for life.

      The thought popped into Mia's mind like a flash of light. She wouldn't focus on the current possibilities. She would try to find someone new. Timing was the only issue. Men weren't well versed on women's bodies, so she could always fudge the due dates or find a plausible explanation to make the right candidate believe the baby legitimately came early.

CHAPTER 4

Blue

The low rumble of Jay's snoring stole into Blue's subconscious and nudged her awake. Her eyes fluttered a few times before eventually catching the light. She blinked away the brightness of the room and woke in a haze. Her chest felt heavy, as if she was being held down by weights. Blue squeezed her eyes, then opened them and looked around the room. The clock told her it was past two in the morning. Jay lay next to her with his arm across her chest. The strong scent of whiskey and stale breath sifted into the air with each snore.

Her mind flooded with flashes of the scene that had led to her current position, laid out on her back. She tasted the remnants of blood on the inside of her lip, and rubbed her temple to soothe the slight pounding. Then she lifted Jay's heavy arm from across her chest and peeled her body off of the floor. The beauty of her cocktail dress was soiled with salty tear stains and hard wrinkles. Dull aches prodded her upper body.

Jay mumbled and rolled over on the floor as if he were in the comfort of their California king-size bed. She stepped over his sleeping body and padded through the penthouse into the master bath. Horrified by her reflection, she forced down the massive lump clogging her throat. The normal brightness of her blue eyes was doused by the surrounding redness. Puffy eyelids overlapped, deepening the crease in her lids. She gently ran her hand across her swollen cheek. The crimson bruise shone easily despite her rich pecan skin. Dried blood crusted her bruised upper lip. She shook her head and turned away as fresh tears added new wet splotches to her dress. She searched the vanity for a hairband and stuffed

the long, natural curls of her unruly mane into a ruthless ponytail. With
her hair out of the way, the swelling became more pronounced. She shook
her head. She would have never imagined their relationship disintegrating
this way.

Blue continued to cry as she quietly crept around the penthouse,
stuffing clothes and toiletries into an overnight bag. She'd already started
mourning the death of their marriage.

* * *

Jay,

*I'll be back in a few days and I want you out! You need help and
I hope you find it.*

Good luck,

Blue

Blue taped the note to the mirror in the guest bath. She fingered
the tape for a few moments, closed her eyes, and sucked in a deep breath
as she pushed back more tears. She knew Jay wouldn't let things go
easily. He owned the rights to the last word, and when he was wrong, he
deemed himself justified. The heaviness in her breath was for the battle
that would ensue since she was the one walking out on him.

Once the stirring in his stomach erupted, she was sure he'd be
incapable of making it to the master bath. And after emptying his insides
in the sink or the toilet bowl in the guest bathroom, he'd wash his face
and stare at his pitiful reflection in the mirror like he always did when
he'd had too much to drink.

Jay was still in a stupor when she tiptoed past him, heading for
the door. When she reached the lobby, Tony, the building concierge,
offered to help her, but she refused. Blue hastened out of the building

with Tony trotting behind her.

"Let me get you a taxi, Mrs. Holiday!" Upon getting a clear view of her face, he stopped walking. "Ma'am, are you all right?" he asked, with accusing, angry brows slashing away his good humor.

"I'm fine, Tony. Please, just get me a taxi. Quick!"

"Surely," Tony replied, and blew his whistle.

Within seconds, a taxi pulled up to the curb. Tony took her bag and gently placed it in the trunk. Almost as an afterthought, Blue reached in her purse to give him a tip, but Tony gently rested his hand on hers and nodded.

"It's all right, Mrs. Holiday. Feel better," he said, then closed the door for her.

"Where to?" the driver asked in a rich West African accent.

Blue didn't answer.

"Miss, where would you like to go?" he asked again.

Blue paused, pondering an answer. Her mother would blow things way out of proportion, she wasn't ready to tell her brother what had happened, and she didn't have many friends.

"Ma'am, please. Where am I taking you?" the driver said, trying hard to mask his annoyance with her.

"Upper East Side. No! Take me to 124th Street and Frederick Douglas Boulevard. Take me there!" Blue said, hoping her cousin, Francois, was home.

She dialed Francois' number, but never heard her say hello upon answering. Instead, in the background, she could hear Fran's giddy laugh and the deep rumble of a man's voice. She disconnected the call.

"Forget it. Take me to this address," Blue said, handing the driver a card.

Minutes later, they pulled up to a building on the Upper East Side alongside Central Park. Blue collected her belongings and tipped the driver. For a few seconds, she stood motionless on the sidewalk with her carryall at her feet. She wasn't sure if it was the right place to be. However, it was where she knew she could feel a semblance of comfort. She touched her cheek, the reminder of why she was here.

The taxi pulled away, canceling out the potential of her getting back in the car and going elsewhere. Blue stood outside the luxurious, mid-century building for a long while before finally making the call. She hated having to bug him, but she was already here. Despite the lateness of the hour, he didn't sound like he'd woken from a deep sleep.

"Hi…uh…are you alone? May I come in?"

Blue dragged her bags off of the elevator and directly into her friend's lavish penthouse overlooking Central Park. She was awash in trepidation. Concern was etched on Gavin's face, which made her remember the past twelve hours as tears streamed down her face. She'd almost forgotten she was crying. The tears felt so normal.

Gavin started to reach for her bags, but stopped suddenly. He stared at her bruised cheek and swollen eye. Blue let the bags slide from her hands and shoulders, hitting the floor with a loud thump, jolting Gavin from his examination.

"He did this to you?" he asked, gently touching her bloated cheek.

Gavin turned her face from side to side with a gentle touch to her chin. His face was tight.

Blue felt naked as he assessed the physical damage. Her body began to tremble under the weight of her emotions. As her silent tears grew into audible cries, Gavin cautiously wrapped his long arms around her.

Moments passed before Blue calmed herself and then stepped out of Gavin's embrace. She suddenly felt uncomfortable in his arms. She didn't want to end up there, but needed to be around someone who understood her and Jay. Gavin had always been around to pick up the pieces when things went awry.

Gavin was tall, but not as hefty as the average basketball player. He possessed a fit medium frame, but not ripped and taut like an athlete. Not physically good enough to make the draft, but intelligent enough to be a sought-after agent and manager. He was nice-looking, but not gorgeous. Jay was over the edge in every aspect of life. Gavin was…average.

"He went too far this time," Gavin said to Blue's back as she walked towards the balcony. "I can't believe this," he continued while pacing back and forth.

"Do you have any tea?" Blue asked casually.

Without responding, he went to the kitchen and put the kettle on. She walked back to the balcony.

Gavin stepped behind her as she peered out over the darkness blanketing Central Park. "What are you going to do?"

"He was asleep when I left. I wrote a note telling him that I would be back in a few days, and expecting him gone."

"Where are you going to stay?"

She let out an exaggerated sigh and shrugged. "I called Fran, but she was entertaining. So, I don't know." She paused. "I probably shouldn't have come here," she said, wringing her hands.

"If you need to stay here, you can," Gavin said after a while.

Blue knew Gavin's offer would require him to give up more than space in his beautiful home. It would possibly cross the line in his loyalty to his best friend.

"I'm going to stay at a hotel. Thanks for the offer, though."

"It's not a problem."

"I'll be fine." She tried to make her voice sound light. "Maybe I can just rest for a little while. Then I'll go and get a room for the night."

"Okay, but just know the offer still stands."

"Thank you."

"Well, you know as soon as he gets up, I'm going to get a call."

"I know," she said, rubbing the back of her neck while squeezing her eyes shut.

"Maybe you should try to get some rest."

"I'll be fine," Blue replied with all the cheer she could gather. "Thank you. Thanks for looking out for me, as always," she said, giving him a big friendly hug. Instead of letting go, she laid her head against his broad chest. "Friends like you don't come easy."

Blue cried and sniffled softly into Gavin's chest. When the kettle screeched, she pulled herself from his embrace, and he headed toward the kitchen. He took his time preparing her tea, then carried the steaming cup out the balcony.

As Gavin turned to leave, the telephone rang. Blue swung her head in his direction. With her eyes, she pleaded with Gavin to keep her visit a secret in case it was Jay on the other end of the phone. She'd expected Jay would lay in his stupor for the better part of the night, giving her time to be long gone before the sunlight hit and he noticed she was gone. Assuming he wouldn't remember much anyway, she rolled her eyes at the thought of him trying to put together all the pieces of his drunken outburst.

"Hello," Gavin said into the receiver, attempting to sound as normal as possible. "Jay...okay...calm down...okay...relax, man. Where are you?" he asked Jay while his eyes locked with Blue's.

Gavin's eyes widened and Blue took a step closer with bated breath when Gavin repeated Jay's response to his question aloud. "You're in the lobby...of *my* building? Right now?"

Without a second thought, Blue grabbed her bags and trudged several flights down the hollow stairwell. The loud clank of her heels reverberated off the cement walls. When she reached the first level, she peered past the door into the lobby for any sign of Jay. Then she hurried past the doorman and through the gold-trimmed glass doors. Once outside, she hailed her own cab. She moved with such haste that the doorman didn't have a chance to open the door for her when the taxi rolled up.

As she climbed into the car, she turned back to the building and locked eyes with Jay as he peered out of the glass-enclosed elevator. His eyes narrowed and then sparked with realization before he exited the elevator and came running toward her.

Blue slammed the door, flung her bag across the seat, and yelled at the taxi driver, "Go! Hurry! Go now!"

"Where to, miss?" the driver asked.

Within arm's length of the car, Jay reached for the door.

"Drive, dammit!" Blue screamed. "Drive!"

The taxi driver caught sight of Jay's lanky, commanding frame and panicked. He threw the car into "drive" and sped off. Blue's heart felt like it would pound right through her chest. She hopelessly tried to catch her breath.

"Where do you want me to take you, miss?" the driver asked nervously once they were a few blocks away.

Blue hadn't given her destination much thought. She wiped her hand down her face and sucked in a deep breath. As her hand pressed her bruised cheek, she winced from the pain. She definitely couldn't go to her family members' house with her face looking the way it did.

"What hotel is close by?" she asked.

"There are quite a few. There's a very nice boutique hotel right along Central Park called The Pierre," the driver suggested.

"Take me there!"

The driver stepped on the gas and made his way toward the exquisite Pierre, a Taj Hotel, while Blue rested back against the seat. Thoughts of the night's events flapped through her mind. Everything about the past few hours blazed through her head so quickly that she thought she actually saw flashes of light. Looking back, she noticed another taxi weaving in and out of traffic behind them.

The car gained on them until it was dangerously close to the rear of her taxi. Blue's driver rolled down his window and began waving rude gestures at the reckless taxi riding closely on his tail. Blue could see Jay in the front passenger seat, directing the driver. Her heart rate increased. There was no getting away. She had to face him or risk him following her all night.

Blue's cell phone sprung to life, playing a jazz tune. The LCD lit up the back of the car. The display told her it was Gavin.

"Gavin!" was all she managed to say.

"Where are you?" he asked.

"I'm on Madison and Seventy-something," she responded, trying to make out the passing street sign. "He's following us in a taxi."

Blue's driver cursed as he cut through the dark misty calm of the city streets. Sweat spread across his forehead and glistened under the passing lights.

"Stop the car!" Blue yelled to the driver.

"Stay in the car!" Gavin yelled through the phone.

"He's not going to stop. Someone is going to get hurt."

"Please, just stay in the car," he pleaded.

Blue pressed the END button on her Blackberry. Then she pulled twenty dollars from her purse and dropped it on the front seat.

"Let me out here," she said.

The taxi jerked to a stop, and the driver snatched the money as Blue swung the door open, grabbed her bags, and jumped out. Blue had barely closed the door when the driver sped away. Seconds later, Jay's taxi screeched to a hard stop in front of Blue. Jay leapt out of the passenger seat and reached for Blue.

"I'm sorry, baby. Let's talk. We need to talk," Jay babbled.

It was clear he was still under the influence of his earlier vices. His disjointed sentences and emotional flux frightened her. Blue had never seen this side of him. Jay grabbed her by the arms, forcing her to face him.

"Let me go, Jay," she told him, trying to remain calm. "We're causing a scene." She looked toward the crowd that began to gather.

Cars whizzed by blaring their horns, demanding they move from the side of the street. Jay continued to babble as he dragged her toward the sidewalk. His fingers felt like they were wrapped around her bones. His pleas made him appear childlike and desperate. As the crowd grew larger, she searched her mind for a safe way to get out of Jay's presence.

"Miss, are you alright?" one gentleman asked.

"Mind your business!" Jay screamed to the onlookers.

"Hey, isn't that the basketball player Jaylin Mack?" another bystander asked to no one in particular when he recognized him.

Jay turned, bore his eyes into the crowd, and screamed again, "I said mind your own damn business!"

Another taxi skidded to a halt beside them, and Gavin jumped out. When Jay saw Gavin, he grunted but didn't release his hold on Blue.

"Jay, let's take this off the streets. You're causing a scene," Gavin said coolly, while slowly approaching Jay's side.

Sirens blared, drowning out Gavin's negotiation. Two police cars barreled toward them and came to a screeching stop. The officers jumped out, barking orders at the crowd and Jay, who still held Blue in his grip. One cop went as far as to draw his gun and command Jay to release Blue. Without letting go, Jay wiped the tears from his face with his shoulder.

"Sir, let the lady go," the officer demanded, approaching closer with his gun still aimed at Jay.

"You're going to shoot me?"

The officer stepped in cautiously.

"You're going to shoot me!" Jay repeated in a higher pitch.

Blue wished she could close her eyes and disappear. The more agitated Jay got, the harder his fingers dug into her arms, his nails breaking her flesh.

As Jay cursed the officers, two of them closed in on him. One held the gun inches from Jay's head, while the other struggled to cuff him as he read his rights to him. By the time they'd stuffed Jay inside the car, the officers' foreheads were speckled with sweat.

After answering a host of questions about the incident, the police officers finally let Blue go. She could feel Jay's eyes glued on her from the rear of the squad car. Blue watched, unmoving, as the police cars sped off along Fifth Avenue. When she turned around, she realized she was once again alone with Gavin, who always seemed to be there for her.

*****

Blue settled into The Pierre, a historic luxury hotel elegantly designed with a marble lobby, towering ceilings, captivating floral arrangements, and gracious white-gloved service. The recently renovated room provided a picturesque view of Central Park. Inviting warmth radiated from the traditional mahogany wood desk, satin headboard, and plush bedding.

Blue soaked her aching body in the hotel's small tub, but longed for the comfort of her own large Jacuzzi. Her jet-black coils floated in the water as tears mixed with the droplets that settled on her face from the steam. Crying, she pondered the abrupt changes in her life, wishing there was a switch she could flick to turn off her heart. She felt sorry for Jay, but she'd grown weary of their taxing relationship. They'd had their arguments, but he'd never put his hands on her. Still, she wondered if it would be fair to leave without at least giving him an opportunity to redeem himself.

Years ago, he'd promised her that he would stop with the drugs.

She had never seen him indulge, but she could always tell when he'd had a hit. His demeanor darkened and his temper flared easily. His lips and eyes would twitch involuntarily. She recalled the time when he'd sneezed and chunks of red tissue and membrane had sprayed the bathroom sink. The cocaine usage had begun to eat away at the flesh in his nasal passages.

Blue realized she had cried herself to sleep when she was shocked awake by her Blackberry playing a cheery tropical tune with steel drums. The melody startled her. She rubbed her eyes and then blinked out of her haze. Her sight settled on her wrinkled fingers; she had shriveled up like a prune. She lifted her sore limbs from the water, dried off, and wrapped her body in the plush hotel robe. She felt a slight pounding at her right temple, the same side of her face that had met the hardwood floor of her penthouse. While holding her face in her hands, she got a sharp reminder of its tenderness.

The steel drums played again, and she reached for the phone. She didn't recognize the number, but against her better judgment, she answered anyway. Hearing Jay's voice froze her to the spot. Tossing the phone entered her mind, but she shook the thought away.

"Blue," he whispered.

He was sober now. She could tell.

"Blue, please answer me. I know you're there."

"What do you want?" She tried to keep her voice steady.

The last thing she wanted to do was cry again or let Jay hear her pain. She swallowed hard and pushed back the hurt before repeating, "What do you want from me?"

"I'm sorry," Jay said and then paused. "Please…tell me what

happened."

Blue lifted her head to the ceiling and blinked back the tears. Jay hadn't even realized what he had done.

"Too much, Jay." This time, the tears came and the pain forced its way out.

"Did I hurt you?"

Blue didn't answer. She drew in a soggy breath, pressed her lips together, and tried to suppress the rest of her anguish. Minutes passed before she spoke again.

"Yes. You went too far this time."

"Baby…I…" A dense silence settled between them again.

"I can't do this anymore. I have to go."

"Baby…can you bail me out?"

Blue pressed the end button.

CHAPTER 5

Gavin

Gavin paced around his spacious living room contemplating whether or not he should bail his friend out. His friendship with Jay had been on the decline for the past few months, starting with Jay's erratic behavior on the court. As his agent, he'd warned him numerous times that his actions could land him in trouble. Jay, being hardheaded, threw aside Gavin's admonitions as idle threats. It wasn't until Gavin dropped him as a client that he realized he'd meant business.

When their friendship survived the business breakup, Gavin was somewhat relieved, even though Jay wasn't the ideal companion. His hardcore competitiveness spilled over from the court into every possible area of life. Simple conversations weren't safe from his need to always be right or to one-up everyone. Gavin wondered how much more their fragile connection could stand. He was still in awe of Jay's behavior the evening before.

Gavin patted his back pocket and checked his wallet to make sure he had everything he needed to get the large sum of money from the bank. Leaving him in that cell crossed his mind several times. Maybe this would be an opportunity for Jay to assess his life and make some much-needed changes. Then again, Gavin doubted it would help.

Gavin headed for the elevator. As he reached to press the call button, doubt clouded his mind again and his hands dropped to his sides. *This is it,* he determined. This would be the last and final time he'd help Jay, and then, just like all the others, he would distance himself. He even decided he wouldn't ask for his money back. It was the price he'd pay to get rid of his so-called friend.

The process of bailing Jay out went more smoothly than Gavin anticipated. He'd expected to spend half the day waiting around the courthouse, and was pleasantly surprised when things appeared to go seamlessly.

Jay came dashing out of the building in haste. Gavin had to look twice to make sure it was him heading in his direction. He looked disheveled. A stomach-churning stench mixed with urine and alcohol littered the air around him. Jay still wore the dress shirt and slacks he'd had on at the reception, which were now stained with blood and liquor. His custom cuff links were missing, and his monogrammed shirt was torn. Gavin thought about giving him cab money to get home instead of letting him ride in his late-model Range Rover.

"Thanks, man! I'm going to get that money back to you as soon as I work things out with Blue," Jay promised as he wiped his dirty hand across his face. He was still moving fast.

Gavin raised a brow. Jay's behavior was suspicious. He'd seen him in this anxious state before and hoped Jay hadn't managed to score while he was in lockup. Being in jail didn't seem to hinder access to illegal drugs.

"Don't worry about it. Consider it a gift," Gavin said, giving Jay a bewildered look. "Why are you walking so fast, man?"

Gavin had to walk double-time to keep up with Jay's pace as they proceeded in the direction of the parking garage. Jay rambled on while the attendant brought the car to them. By the time they got inside, Gavin had stopped listening.

"Can I use your phone for a minute, man? I need to call Stan," Jay said.

The mention of Stan's name confirmed Gavin's suspicions. Gavin shook his head. He couldn't believe that after getting out of jail, the first person Jay wanted to call was a damn coke dealer.

"Better yet, can we stop by there on the way to the house? I need to—"

Gavin slammed on the brakes. "After what you've been through in the past twenty-four hours, you get out of jail and the first thing you can think of is getting high. Isn't that what got you into this situation in the first place?" Gavin eased off of the brakes. "You need to focus on working things out with Blue."

"Don't worry about me and Blue. We'll be fine. This is not the first time we've had problems," Jay replied like it was no big deal.

Gavin snapped his neck in Jay's direction. "You hit her!" His brows were knitted. "Is yesterday a total blur to you?" He waited for a reaction from Jay. "You need to get your head straight, man. I'm not taking you to Stan's. I'm taking you home."

Jay slammed his fist down on the dashboard and then stared out the window, while taking hard breaths. Gavin shook his head again.

"Fine. Don't take me to Stan's. I can handle my business on my own. Just drop me off. I'll get your money. Don't worry about that."

"Jay, this is not about the money!" Gavin said. He was on the verge of saying more but stopped. Getting through to Jay during a normal conversation was a daunting task, so he knew his efforts would be especially fruitless now. Gavin resigned himself to focusing on getting Jay home as fast as possible.

"Why are you worried about it? I bet you just want her for yourself. I see how you look at her. You've always been mad because I got her instead of you."

"What!" Gavin's face was tight from Jay's insinuation. A vile response lingered on his lips, but he held his tongue. Instead, he looked at his watch and then checked the street to see how close he was to Jay's building. He even thought about putting him out right where they were.

"You've wanted Blue since the first day we all met, but I got her. That incredible body, nice hair, and blue eyes against her pretty brown face. You're jealous!"

Gavin smashed his brakes, shifted into the right lane, and brought the car to an abrupt stop. It took all of his inner strength to refrain from punching Jay right in his mouth.

"Get out!"

"You're putting me out? I don't live here," Jay said, repositioning himself in the seat.

Gavin shut his eyes briefly and gnawed on his bottom lip.

"How can you just put me out of your car? You can't be serious!"

"I'm going to say this one more time." Gavin clenched his fist, took a deep breath, and centered his heated gaze on Jay's eyes. "Get. Out!" He pointed to the door.

Jay looked at Gavin like he didn't understand.

"Man, just drive. Stop playing games."

Gavin turned off the ignition, sat back, and folded his arms.

"So you're just going to sit here?" Jay asked when he realized Gavin wasn't going to move. "Come on, man. I don't have time for this."

Gavin closed his eyes to focus on reeling in his anger. He wasn't a fighter, but he could already feel the satisfaction from striking Jay one good time. Jay wouldn't go down easy, and that one punch would quickly evolve into an all-out brawl. Gavin toyed with the possible outcomes as he sat there.

"All right! I apologize. Now can we just go home?" Jay huffed.

Gavin shifted the car back into drive and raced to Jay's building in silence. The car door had barely met the frame before he peeled off, filling the air with the high pitch of his tires.

When he arrived home, Gavin wore down his natural wood floors pacing off his anger. The conversation with Jay played over in his head. He wasn't surprised at his friend's uncharitable ways, but he'd at least expected a semblance of appreciation for bailing him out.

Snatching a glass from the cupboard, he set it down with a clank and popped open a vintage bottle of red wine. Stepping out onto the sun-soaked patio, he settled into a chair. With no other obligations for the day, he was free to rest his mind. He couldn't imagine having to go back to the office after his encounter with Jay. He'd made the right decision by clearing his work schedule.

Undoubtedly, it was time to cut the ties on their taxing relationship. Gavin had tolerated Jay long enough, having been friends since high school. Over the years, he had witnessed many of Jay's other friendships disintegrate and wondered how theirs' had lasted. By the time they'd reached their thirties, Gavin had expected more growth from Jay.

Gavin blamed Jay's mother for his destructive ways. She was the guilty type who used materials things to fill voids that should have been sustained by basic nurturing. She was hard, made bitter by his father's absence. Their relationship had stripped her of softness, leaving a shell of a woman to serve as Jay's only parent. A single mother with multiple jobs, she barely had enough of herself to give. Jay's interaction with his father had been minimal, spanning years at times, with occasional visits that induced momentary excitement from vacant promises. Together, they'd succeeded in creating another bottomless shell who desired from the world what his parents were unable to give.

Certain of his final decision, Gavin rose from his chair. It was time to end their friendship. He huffed as his resolve clashed with his conscience. He no longer wanted to be bothered, but who else did Jay have?

CHAPTER 6

Mia

Mia used shopping as therapy to take her mind off of the fact she was having difficulty finding the right man to trap into being father to her child and pay her what she deserved. She found herself being drawn to the children's stores inside the mall. The French-inspired designs at Jacadi, along with the colorful and whimsical selections at Gymboree, sparked a little excitement. Mia touched her stomach while fingering the small items. She decided most of her baby's clothing would come from these two stores since they were more upscale and unique than Baby Gap or the department stores.

"Damn!" she said out loud when her phone rang. Then she looked around to see if anyone had noticed she was talking to herself.

She dug into her designer bag in search of her cell phone. It had been at least a week since she'd spoken to her mother. Just the other day, she'd seen her mother's number appear on her phone several times, but she hadn't bothered to answer. Mrs. Reynolds' meekness annoyed Mia. Times had changed drastically; there was no need for her mother to seem so feeble and domestic, and act like the world revolved around her unaccomplished husband.

Mia patted her stomach. This baby was a sacrifice Mia had to make. Of course, she would have to slow down a little, but the child support payments would allow her to maintain her lifestyle. She anticipated being able to get at least a few thousand a month to secure her finances and help start her decorating business. As stylish as she was, she knew she could be a dynamic interior designer, despite the fact she had no experience or formal training.

Still searching, Mia finally retrieved the phone from the bottom of her large bag, rolled her eyes toward the ceiling, and sighed. Red stars indicated she had messages on her Blackberry. Mia checked her emails, replied to a few text messages, and started to go through her Facebook notifications. None of the messages were of any importance, so she stopped procrastinating and dialed her mother's number.

"Hey, baby," her mother answered with excitement.

"Hey."

"I called you the other day. I know you're a busy woman, but you can't tell me you don't have time to at least call your mother back."

Can we just cut to the chase? Mia thought. "I've been very busy lately," she lied.

Mia couldn't care less if she only spoke to her mother once a month, but she made a point to call her once a week so she wouldn't have to hear her rant about her lack of communication.

"Are you coming up for Clarence's retirement party? He'd love to see you. It's been so long since you've been home."

"I'm not sure. I've got a lot on my plate." Truthfully, she didn't give a damn about Clarence or his retirement.

"You need to stop being so selfish, Mia. He may not be your biological father, but that man gave you his name, raised you, and kept a roof over your head and food on the table. You should appreciate him a little more. He cared for you, your sister, and your brother like you were his own children," Mrs. Reynolds said with a hint of annoyance in her voice.

The comment made Mia wonder for the hundredth time if her

mother was a mind reader. Psychic or not, she still wasn't making a trip all the way to New York just for Clarence.

Mia thought about telling her about the pregnancy, but then decided she wasn't ready to share the news with her family.

"Okay, Ma. I've got to go. I'll call you later. Love you." Her weekly obligation had been fulfilled.

A slight strand of guilt came over her, but quickly dissipated like a thin spiral of cigarette smoke. She had to admit, Clarence was a decent stepfather and provider for her family, but he was cheap as hell. His frugality had always incensed her as a teen. Growing up, they were never allowed anything exciting. Everything they had or did was basic, and never exceeded the bare minimum. Excitement for Clarence translated "special" into spending unnecessary money. She couldn't fathom how her mother was able to put up with his stingy ass for all of these years! If she had learned anything from their union, she knew she didn't want any part of a relationship with a penny-pincher like her cheap stepfather.

Getting stuck with a man of meager means wasn't in the cards. With that in mind, she needed to figure out how she was going to break the news to the real daddy. Each of her options failed. The remaining possibilities weren't solid enough to act on them. Mia didn't think her targeted athletes were stupid, but she knew most of them would pay to keep her quiet for the next eighteen years. Either way, silence came with a price.

CHAPTER 7

Blue

Blue longed for her own space again. The hotel served its purpose, but it was time to go home. She hadn't heard from Jay since she'd hung up on him a few days before, but she wasn't sure if that was a good or bad thing. As her Blackberry danced a muffled jig across the hotel's desk, she wondered if it was Jay. She let the phone ring. Since she'd been working from her hotel room—the only calls she took were from the office. Her bruises hadn't completely healed, and she didn't want to deal with the scrutiny of curious stares from her coworkers.

Trepidation slowed Blue's pace as she gathered her things to head home. That same apprehension encouraged her to take her time getting in and out of the taxi. She moved like she was trudging through cement.

Blue slipped her keycard into the slot inside the elevator and headed up to her home. Walking through the door wasn't as hard as she thought it would be. The apartment was spotless. No broken sculptures, strewn golf clubs, or overturned furniture. Jay had obviously gotten out of jail and called up the cleaning lady. She closed the door, took a deep breath, and contemplated leaving. She stepped further in the penthouse as she fought against the desire to turn away and run. If he was there, she at least hoped he was sober.

Blue slipped through the house like a cat burglar, praying for his absence. She checked for signs of him as she walked toward the master bedroom at the back of the house. She heard a bang, flinched, and then froze. Jay grunted. She held her breath. Mentally, she saw herself retreat, but her body remained motionless. Her heart thrashed against her chest, and her palms grew moist. Her mind told her to stay, while her heart urged her to go.

"Deal with this now," she whispered.

Blue still loved him and wanted things to be different. She wished she could flip those feelings off with a switch. For days, she'd tried to understand the rationale behind his actions, find some kind of justification. What did she do to provoke him? He'd seriously violated their union, yet she still loved him. Being away made leaving him possible. Contemplating her departure from her life with Jay at a distance was one thing. Facing him would be her test.

"Stay and deal with this," she chastised herself.

Blue heard another bang and almost took off running, but instead, she stood still. She drew her chest up, lifted her chin, and stood board straight, prepping her will for the encounter with Jay. Just as she started toward the bedroom, the phone rang. So, Blue tiptoed over to the cordless in the kitchen. The phone stopped, but after a moment, it rang again. She wondered why Jay didn't answer. Blue peered at the ID display and saw a Georgia area code. The number looked familiar. As she peered at the phone, her memory snapped into place. Mia was calling. She hadn't spoken to her in the past few days.

"WHAT do you want now?" Jay yelled from the bedroom.

His prickly tone startled Blue. She stood quietly, straining to hear him through the walls. He was obviously irritated. Whenever Jay was angry, his rancor extended to everyone who crossed his path.

Quietly, Blue picked up the phone. She was shocked when she heard Mia's distressed, tearful voice.

"Why are you treating me like this? You know I haven't been with anyone else."

Blue's heart dropped along with her jaw. Did she just hear Mia right? She stood paralyzed by her outrage.

"Mia, I don't have time for this shit. How am I supposed to just believe that baby is mine, huh? Be honest! Who else have you been with? I know how you love men with lucrative contracts."

Mia's gasp allowed Blue's to go unnoticed.

"Stop it! This baby *is* yours and you know it!" Mia yelled.

"I don't want kids!" Jay shouted back.

"All you think about is yourself. I should hang up and call Blue right now and tell her everything."

"Do it and I'll come to Atlanta on the next flight and kick your ass. Without a contract, Blue is all I have."

"Enough!" Mia yelled. "I didn't intend to get pregnant, but now that I am, what are we going to do about this?"

"Figure that out on your own!"

Blue's jaw dropped. "I've heard enough," she croaked through the cotton clump lodged in her throat.

"Hello?" Jay and Mia said in unison.

Jay spent a lot of time on the road as a ball player. Blue didn't exactly keep track of all his trips, but clearly recalled the times she'd offered to travel with him and he'd found reasons for her to stay home.

A rhythmic pounding drummed at her temples as she wondered just how long the affair between her husband and best friend had been going on. Blue threw the phone down and ran to the door. As Jay dashed out of the bedroom and chased after her, she slammed the front door in his face and ran as fast as she could.

Blue raced down the hall, leaving her purse and keys behind. Just as she approached the elevator, the doors opened and she collided with a gentleman from her floor. He grabbed her by both arms to keep her from falling and stared into Blue's wet eyes. She tried to pull away, but the man held his grip. She glared at him.

"Mrs. Holiday, are you okay?"

Blue's glare softened. For a man, his face was a work of art. Jay was tall, dark, and handsome, but this man was beautiful. The deep olive tone of his skin appeared to glow. A wisp of straight jet-black hair fell over one of his steel-gray eyes. His lips were slightly fuller than that of any white man she could ever recall. He looked exotic. Blue realized why she felt like her neck was going to break as she stared up at him. He had to be as tall as Jay, standing around six feet, five inches.

His grip on her was firm, but not harsh. He still hadn't looked away from Blue's eyes. Nor had she responded to his question.

"Are you okay?"

Blue wondered how he knew her name since she didn't remember ever speaking to him before. She pulled away and nervously straightened her clothes. While wiping her eyes, she saw concern in her neighbor's face.

"I'm fine. Thanks!"

"Do you need help, Mrs. Holiday?"

She wished he would stop calling her that.

"No! And my name is Blue."

The man smiled, exposing a perfect row of pearly whites.

"No, thank you. I'll be fine," she answered again.

"You look quite upset. Are you sure there's nothing I can do for you?" His words carried an accent, but Blue couldn't place its origin.

She wondered if the beautiful man was just trying to pick her up. As she studied him, he tilted his head and offered another smile. She noticed the innocence. Blue looked down the hall towards her apartment. Jay hadn't even come after her. She looked back at him. For as long as she and Jay lived in that building, it was a shame that she still didn't know her neighbors' names, especially since there were only three units on the entire floor.

"Thank you, but I'll be fine," she repeated, then pressed the elevator call button.

"Okay, but if you need me—ever—I'm right down the hall."

"Sure. Thanks," Blue said, turning away. She didn't miss the implication in his tone.

He smiled at her again before walking off.

"Oh, by the way…," he turned back and stretched his hand towards her, "…my name is Kalisto Diodorus."

"Oh. Okay. Nice to meet you." She halfway shook his hand while casting her eyes down the hall. She returned to thinking about the fact that her husband and best friend were going to be parents of the same child. A crushing feeling settled in her chest. Her world was spinning out of control. The elevator doors opened, and she stepped in as Kalisto waved goodbye. She pressed the button for the lobby but by the time she made it half way down, she decided to go back to her floor. She couldn't run from the situation. As the elevator ascended back towards her floor she grew angrier. Jay had to know their relationship was over and it was time for him to go—not her.

Blue breezed down the hall, charging towards the penthouse, and banged on the door. When Jay snatched the door open, she charged to the storage closet, pulled out Jay's large Tumi luggage, and began filling it with all his clothing from the room-sized walk-in closet. Jay took his time getting to the bedroom.

"We need to talk."

"There's nothing left to talk about," she said, breathing heavily as she snatched clothes from the closet and threw them into the suitcase.

"Well, at least tell me where you're going," She stopped abruptly, tilted her head to the side, and looked at him.

"I'm not going anywhere. You are," she replied, then continued jamming his clothes into the bag.

"Damn you!" Jay yelled and punched the wall.

Blue flinched and glared at him for a moment before resuming the packing. She kept a sideways watch of his movements.

"I don't want to leave, Blue. I didn't mean for this to happen!"

"You didn't mean to get my friend pregnant? You didn't mean to violate me? You didn't mean to cheat on me with God knows who else? Just what didn't you mean?"

Jay looked surprised and then held his head on both sides as Blue continued stuffing his clothes in the bag. She remained watchful, but refused to allow him to rattle her.

"I love you, Blue. I'm sorry."

Blue stopped, and despite her fight to hold them back, unwanted tears rolled down her cheeks. She didn't want to be affected by words. It was hard enough dealing with the lies and betrayal. She'd rather him run around yelling and cursing instead of declaring his love for her. Blue also wasn't going to let his pleas weaken her. She paused. She couldn't recall the last time he'd said those words and actually meant it.

"You sure have a funny way of showing it," she said, standing still.

"We can work this out, baby. People go through stuff and work it out all the time," Jay pleaded.

After a long pause, Blue said, "So, how do you propose we fix this? I hit you upside your head, then have sex with Gavin, become his baby's mama, and call it even?"

Jay bit his bottom lip and glared at her.

She was proud of herself for standing up to him. Blue felt fearless for a moment, hoping her words stung.

"That's not funny, Blue. I'm serious. We need to work something out. I can't leave; I have no place to go and I need you," Jay said.

"Need me? For what? Money?" Blue smarted.

Jay looked aggravated and turned away. "Baby Blue?"

"Don't call me that!" Blue screamed, referring to his pet name for her. That was reserved for good times. "Leave! Get out!" she cried as she pushed Jay in the chest, backing him towards the door. She ran back to the bed, closed the suitcase, and tried to toss it at Jay, but it fell to the floor and cracked open. She kicked the luggage and then ran back to the walk-in closet, grabbed another pile of clothes, and tossed those directly at Jay. He stayed calm while she cried as she flung his belongings across the room.

"Get out! Now! Don't bother leaving the key because I'm changing the locks. Call your baby's mama and tell her to make room for you down there in Atlanta. I'll even pay for your one-way ticket!"

As Jay stepped toward Blue, she closed her eyes and held her hand up to let him know not to come any closer. He picked up the suitcase after closing it and walked out the door. She felt the urge to jump on his back as he exited. Blue wanted to see him hurt, even if it was just to experience a small taste of her pain.

CHAPTER 8

Mia

Mia cried until she could barely breathe and her hazel eyes were red and swollen. Blue was never supposed to find out about the baby. She looked down at the cordless phone still in her hand and tossed it across the room. With a loud bang, it separated from its back. The batteries fell out and rolled under the bed. She didn't even bother to pick them up.

Mia closed her eyes and tried to imagine what Blue would say to her once they were face-to-face. Then she tried to put together words that would possibly make Blue understand how this whole situation came to be. She wouldn't expect immediate forgiveness, but maybe eventually, they could be friends again.

Her mind raced as she cried. The walls felt like they were closing in on her. Mia ran downstairs to the living room for more open space. She plopped down on her pink loveseat, curled her body up like a ball, and covered herself with one of her chenille throws. *Sleeping with Jay was something that just happened. I never intended for it to go on as long as it did.*

Restless, Mia stood up from the loveseat and then sat back down. She had forgotten why she stood up. The words *I've heard enough* rang out in her mind. It's the last thing Blue had said before hanging up the phone when she called to tell Jay that she was having his baby. She heard Blue's voice again as clearly as if she was in the room.

Mia went into the kitchen to pour a glass of wine. The semisweet mixture turned sour in her mouth, and she launched the glass against the wall, shattering it to pieces. Shards of glass sparkled across the floor and counter. Blood red stripes scaled the maple cabinets. Her defiance had gotten the best of her.

After a while, Mia wiped her face with her hands. She hated rejection. That was one of the main reasons she dealt with married men. Having wives and children, they never really belonged to her, so she never had to worry about abandonment.

Jay's reaction was harsh and had caught her by surprise. She hadn't expected him to be excited, but she also hadn't anticipated that he'd be so vile. Even though she didn't love Jay, his words had cut deep. Then there was the guilt, which ate at her conscience.

The idea of Jay speaking to her in such a nasty way made Mia livid. She never let anyone disrespect her, especially a man. She wanted the baby to belong to one of the other husbands, not the spouse of her best friend. She'd tried to protect Jay. However, she couldn't guarantee the proof these men sought, so she'd decided to go ahead and tell Jay the news. At least he was an athlete with money.

Now the truth was out, and Mia was dejected and culpable without a willing father for her unborn child. Blue was sure to write her off as a friend forever. Blue didn't necessarily deserve to go through this, but Jay had it coming because he'd tried to deny their child.

She pushed the tears from her cheeks and began putting together the pieces to her plan. With Jay denying the baby, she'd have a fight on her hands. Finding someone to fill in as her baby's caretaker and serving as a backup father was a top priority.

Mia picked up her cell phone and thumbed through her contacts. Princeton Manning, an NFL star player, had been trying his best to woo her. Recently, he'd made frequent trips to Atlanta and had asked Mia out several times. She'd always made an excuse since she was working on securing her baby's financial paternity. Now with Trent out of the way and Jay acting out, she could make time for Princeton. His new multi-million dollar contract was making headlines across the country.

Mia traipsed up to her room, taking two steps at a time. She grabbed her laptop and started her research by Googling all of the recent articles about Princeton's new contract. Sports magazines and websites reported his eight-year, 103 million dollar deal as one of the ten highest in football history. She came across a picture of him with his wife and three kids. Mia smiled at the cozy image of the happy family. The interviewer congratulated them on their seven years of marriage.

"He could be the one," she said.

When the men were married longer, they did more to protect precious information from getting back to their wives. She smiled again, thinking of the leverage she could gain.

Mia dropped her robe on the edge of the bed and stepped to the full-length mirror resting against the bedroom wall. Looking over her toned body, she smiled, feeling sexy again. Full of herself, she sauntered over to her phone, dialed his number, and lay across the bed.

"Hello!" his low voice bellowed.

"How've you been?" Mia crooned.

"Hold on," he said and then she heard silence. After a few seconds, he returned to the phone. "Mia?" he asked with a smile in his voice.

She heard an echo in the background, indicating he had moved to covert quarters.

"So you know my voice. I'm impressed," she said, tracing circles on the duvet with her fingers.

"What's up, baby? Now that you've finally called me, are you going to let me take you out?"

With a sultry chuckle, Mia replied, "I've been thinking about it."

"Well, I'll be in the A.T.L. for a few days looking at a couple of places. I'm working on a few things and want to get a pad there. Free up some time. I'll make it worth your while."

Mia was intrigued and simultaneously taken aback at his directive. "I'll have to check my calendar."

"I'm coming to town, baby. That's a reason to clear your calendar," he boasted.

Mia rolled her eyes. "We'll see about that. I have to run. Give me a call when you get to town."

"Will do!"

"Okay." Mia released a sweet giggle. "See you then."

"For sure, baby girl. You won't be disappointed."

"Neither will you," she said, and hung up before he could respond.

CHAPTER 9

Blue

Blue woke with a start as the pilot announced their descent into Atlanta's Hartsfield-Jackson International Airport. Her first-class ticket was a total waste since she'd slept the entire flight. She stretched her back and then twisted her neck to remove the kinks.

After taking a few days to absorb the shock of Mia's pregnancy, Blue was now anxious to face her. As promised, the rental car she'd reserved was waiting. Blue signed the papers, jumped in, and headed for I-85, toward her townhome in Buckhead. The closer she got to the house, the more excited she became.

Blue parked her rented Chrysler Sebring down the block and walked up to her house. The darkness of the south coated the streets like molasses. Blue was disappointed when she approached the house and saw it appeared to be empty. She wondered if Mia had relocated after her secret got out. A single light shone from the first floor bathroom.

Carefully, Blue entered and took a seat in the dark living room. Minutes passed before she realized the bathroom was also empty. She surveyed the house through the shadows. She didn't want to alert Mia to her presence, so she tipped to the garage, found a flashlight, and then tipped upstairs. The bedroom was in disarray. It looked like Mia had left in a rush.

Blue stepped into the large master bathroom and looked around. Hair products and a curling iron wire were strewn across the vanity top. Mia's fluffy pink robe hung lazily across the glass shower door. Blue opened the medicine cabinet and then ran back to the bedroom to check the drawers. The bottom drawer held one of Jay's jerseys and a few pieces of underclothes. A pair of sneakers from one of his short-lived endorsements sat in the back of the walk-in closet.

Seeing Jay's belongings in the townhouse made Blue's knees weak. She continued searching the bedroom. Near the edge of the bed she noticed a half opened storage box decorated with fancy shoes and tubes of lipstick. She pushed the top aside and peeked in. Fluffy white handcuffs, sex toys, and DVDs were all inside the box. The writing on the DVDs piqued Blue's curiosity. Initials were scribbled on each one. She continued searching through the box, paying close attention to the labels until she found one with the letters J and M. Blue snatched that DVD, along with another marked R.J., and tossed the others to the side. She turned on the TV and slipped the DVD into the player.

Mia appeared on the TV donning only a pink boa, thong, and silver stilettos, dancing in front of Ray Johnson, Jay's former teammate in Atlanta. Fast-forwarding the video, it jumped to a scene where Mia was grinding on top of Ray. Blue was shocked. Ray was married, and Mia knew his wife well. They'd hung out together a number of times. She stopped the DVD and stared at the other one in her hand. The one marked with her husband's initials. She turned back to the box and looked through the other initials. From what she could figure out, all of them were married. Now Blue knew how Mia lived so well.

She took a deep breath and slipped in the DVD with her husband's initials. Just as she expected, there was Mia on top of Jay. After a few seconds, she tried to stop the DVD with her shaky hands. Instead of the screen going black, it paused with Mia staring directly into the camera. Blue walked to the TV and slammed the remote against it, cracking the screen.

Her heart slammed against her chest. She backed up to the wall, slid down to the floor, and then flung the remote across the room. The crash confirmed she'd made contact with something fragile, like a lamp or vase, but she didn't care. Burying her face in her hands, she cried.

The whining of the garage door opening jarred Blue awake. She'd fallen asleep on the floor. She ran to the window in time to see Mia pull up in a shiny new Infinity G convertible. Grabbing the DVDs, she raced downstairs and put them in her bag before Mia could get inside. Then she hopped onto the granite island in the kitchen nearest to the entrance from the garage, crossed her legs, and waited patiently for Mia to enter.

"I'll talk to you tomorrow, okay?" Blue heard Mia talking on her cell phone as she opened the door to the kitchen. Mia giggled as she removed her shoes. "Yes, he's on his way. He should be here any minute, and I need to get ready for him. I'll talk to you later."

Mia continued chatting as she came into Blue's sight. When she flicked on the kitchen light, her jaw dropped, as well as her purse and doggie bag. Blue delighted in Mia's shock for a few moments and then jumped down from her perch.

"Hey, Mia. Surprise, surprise! You were right. You've got company," Blue said, and mocked Mia's giggle.

"Blue!"

"Yep, it's me. Your *friend*," Blue sang.

Mia reached out to Blue, but she jerked away. She scowled at Mia, and then smirked.

"I guess I can see how you would be at a loss for words. Don't worry. I have a few words for you while you think of something insignificant to say. Oh, and I have a few more surprises for you, too." Blue could hear Mia swallow. "I'll give you about five minutes to go upstairs, grab some of your clothes, and get the hell out of *my* house before I call the police." Blue spoke slowly as she fought a burning urge to wrap her fingers snugly around Mia's neck.

"Please. Don't do this, Blue." Mia petitioned with her hands up.

"Why not!" Blue said, looking puzzled.

Mia took cautious steps in Blue's direction. "I know you're upset. I didn't mean for this to happen."

Blue scoffed at Mia's insincerity.

"Well, you did it." Blue looked down at Mia's stomach. "Some friend," she spat.

"I'm sorry," Mia said, as a single tear trailed down her cheek.

"It's too late for that. Get your sorry ass out of my house!"

Mia took a step towards her, but Blue raised her fist. Mia backed away and then stepped past Blue on her way upstairs. Blue sauntered to the bottom of the steps and listened to Mia as she dashed around gathering her belongings.

"Dammit, Blue!" Mia yelled from upstairs. "That TV was a gift!"

"You've got four minutes left," Blue said. "Don't bother looking for those little home movies of yours either. I've put them away in a safe place!"

When Mia ran halfway down the stairs, Blue challenged her with tight eyes, ready to fight. Mia stayed on the steps, spurting quick, short breaths. She glared down at Blue as her chest rose and fell.

"You're taking this too far," Mia said.

"*I'm* taking things too far?" Blue jabbed her finger in Mia's direction. "Ha! I can't believe you fixed your lips to say that!"

Blue was ready for battle, but the doorbell rang. She looked towards the door, and then turned back to Mia. "I guess that's your date. I wonder which wife he belongs to."

CHAPTER 10
Gavin

"I'm having company tonight, so I need for you to find somewhere to go," Gavin said without looking directly at Jay, who had taken up residence in one of his spare rooms.

"Come on, man! Where am I supposed to go?"

Gavin shook his head. He was tired of Jay's shiftlessness. Gavin wanted him out, but right now, he just needed Jay to find someplace to go for a few hours while he entertained Lisa over a candlelit dinner.

"I'm sure you can find something to do. I want to be alone with my company," Gavin told him.

In the days that had passed since Jay had moved in with Gavin, all niceties had vanished. They'd ceased being cordial to one another. Gavin's frustration with Jay settled between them like a thick fog. Jay barely acknowledged him when he trudged into the house each day. He would leave for hours and return wide-eyed and frazzled. Gavin hoped some of his time spent outside was being used productively rather than just getting high.

Jay frowned, tossed the remote, and stood up. The room was littered with crusted food containers, empty liquor bottles, and clothing tossed across the furniture. Staleness hovered in the space, making the air foul and thick like a locker room after a laborious game. Even the cleaning lady refused to enter Jay's room.

"I'd appreciate it if you cleaned up a little, too," Gavin said, his lips twisted toward his nose.

"Whatever, man," Jay responded, waving Gavin off as he

grabbed his keys and pushed past him in the doorway.

Gavin bit his lip, and then looked sideways as Jay stomped to the kitchen and back with a glass in his hand. He took a deep breath and stood still, reeling in his anger.

"Have you started looking for a place yet?" Gavin yelled over his shoulder, already knowing the answer.

"No," Jay tossed back as he grabbed a new bottle of scotch and poured half a glass.

Gavin shook his head and walked away, leaving Jay to his vice.

"Well, you have until Friday, remember?" Gavin said over his shoulder, wishing the very next day was Friday.

"I heard you. You don't have to keep reminding me."

Gavin walked back towards Jay's room. "My company will be here in an hour," he said in an attempt to rush Jay along.

Jay frowned, shook his head, and huffed before opening a duffle bag full of money to dump clothes on top. Gavin knit his brows.

"What's up with all that money? I thought you said you were broke," Gavin asked, feeling the heat of irritation rise again.

"Don't worry. I'm going to pay you back for my bail. I told you that," Jay said.

"I didn't ask about that. What's up with all that cash? Did you clean out your accounts?" Gavin threw question after question at Jay.

"You sure do have a lot of questions. I didn't steal it, so don't worry about it," Jay stated, frustrated.

Gavin looked confused. "You've been walking around with all that money? What if something happens?"

"Does it matter? I have to take care of myself. I can't wait for someone else to do it." Jay drew in a long breath, then tossed in a pair of socks, zipped the bag, and flung it across his shoulder. He stopped in front of Gavin as he walked out of the room. "Just don't worry about it," Jay said and left.

As Gavin watched Jay leave, he wondered if he would see him again. A part of him wished he wouldn't. He couldn't help but wonder about the bag of money, hoping Jay didn't get himself into too much trouble.

Gavin forced his thoughts back to the present and focused on getting the house ready for his date with Lisa. Looking at his watch, he realized he had less time than he thought. After grabbing a can of air freshener, Gavin misted Jay's room with the pine-scented aerosol, even spraying the clothes and shoes he'd left behind. He then closed the door, hoping to trap the overpowering scent in the musty room.

He ordered an exquisite meal from a nearby restaurant and pulled a few bottles of wine from his custom cooler. By the time Lisa arrived, the penthouse was filled with a fragrant mix of exotic spices from Gavin's favorite Indian restaurant. Soft, melodic tunes seeped from the speakers installed in the ceilings of every room. Several aromatic candles flickered under the dim lighting, cloaking the combined living/dining room with a romantic ambiance.

"Wow. It smells wonderful in here," Lisa said as Gavin led her inside by her hand before bending down for a sweet peck on her plush lips.

He twirled her around like a ballerina, admiring the strapless number draped perfectly on her small but curvy frame. With their stark differences in height, Lisa's stilettos didn't seem to have much of an impact, but Gavin appreciated what they did for her toned legs and round behind.

"This is just the beginning. Maybe I'll get lucky tonight," he said, and flashed Lisa with two quick lifts of his brows.

Lisa rolled her eyes upwards, smiled, and shook her head. "You're bad."

"I know!" Gavin waved her over to the seat he'd reserved for her and pulled out her chair. "I bet you like it when I'm bad," he whispered into her neck as she sat.

Gavin saw the glimpse of sultriness in Lisa's eyes after his comment and looked forward to an eventful evening. He enjoyed impressing women in a confident, yet understated way, but reserved pulling out all the stops until he was completely certain she was a keeper. Things were looking up with Lisa, but there was still more to explore before Gavin would consider her on a more permanent level.

After dinner, Gavin served Lisa dessert on the moonlit patio. Barefoot, they carried a bottle of Merlot with them. The night air caressed their skin with a coolness that awakened an unruly desire in Gavin. Lisa's smooth dulcet voice, the curvature of her thighs, the sway of her hips, and the floral scent that wafted from her supple auburn skin, all united to fuel his craving.

Gavin licked his lips as he watched Lisa eat her cheesecake. He felt his blood pulsing inside his pelvis. He drank her in as she sauntered toward the railing, tilting her long neck back to gaze at the speckled sky.

He drew close to her, his body moving as if it were compelled. Wrapping his arms around her from behind, his manhood rose to the occasion, pressing against the small of her back. He leaned over and kissed her bare shoulders, tasting the salted heat as his lips met the inset of her neck, and she turned in to him.

Before she could protest, Gavin covered his mouth with hers. Lisa rose on her toes and met his fervor, pressing her body into his. Lifting her into his arms, he carried her across the starlit patio with her legs wrapped around his back. Their lips never parted. He laid her across the picnic table, then paused to admire her for a moment. The aching in her eyes summoned him closer. She grabbed his shirt, pulled him in, and locked him into another heated kiss as their hands explored each other's bodies.

The fire between them rose quickly. Lisa began carefully unbuttoning his shirt before she resorted to yanking it, expelling his buttons into the air with a snap. Gavin unzipped her dress and tugged on it, freeing her bouncy breasts. He sheltered them with his hands, twisting her nipples between his thumb and forefinger before teasing them with his tongue. Lisa's body wrenched, and simultaneously, as if their needs met at their minds, they reached for each other's core. Their bodies entangled with such intensity, it took no time at all to reach their mutual peak.

They allowed their bodies to cool before taking it slower the second time around. Stretching their naked bodies across one of Gavin's lounge chairs, the cool of the night lulled them into a pleasant sleep like a mother's lullaby.

CHAPTER 11

Blue

Blue's upper body thrust upward, pulling her from her sleep. Her arms flailed about like she was drowning. With cheeks soaked with tears, she willed herself toward clarity. Slowly, she got her bearings and began to float back to reality, finding her way through the blackness that coated the room. The feeling of being pulled under gradually washed away.

Ragged breathing gave way to calmer, deeper breaths. Blue placed her hand on her chest to help gain control of her breathing. Once the fog cleared, her emotions took hold. Now that she was fully aware of herself, images from her nightmare scuttled across her mind. She cringed at the remembrance of Mia and Jay making love. But in her dream, both of them leered at her as their naked bodies merged on a huge screen, large enough for viewing at a drive-in movie. Grudgingly, tears spilled down her face again.

She shut her eyes hard and screamed, trying to force the images away. An ache thumped in her chest like angry drumming. She thought her heart would explode through her chest. Giving up her fight to stop the tears, she sat in the center of the bed, rocking. Suddenly, she thought about the fact that the betrayal had happened in the same bed where she now slept. She jumped out of the bed, stumbled through the covers, and curled up in the corner by the bedroom window.

Feeling her insides twist, she held her stomach and hunched over. The pain felt like someone had fastened weights to her shoulders and heart. She sobbed until her eyes were drained and swollen.

"I don't deserve this," she cried into the night.

Blue looked at the clock. It was 3:10 in the morning. She continued to sit on the floor long enough to produce a fresh batch of tears. They flowed quietly this time, unaccompanied by outcries and haunting images. Despite the late hour, Blue lifted her body from the floor and searched for her cell phone. The carpet quietly received the tears leaking from her eyes. She dialed a number, then dropped her shoulders and put the phone down.

Blue went downstairs to get a glass of water. Looking around the townhouse, which resonated with Mia's personality, anger rose in her throat like bile. Placing her cup on the counter, she raced toward Mia's self-portrait, snatched if from the wall, and put her foot through the canvas, leaving a gaping hole where Mia's face used to be. She flung the remnants across the room, knocking a lamp to the floor with a crash. Next, she marched to the front closet and yanked Mia's coats from the hangers. Taking two steps at time, she raced upstairs and pulled all of Mia's remaining clothes from the closets and drawers, threw them into the circular whirlpool tub, and turned the water on. She looked around in search of something to stain the water and settled on a bottle of tile cleaner. After removing the spray top, she emptied the liquid into the tub and then walked away.

Blue sauntered back into the master bedroom, proud of her wickedness, but the pain hadn't dissipated. The loneliness she felt was stifling, carrying the weight of abandonment. She reached for the phone when she felt like she couldn't breathe anymore.

"Gavin," she whispered in a soft cry, her voice saturated with distress.

"Blue?" Gavin croaked and cleared his throat. "What's wrong?"

he asked. His voice was clear, yet quick with alarm. "What happened? Where are you? Are you hurt?" His questions flashed like the urgent blaze of lightning.

"Why?" Blue's cry developed bravado. "Why did they have to do this to me?" Blue sniffed, sopping up her cries.

"Hold on." After a few moments of silence, Gavin returned to the phone. "Where are you? Do you want me to come?" Gavin's heart was in every word. "I'm getting dressed. Where's Jay? Is he there?"

"I'm sorry. I shouldn't have called you this late."

"It's not a problem. Just tell me if you're hurt."

For minutes, soft cries were all the sound she could manage.

Gavin waited patiently for a response.

"I'm in Atlanta," Blue finally said.

"Oh!" Gavin said, relief and surprise registering in his tone.

Blue suddenly found herself wondering who Gavin had in his company.

"When do you get back to New York?" he asked.

"Tomorrow night," she replied, sniffling again as she sat on the bed and eased her body down. She stared blankly at the ceiling, listening to Gavin, noting his concern.

"Do you need me to pick you up at the airport?" Gavin asked.

"Would you?" She asked, already looking forward to being in the presence of someone who genuinely cared about her.

"Text me the info, and I'll be there," he offered.

Silence fell between them again, but she no longer felt alone.

"Gavin," she called gently.

"Yes?" he asked.

"Just stay on the line with me for a little while, please. I know it's late, and I apologize for calling you at this time of the morning, but I just needed to talk."

Blue took a deep breath and let her head sink into the plush pillow. The remaining tears slid from the sides of her eyes. Blue wiped them away before they could pool in the crevices of her ears.

"No problem," Gavin said.

Blue tried to think of lighter subjects, but thoughts of Jay wouldn't relent. Jay had siphoned love, trust, help, and support from his friends and her. All he gave in return was grief and heartache. She decided it was time for Jay to get back some of the anguish he'd so often imparted.

"You know what, Gavin? I feel a little better now. Try and get some rest. I'll see you tomorrow night," Blue said as her mind spun with possibilities. "And thanks for being here for me—like always."

By the time Gavin could say goodbye, Blue had already hung up the phone. Her mind was made up. Instead of moping and crying, she needed to plan and plot. Mia and Jay were going to pay for what they had done to her.

She packed her things and checked for earlier flights leaving for New York. Blue had plans for Gavin, too.

CHAPTER 12

Mia

Mia sat in Princeton's luxury rental, eyeing her front door from a few houses down. Blue finally emerged from the townhouse just after the break of day. Mia watched as she locked the door and then tossed an overnight bag into the backseat of her rented Sebring. While gnawing on her bottom lip, she charted every move Blue made through tight eyes. She knew Blue had her DVDs in that bag.

She wished Blue would go back inside. Mia was willing to take a chance and snatch the bag from the back of the car to recover her home movies. She sucked air and flung her hand in a dismissive wave. The thought of her escapades being out of her possession made Mia uncomfortable, but then she surmised Blue was no threat.

What is she going to do with those DVDs besides get mad about the one Jay starred in? She thought.

Mia had nothing to lose. She wasn't the one cheating. It was the husbands who had to worry, not her. She may end up running into a bitter wife somewhere, but other than that, what would happen? Their homes would be broken, not hers.

Mia snapped back to focus on spying when she heard the revving of the engine as Blue started the car. Finally, Blue pulled out and sped right past Mia without as much as a sideways glance. Mia had succeeded in keeping her presence low key. She was about to push the ignition button, but decided to wait in case Blue came back. So, she sat back and scouted the place for another half hour.

When she was convinced Blue wouldn't return anytime soon, she eased to the front of the house, looking over her shoulder with every step. Mia hurried to the front door and fumbled with the keys until she was able to get the door open. She had never been afraid to fight, but Mia simply didn't have the emotional, mental, or physical capacity to deal with another encounter with Blue. Now pregnant, she had to proactively avoid potential confrontations since she couldn't physically defend herself anymore.

It took several attempts to get the door open because of Mia's clumsy hands as she kept looking over her shoulder in case Blue returned. Once she finally flipped the locks, Mia pushed the door open to suspiciously look around, not knowing what awaited her on the inside. Mia stepped in and then became stuck in her tracks. Heat tingled at the surface of her skin, generating from the inside out. Her mouth fell open as she surveyed the damage. Picking up her broken lamp, she noticed her busted portrait. The rest of the destruction seemed diminished compared to the assault on the prized painting.

"You bitch!" Mia yelled and tossed the canvas bearing her torn image across the room, knocking down a tall vase filled with an earthy spray of dried flowers. "This is how you want to play this game. You'll never win!" She screamed as if Blue were there to receive her threats.

She stomped up the steps, huffing as her mind raced. Her mouth dropped again at the sight of her clothes strewn across the room in a heaping trail towards the connecting bath.

"Ahhhh!" Mia grappled at her discolored wears, and then gagged at the release of the strong odor wafting through the tight space.

The harsh cleaners had turned her expensive garments into spotted scraps. She held her belly with one hand and her mouth with the other as she tried to keep the contents of her stomach down. With fumes overwhelming her, she threw the dress she had in her hand back into the tub and ran out of the bathroom. Mia raced to the bedroom window, opened it wide, and desperately sucked in fresh air. When her breathing returned close to a normal rhythm, she held her nose, tiptoed back to the bathroom, pulled up the window in there, and dashed out.

The air upstairs was too toxic, so she went back downstairs and plopped on the couch. Rocking back and forth, stewing in her anger, Mia contemplated getting back at Blue. At a glance, she counted at least ten thousand dollars in damage to her belongings, including fur jackets and couture dresses. She knew once she took her time going through everything, that her assessment would be much higher.

Mia hated to feel like someone had gotten the best of her, and she felt like Blue had gotten the final word. Even though she was wrong initially, Mia had a hard time accepting any semblance of defeat. She had been that way since childhood, harboring a need to at least appear like she came out on top in every situation. Even when her biological father walked out on her family, she refused to give him the satisfaction of knowing how much his absence hurt. She claimed to be happy when he stopped showing up, while her mother, sister, and brother openly mourned the breakdown of their family. When her mother remarried, she tried to act unmoved, refusing to acknowledge her stepfather's good qualities. She preferred to focus on what she presumed was his flaw—his frugality.

She despised feeling like she was the underdog. It made her feel weak, and she despised weakness even more than she despised defeat. Somehow, she was going to make Blue pay for her soiled wardrobe.

Mia shot up from her position on the couch and marched back upstairs. She loaded everything she could salvage into the trunk of the car and headed to a nearby hotel. The whole time, her thoughts were entangled with vindictive acts of retaliation, such as breaking out all of the windows of the townhouse or flooding it. She shook those thoughts out of her head.

Her relationship with Blue was ruined, with nothing left to salvage. Mia's emotions were bound into a gang of twisted knots. Feelings of empathy gave way to anger, hurt, resentment, and somehow reverted to guilt. She felt like crying, but sulking wasn't her style. She would have to get used to the fact that Blue would no longer be considered a friend, and after this episode, it would make it a little easier to put Blue out of her life.

Jay was another story, though. In addition to paying for her things, someone was going to take care of this baby. She didn't work so hard and risk so much to get pregnant for nothing.

Mia pulled over, grabbed her cell phone, and dialed Jay's number. The first two attempts went to voicemail. She called again and planned to continue calling until she got an answer. Jay picked up the third time.

"Who is this?" Jay snapped.

"You know who this is. You never answer unknown calls," Mia snapped back.

"What's so important that you had to call me so early in the morning?"

"This baby, that's what. We need to talk, Jay! How are we going to work this situation out?" she asked.

"That's your problem. You figure it out."

Mia's ears grew hot, and she could almost feel the steam seeping, ready to blow.

"Jay, this baby is yours! You hear me? I didn't want this to happen any more than you did." She choked back the unexpected surge of emotion that caused the end of her sentence to waver.

"Why do you want to try and pin this one on me?" he asked.

"You are an arrogant bastard. We both know what we did was wrong. Don't try to lay all the blame on me. You crawled into my bed while knowing your wife was my best friend." Mia sucked her teeth. "And to think I've been trying to protect you from this since the day I found out." Mia paused. "Either we work together to deal with this, or I'll have to become the bitch you know I'm capable of being, and you will really have problems."

Silence.

"Yeah, I thought so. I'm not Blue. I was never that nice!" Mia paused and thought about the bathtub filled with her speckled belongings. "So what's the plan?"

Jay remained silent, and Mia allowed him to wallow in the depth of the uncomfortable moment.

"Damn!" Jay said.

Mia could hear the rustle of the covers and pictured Jay getting out of bed naked. He was never an early riser, and he refused to cover his taut body with pajamas. His self-admiration was fanatical. Admittedly, his physique was a work of art; Mia had to give him credit for that. The vision of his dark chocolate skin poured over his muscular frame flashed before her eyes. She pictured his deep-set eyes sparkling like black pearls.

Jay was a lot of man, and both he and Mia knew it.

"What makes you so sure this kid is mine?" he asked, broaching the subject again.

"Because I know, Jay!"

"So just because you say it is, I'm supposed to believe that? What's your angle?" He lowered his voice. "Is it that you want me for yourself?" he asked rhetorically.

"Please, Jay. Don't flatter yourself," Mia lied, knowing she always believed she was a better match for Jay. His personality was far too big for Blue. "You would've been mine a long time ago if I'd wanted you. Right now, it's about this baby."

"I don't even want kids. I think you should get rid of it," he stated casually.

"I'm not getting an abortion!" Mia shouted, surprised he even made the suggestion.

"Well, I'm not doing shit until I know if the kid is really mine," he retorted.

"Well, it's yours, so now what? Are you going to be there for this kid or just throw money at me to take care of it? I need to know."

"That's all you want—money. Well, guess what? All the money I have is with me right now. So, if you're looking to get paid, you've got the wrong man!"

"What the hell is that supposed to mean?" she asked.

"You know." Jay chuckled. "I'm no longer on the team, so that fat paycheck you were looking to get your hungry hands on won't be coming my way. Now do you still want me to be your baby's daddy?" Jay's laugh was riotous.

It was Mia's turn to be silent. She always knew what was going on behind the sports scene down to the exact figures of an athlete's salary in his contract. That was how she picked her prospects. Now Jay was cut, and she was pregnant with his child. What had she missed?

"That's not funny. Stop playing games with me, you cheap bastard. You just don't want to pay. I'll prove this baby is yours, and you will take care of it," she threatened.

Jay laughed harder.

"How? You can't get money from a rock! With no contract and Blue out of the picture, where's the money coming from, genius? Oh, I'm sorry. You messed around and picked the wrong baby daddy." Jay cackled uncontrollably. "You still want to put this one on me?"

Mia jabbed the cell phone, ending the call, and then threw it down on the passenger side floor. Jay was broke! After all she had done, she'd ended up getting pregnant by her best friend's broke, unemployed husband!

Then she thought about her situation. Jay didn't have anything, but Blue did! Mia retrieved the phone and called Jay back. Jay's greeting was more laughter.

"What d—"

"I'll be in New York in a few days. We can talk then. I have a plan," Mia said and ended the call before he could respond.

CHAPTER 13

Blue

Blue arrived at Atlanta's Hartsfield Airport with two hours to spare before her flight back home to New York. Getting through security was a breeze, leaving her with well over an hour to wait before boarding. She busied herself in the shops near the boarding gate to avoid thinking about her plight. Earlier that day, she had painted a facade with foundation, eyeliner, and shadowy eyes, but when she looked in the mirror, her pain still managed to seep through the veil.

She looked at the magazines in one of the shops and picked up a few to read during the flight home. The cover of her favorite fashion magazine caught her eye just as someone called her name. She hoped it was her imagination. She didn't feel like playing masquerade. Blue's eyes locked with Peyton King, wife of Kendrick King, who was a fellow NBA ball player and former friend of Jay. Peyton was smiling and waving wildly. Blue hoped Peyton wouldn't see past the veneer she'd carefully constructed.

Peyton trotted toward Blue, excitement steering her forward. She pulled Blue into a warm embrace, and the sweetness of her fragrance charmed the air.

"Hey, honey! Long time no see. How have you been?" Peyton asked in her thick Southern drawl. "Are you on your way back home?" Peyton's words linked together like a slow melody.

Peyton's blue eyes sparkled, and her naturally curly blonde hair bounced as she smiled and pulled back to look Blue over. For a petite woman, Peyton's sweet demeanor made her presence larger than life, and her warm smile was the picture of Southern hospitality.

"Give me some sugar, girl!" Peyton said as she leaned in, gave Blue another hug, and kissed her cheek.

"Hey, Peyton. It has been a while." Blue smiled, genuinely happy to see her old friend.

Kendrick and Jay had played on the same team in Atlanta for a short while before Jay was traded to New York.

"Girl, what are you doing in Atlanta, and why didn't you call me? We could have had dinner together," Peyton said, one hand on her hip. "Looking sharp as always on the outside. Not so hot on the inside, huh, baby girl? Your eyes are looking kind of worn," Peyton surmised. "Want to talk about it?"

Blue turned from Peyton's concerned countenance.

"There's a lot going on. How's Ken doing?" Blue asked, diverting the attention from her telling eyes.

"Oh, he's doing just fine. He's sending me to New York for a quick weekend getaway to do some shopping and get a little R and R. I can't stand shopping with him, so I'm going first and he's going to meet me out there in the morning so we can spend the rest of the weekend together. Things have been so crazy," she said, stretching out the word "crazy" as she flipped her hand in the air. "Couldn't wait to get out of Atlanta, even if it is just for a minute. I'm happy to say that life has gotten much better for Ken and me."

"Wow, Peyton. I'm so happy to hear that. Too bad I can't say the same for me and Jay," Blue said and paused. She caught the look of concern in Peyton's eyes. "Let me pay for these magazines, and we can get out of this store. How long before your flight? Maybe we can get a drink," Blue offered.

"Honey, I got more than an hour before my flight takes off. Check your ticket," Peyton said, examining her own ticket and then looking at Blue's. "Well, looka here. We're on the same flight. Maybe the agent can seat us together. I can ask." Peyton paused for a moment before continuing. "That's if you want me to."

"Works for me," Blue replied, even though she preferred to sit alone.

The more she thought about it, she reasoned the company would do her some good. She would manage to avoid the vengeful thoughts that clouded her brain if she chatted with Peyton during the flight. Maybe the tears would stay at bay in the face of company.

Together they browsed a few more shops before sitting down for a bite to eat.

"So what's up with Jay now, Blue? That look in your eyes tells it all," Peyton asked as she pushed a French fry into her mouth and sipped on a Diet Coke.

"I don't even know where to begin," Blue responded, not sure if she wanted to tell anything at all. She looked down at her tray of uneaten food and pushed her fries around.

"I know. Ken has put me through some crazy ordeals since we've been together. But, one day, things just changed." An amazed expression appeared across Peyton's face. "He stopped hanging out as much as he used to. I don't hear any more crazy stories about him out there running around with all these different women. And can you believe that after all these years, he finally decides he wants to have some babies." Peyton's southern lilt laid heavily on her last sentence.

"Wow! What's gotten into him?"

"I don't know, but I hope this time its permanent. The funny thing is I'm not sure how to take it. I've lived with so much mess for so many years. I never really knew what it was like to have a real relationship with a man who was solely focused on me. Seeing all the other wives dealing with this same mess, I simply assumed it came with the territory. Now don't get me wrong," Peyton waved her hand, "we fought like cats and dogs. I may have accepted all his behavior, but I never really wanted to. It's sad, but spending money was my solace. But now, I can finally say I am truly happy."

Peyton's smile made Blue happy and envious at the same time. Now that she and Jay were done for good, she'd never know the feeling Peyton just described. A lump grew in her throat as she sipped her drink.

"That's good to hear. I wonder what triggered the change," Blue said, her voice and thoughts trailing off.

"Oh!" Peyton said, like she just remembered something. "What's up with your little heifer-friend?"

Blue busted out laughing. She knew Peyton was referring to Mia, whom she'd never liked.

"Is her conniving ass still living in your place here in Atlanta?" Peyton asked, taking another sip of her Diet Coke.

"Not anymore."

"Good! Are you still friends?"

"Not anymore."

"Whew! As my preacher-daddy would say, 'There is a God!' I knew it would only be a matter of time," Peyton said, shaking her head and raising her hand in the air. "Let's get our behinds to the gate," she suggested, looking at her watch. "They should begin boarding our flight soon."

Blue and Peyton grabbed their belongings, threw their trash in the bin, and headed to the gate. Peyton worked on the attendant and was able to get her and Blue's first-class seats changed so they could sit next to each other.

"Let's get back to heifer-girl," Peyton said. "I hear she's pregnant now. I just wonder whose husband that baby belongs to."

Blue looked surprised. Did everyone know about Mia's trysts but her?

"What makes you say that?" Blue asked.

"That woman has been through just about every man in every sport throughout Atlanta, including the sportscasters. When she's done with that mattress, it needs to be burned!" Peyton said. "She went after Ken for a while. That's when we fell out. I told her that she better sniff after someone else's man. The wives can't stand that girl. And the worse part about it, she would pretend to be your friend while sleeping with your husband. She's so conniving."

"Believe me," Blue said, "I know what she's capable of."

Peyton's eyes grew big. "No, Blue. Don't tell me…"

"Yes, Peyton."

"That bitch!" Peyton said, sitting taller in her seat and looking around to see if anyone heard her outburst. "I can't believe that." Peyton paused and shook her head. "And *you*…were truly her friend. I guess it's true what they're saying."

"What are *they* saying?" Blue asked.

"Another one of her former friends—or rather one of her latest victims—said she thinks Mia got pregnant so she could collect a guaranteed check. You know all these men give her money. It's because of them that she lives so well. That's just crazy to me."

It didn't sound so crazy to Blue. Mia must have been in jeopardy of losing her lifestyle, so she decided to pull out all the stops. The baby could belong to Jay. Then again, it could be any one of the men she'd been sleeping with. Blue figured it out. If Mia's baby belonged to Jay, then Mia could gain access to her and Jay's money—actually her money. She'd just never expected to be a part of this wily scenario.

The flight attendants asked for their attention to communicate the flight's safety precautions as Peyton continued to witness about Mia's scandalous ways. Blue couldn't focus on either. Her thoughts were consumed with the idea of being a target in Mia's get-rich-for-eighteen-years scheme.

All of Atlanta had come to know what Mia was up to, but Blue didn't live in Atlanta. How could she have ever known the truth all the way in New York?

Blue knew the truth now, though.

CHAPTER 14

Gavin

Gavin took a deep breath before dialing Lisa's number. Ever since Blue's call the night before, Lisa had been giving Gavin the cold shoulder. He'd taken his conversation with Blue into the living room, but realized that didn't look good. He didn't want Lisa to think he was playing games with her just as their union was heating up.

"Hi," Lisa answered casually, devoid of her usual enthusiasm.

"Hey. How are you?" Gavin asked cautiously.

He'd called her several times throughout the day, but after the first call, she'd ignored the rest. He recognized the clipped rings when his calls were being forced to voicemail. The fact that she answered this time surprised him a little.

"Fine." The edge in her voice was ragged. She sucked her teeth in the receiver.

"What are you doing…later? I want to take you out to dinner. I know a nice sushi place. They have good food and a cool atmosphere. I can meet you at your job after work, and we can head over there together."

"I don't know," Lisa said.

"Lisa, come on." Gavin wasn't interested in playing the game.

"What?" she asked.

"How long do you plan to keep this up?" he asked, getting bored with her act.

"Until you tell me what's really going on with you and your damsel in distress," she said with a drizzle of emotion and a typhoon of attitude.

"Finally! I got a rise out of you. Now what do you mean by *my* damsel in distress?"

"That was not the first time we've been together when she's called and you forget that I was there. After what we did last night, I don't want to… I don't feel like discussing this right now."

Good! Gavin thought. "Listen! It's not what you think. Blue is my friend's wife. They are going through something right now, and I'm just being a friend like I've always been." Gavin drew himself in and huffed. "Are we going to dinner or what?" Gavin asked with a smile in his voice, hoping to lighten her mood. He didn't feel like discussing Blue anymore. "What are you wearing?" he inquired, trying to change the subject.

"Why?"

"I just want to know."

"Work clothes. What do you think? I'm at work, aren't I?"

"Well, what are you wearing under those work clothes?" Gavin asked in a lower octave. He could almost hear her smile.

Lisa sucked her teeth but didn't respond right away. Gavin could tell her tenacity was waning.

"Underwear. What do you think?" She said.

"Damn. Why!"

"Oh my goodness, I'm at work! What's wrong with you? "She said through her titter.

Gavin was sure she was smiling.

"Well, I can't take you out like that? You need to go home and get rid of those things. Don't you know they're bad for dates?"

Lisa shrieked. Gavin had successfully fused the icy distance between them with sexy banter. His load was heavy enough. There was no need to add the weight of Lisa's reproach.

"I'll pick you up at seven. Be ready. And remember, no underwear. They're bad for your health!" Gavin said with mock concern. "Get sexy for your man. I'll see you later."

"Oh, my man, huh! Now you're my man?"

Gavin wished he could take back those words. She'd read too far into his statement. Women always did.

"Just be ready at seven. I've got to run, so I'll talk to you later," he said, rushing off the phone, hoping that part of the conversation didn't resurface.

"Well, don't be late. Your *woman* will be waiting," she replied.

He hung up without saying goodbye and then pinched the bridge of his nose. He'd listened to himself say the words "my woman." It had sounded innocent enough to him, but he knew the words carried more weight when Lisa heard them. Gavin liked Lisa and hoped his 'claim' wouldn't turn into an obstacle, along with the other thing that stood in his way. Gavin tried to force the second complication out of his thoughts. At least he tried to by attempting to refute the idea of being there for Blue.

Gavin didn't want to abandon Blue in her time of need. He knew how much of a jerk Jay could be. She didn't have many friends, and the one woman that she was closest to had betrayed her. She couldn't reveal this mess to her family because of the possible repercussions. Her brother would surely end up in jail for retaliating on behalf of his sister. He was the only person in Blue's corner. Either he would have to get Lisa to understand that or simply keep her in the dark about his interaction with Blue.

CHAPTER 15

Mia

Mia hoped her funky new pixie-styled haircut hadn't become too undone by the sharp winds as she marched through the thick foot traffic along Seventh Avenue. Evening had graced the city, and the temperature had dipped significantly for late summer. Mia's faceoff with Blue the previous week had helped to put her future in focus. She'd come to New York to meet with Jay about her plans over dinner. As she pulled open the door to the restaurant, the wind snatched it from her grip and swung it back. She reached for the door and yanked it closed.

Mia had only walked a few blocks, but it felt like she had trudged across the Mohave desert in a sandstorm. Between dodging the tourists, the fast-stepping New Yorkers down Fashion Avenue, and pressing against the forceful winds, Mia felt like she had been whipped.

The popular restaurant bar was filled to the brim with professionals and urbanites, just as she'd expected. Mia excused herself through the tapestry of colorful city folk and headed toward the hostess.

"Reynolds, party of two, please. How long is the wait?" she asked the hostess.

"About twenty minutes," she said with a smile. Her Botox-filled lips appeared to get in the way as she tried to speak. She dismissed Mia with a shift of attention to the next guest, which appeared to be professional but bordered on rudeness.

"Thanks," Mia tossed back and headed for the restroom.

From the moment she stepped into the small bathroom, women checked her out. She knew she looked good. She had to. No way would she meet with Jay and not look her absolute best. Mia adjusted the collar of her black leather jacket and pulled up her leggings, snapping them at the waist. Then she turned slightly in order to catch a glimpse of her round bottom. She brushed the back of her leggings, smoothed her shirt around her small baby pooch, and pulled at the top of her patent leather boots. After teasing her hair and adding gloss to her full lips, she tossed her oversized Gucci bag over her arm and headed for the door.

Mia's eyes caught sight of a snake-skinned Gucci bag and looked up to assess the average-looking girl carrying it. *Cute, but no competition,* she thought.

"Love your hair and boots," the girl commented.

"Thanks!" Mia said and threw her a thankful but fake smile. She pranced out the door, making a mental note to look up the woman's purse online.

Mia managed to kill about ten minutes on her trip to the bathroom, but Jay still hadn't arrived. Her impatience made her back rigid. She took a seat at the bar and ordered a cranberry spritzer, wishing she could have a dirty martini instead. Jay was now twenty minutes late. Frustration tightened Mia's lips. Another ten minutes and she was leaving; she had other plans for the evening. Mia ordered another spritzer. When that one was done, she would be, too.

Just as the bartender set the second glass in front of her, Mia witnessed a large, dark hand reach from behind her and placed a twenty-dollar bill on the counter. She spun around to find Jay standing so close, she could feel his breath on her face.

"You're late!" she snapped.

Jay flashed a brilliant smile, revealing a perfect set of stark white teeth. She rolled her eyes and pushed him aside with the back of her hand.

"Let me check on the table. We need to hurry. I have other things I need to take care of," she said.

Still smiling, Jay gracefully stepped out of her way. Mia knew he was watching her backside, so she put her stiletto boots and leggings to work, offering Jay and any other lucky patron an eyeful.

As they were being shown to their table, Jay grabbed Mia's elbow, stopping her. When she turned, she spotted the average-looking woman with the snake-skinned Gucci bag coming toward her while holding Gavin's arm like a trophy. Mia dropped her head and turned back towards the door, leaving the hostess behind. Jay followed her lead.

"Do you think Gavin saw us?" she asked when they got outside.

Jay looked frustrated. Without acknowledging it, they both agreed that being seen together wouldn't be the best thing.

"I don't know."

"Listen, I don't have much time. You were late, and I have other plans. We need to talk so I can get going," Mia said, then huffed because Jay was eyeing her hips. She threw her hands up and asked, "Are you even listening to me?"

Jay licked his lips. Mia pretended like his attention annoyed her.

"I know where we can talk and get food without worrying about running into people. Come with me," Jay said, brushing her behind as he reached for her arm. As soon as they reached the nearby W Hotel, they ordered drinks at the bar.

"So what's your plan?" Jay finally asked.

"You need to work things out with Blue," she said casually, while sipping her fourth juice in the past hour.

"What! What kind of plan is that? Don't you think I've already tried?"

"I know, but without Blue, what do you have? If she doesn't take you back, there's only one other option. However, with this other option, I will have to coach you, and you will have to listen and do exactly what I say in order for it to work."

Jay raised his brows. "What are you talking about?" Mia had piqued his interest.

"You have to divorce her and request spousal support."

Jay shook his head. "I wouldn't want you for a best friend."

"Listen. If you do it right, you'll be set up for life, but you have to follow my instructions to the letter. I can help you gain access to some of the money and keep the house in Atlanta."

She knew what she planned was devious, but she needed money. Her funds were dwindling, and this was her only way to avoid her own financial meltdown. She needed a security blanket for the future, and the baby was it. There was no room for hard feelings. This wasn't personal for her. This was business.

"Do you want my help or not?" she asked.

Jay sat back and gestured for her to keep talking. He listened intently as Mia disclosed the rest of her plan.

"Let's finish this conversation upstairs where there are fewer ears," Jay said, downing the rest of his scotch with one swallow.

"Upstairs?" she asked.

"Yes. I have a room here till tomorrow," he said, dropping money on the bar to cover their tab.

Mia hesitated at first.

"I'm not having sex with you," she told him flat out when they entered the empty elevator. "I'm here to handle business."

"Yeah. Business."

When they reached the room, Jay opened the door and stepped aside to let Mia in. He slapped her on the ass as she walked past. Mia stopped and narrowed her eyes at him. Jay held both hands in the air.

"I'm just joking!"

Mia stood by the window, taking in the view of the city as she explained what he had to do for their plan to work. Jay poured himself a small glass of cognac before plopping down on the chair and turning on the TV.

"Are you paying attention?" Mia asked, her hands on her hips.

"Yes. I'm taking it all in," he said, then licked his lips.

Jay's eyes followed Mia around the room. She swatted at him.

"So are you in or what?"

"You really think this will work?"

"I know it can if you play your cards right. I've seen it happen before, and I have the perfect attorney for you."

Jay's expression questioned her.

"Don't worry. He's one of the best," she assured him.

The thought of things working out the way she planned made her adrenaline kick into high gear. Mia daydreamed as her eyes washed over the lights of New York City. Her dreams were interrupted by Jay's hand between her thighs. Jay's other hand found its way to her breast, and he pulled her close. She wanted to resist, but the grunt that escaped her lips told Jay another story.

"No. Jay…," she said with her mouth, while her body showed no sign of protest.

"Why not? We have nothing to lose now," he said, breathing heavy while kissing the back of her neck.

The fresh smell of cognac filled the air when he spoke. Moist traces of the liquor were left on the back of Mia's neck.

"You looked so damn good at that restaurant. I don't know why you're playing with me. You knew what you were doing when you put on those leggings and boots."

Mia moaned as Jay explored her body. When he dipped his hands inside the front of her leggings, she bent her knees, giving him more access. Jay ground his hardness against her backside. He guided Mia forward, giving rise to her ample behind, and gently tugged her leggings down.

"Wait!" Mia said out of breath.

She removed her boots, took off her clothes, and lay on the bed.

Jay, now also naked, pulled her off of the bed and led her over to the massive windows overlooking the city. As she faced the beautiful dimly lit skyline, he planted her hands against the window and bent her forward. From the back, he teased her smoldering wetness with his manhood.

As he entered her, she winced from his expansiveness, and then tightened her walls snugly around him. He pounded against Mia until ecstasy had them howling and drenched in sweat. They were so caught up in the moment, they never heard the first few knocks at the hotel room door. It was the police-like pounding and the commanding voice of the security personnel that finally stole into their consciousness, forcing them to float back to Earth.

Leaving Mia with her hind quarters exposed and still up in the air, Jay slowly walked to the door. Sweat and fresh sex juice clung to his body. He opened the door without shielding himself.

"Sorry. We promise to keep it down," he said casually, and then slammed the door in their faces, but not before Mia's eyes had a chance to lock with her sister's…Myra.

CHAPTER 16

Blue

Vengeance was easier to deal with than hurt. She wanted no part of either, yet they both nipped annoyingly at her like frenzied puppies biting at her ankles. Consuming thoughts of Mia and Jay stole into her sleep and daily focus, robbing her of emotional serenity, resolve, and rest. Blue sighed, plopped onto the couch, and snatched her phone from the side table.

"Hey, it's me," she said immediately after Gavin said hello.

"I thought I would have heard from you before now. You never called me to pick you up from the airport last week."

"I caught an earlier flight." She hesitated before saying, "I need to talk to you." She paused again. "Will you be busy after work? I found out a few things while I was in Atlanta, and there's no one else with whom I feel comfortable enough to discuss this stuff with."

"I'll be around. But—"

"Okay, good. I have to run now because I have another call," she said, looking at her mother's number on her display. "Thanks, Gavin. I'll see you later."

Instead of clicking over to answer, she just stared at the phone. Blue hadn't been in contact with her family since her life started falling apart, especially her mother. The screen told her that she had a missed call. Shortly after, a red star appeared next to her message indicator. Blue had no intention of calling her mother back anytime soon.

Just as she was about to drop the phone into her purse, it rang again. This time, her brother's number appeared.

"Hello."

"So you'll answer for him, but not for me," Jean Holiday said.

After a long sigh, Blue answered casually, "I didn't get to the phone in time. It was in my bag."

"Um hmm. I'm sure that's the reason."

Jean's sarcasm never moved Blue.

"What's going on with you? No one has heard from you. You aren't answering calls or replying to any messages. Richard said he hadn't heard anything about you taking any business trips, so what's up?"

Blue wanted to tell Jean to mind her business, but she would never be that rude no matter how fickle their relationship was. Jean learned most of what she wanted to know through Richard anyway. What more did she want?

"I just have a lot on my plate, that's all."

"Yeah? Well how's my son-in-law doing? Richard heard about him being cut from the team on one of those sports channels. How's he taking it?"

Blue's eyes rolled up, and she let them hang there for a moment. Her sigh was heavy. Jean hated when she sucked her teeth, so she sucked them as loud as she could. That was the extent of her defiance. Regardless of the fact that they didn't get along, Blue was never overtly disrespectful.

"He's getting on my nerves. That's all I know."

Jean's gasp was Oscar worthy. Her performances often garnered notoriety. Blue pictured Jean's hand across her heart as she slightly turned away.

"How insensitive! That man lost his job—his career—and all you can say is that he's getting on your nerves? You've always been a selfish little bitch."

Is she serious! Blue touched her temples, anticipating the headache she'd have by the time she ended this conversation.

"I'm not being insensitive or selfish. He's been pretty nasty since the cut. It hasn't been easy," Blue responded, cutting her explanation short. Filling Jean in on the details wouldn't benefit her in any way.

"You need to be more understanding towards his situation, Blue." Jean paused, but continued when Blue didn't bother to comment. "Think of how you would feel if your dream was snatched from under your feet. That's horrible. What about his pay? Do they plan on paying him for the remainder of the season?"

Finally, Jean got to the point of her call. Blue had anticipated the question.

"No!"

"Oh my! So what's going to happen?"

"Not sure right now."

After a long pause, Jean asked, "Well, what about your money? You aren't using your trust fund to take care of him, are you?"

"Jay's name isn't associated with my trust fund."

Thanks to the basketball contract, Jean had adored Jay, despite the fact that he wasn't exactly Prince Charming. She'd wanted Blue to marry Jay because of his presumed fame and fortune, but now that his funds would begin to fade, all her mother could think about was keeping the trust fund money out of his hands—the same money that was partially the cause of their estranged relationship. Jean wanted to have control over it, but she couldn't because Blue's wealthy grandfather, Gabriel Dufour, had set up the fund with specific guidelines. He didn't want his favorite grandchild to suffer because of her father's absence and her mother's resentment. He'd put some of his wealth aside for each grandchild but had left a special helping just for Blue.

"Well, what's he going to do?"

"I'm not sure."

"Why don't the two of you come by for dinner this weekend?"

Since they'd wed five years ago, Jean had never offered them even a cup of tea. Jean's only interest was to pry, and Blue wasn't falling for it.

"Like I said, Ma, I have a lot on my plate. Chances are we won't be able to make it this weekend."

"Okay, well maybe next weekend. Call me if you need anything."

"Sure. I've got to go. Please tell Rich to call me. Bye." Blue ended the conversation abruptly.

Jean's offering to help made Blue chuckle. Since when did Jean offer to help her with anything?

Blue stepped over to the hall mirror and stared at her reflection, looking directly into her sullen eyes. Those same eyes had caused her father, Fredrick Holiday, to walk out of their lives the day she was born, creating a void in Jean that she'd filled with bitterness. With her crinkly hair and startling blue eyes, Freddie had insisted Blue couldn't have been his child. No one could convince him that Blue may have possibly inherited those bright eyes from Grandpa Gabe and his side of the family. Freddie accused Jean of cheating and ordered her to let Blue's "real" daddy take care of her, because he was nobody's fool. His absence had formed a heavy presence in their home. For years, Blue had searched for him in the men she dated, finding herself attracted to traits she imagined her father possessed. He had to be gutsy to walk out on their family the way he did.

"This isn't about him," Blue said out loud, pulling her focus back to the present.

Then Richard entered her mind, her only brother and one of her few true friends. What had her mother said to make him feel guilty enough to allow Jean to call Blue from his phone? They shared a much better relationship, and unfortunately for Richard, that always placed him at the center of their problems. Blue always felt like the thorn in Jean's side, a keepsake of uncomfortable memories. She'd deal with Richard for putting her on the spot, later. Now, she needed to focus on a plan.

Blue promised herself that Jay would never get a hold of her money. First thing the next morning, she planned to check in with the family lawyer and her financial consultant. She wanted to make sure Jay wasn't entitled to have access to her funds.

Blue gently touched her face. The bruises were healed and the tenderness long gone. Yet, the memories of that night made her skin tingle as if the pain was fresh. Her lips tightened as she remembered it with vivid clarity, like she had witnessed the abuse instead of being abused herself. She felt the heat of anger rise in her chest. She closed her eyes, willing her temperament to remain stable.

"And he wants my damn money?" she said aloud while pacing her living room floor. "I will fight you tooth and nail before I let up on a dime," Blue continued as if Jay was right there with her.

* * * *

The doorbell rang, waking Blue from her slumber. At first, it sounded far away, and then became louder and closer. Blue realized she had fallen asleep. She stretched and looked for her cell phone to check the time. More than an hour had passed. The door chimed louder, invading Blue's senses. For a moment, she contemplated leaving the uninvited guest outside, but realized this person had to be familiar enough to get past the doorman. *It must be Jay.* She was mad enough to challenge him for his audacity and ready to face him. She marched to the door, flung it open, and swiftly stepped into the person's face, ready to give Jay a solid piece of her mind. Blue nearly jabbed her mother in the eye with her index finger. Her mouth fell open and she rolled her eyes, bracing herself for a verbal confrontation.

"What are you doing here?" she asked.

Her mother's timing was off. Blue preferred to seethe in private, and the last person she wanted to deal with, besides Jay, was her mother.

"Are you going to let me in?" Jean asked.

Blue huffed, stepped aside, and moved her arm in a wide sweeping gesture, directing her mother inside. Jean shook her head as she walked past. Blue cut her eyes at her mother's back and shut the door hard. She watched as her mother's tall, slender body sauntered through the living room and examined the area before taking a seat on the couch. Blue remained at the door with her arms crossed over her chest, hoping the impromptu visit would be quick.

"What made you decide to come for a visit…without calling?" Blue made an honest attempt to suppress the sarcasm in her tone.

Her mother chuckled. "You don't seem happy to see me," she said as she wiped her hands across her lap, straightening her ivory slacks.

Blue stared at her mother a moment before answering. Jean always looked regal in her all-ivory attire, with her long, fine hair pulled back into a sleek ponytail and clasped with a decorative barrette at the nape of her neck. She was infamous for the bright red shade she painted across her collagen-injected lips. The color popped against her fair mulatto skin tone. Blue was the spitting image of her mother, save for the springy coils of thick hair and nut-brown coloring, complements of her father's deeper complexion. Another reminder—she assumed—that caused her mother grief.

"This is just not a good time." Blue finally responded to her mother's comment.

"The place looks so different. What's missing?" Jean asked as she continued to survey the room. She stood and went to the opposite side of the room near the window overlooking Park Avenue. "What happened to Jay's bust?" Her brows creased.

Without answering, Blue moved around the apartment in a hurry. "It broke," she said dismissively. "Ma, I'm sorry your visit has to be so short, but I have an appointment and don't want to be late."

Blue left the room and returned with shoes and her purse, hoping to make her story appear real.

"You're working on a Saturday?" Jean asked.

"Well…yeah. It's a potential private client," Blue replied quickly. She was sure her mother didn't believe her lies, but she stuck to her false account.

"Client or not, I came here to talk about this thing with you and Jay," Jean said, waving the apparent dismissal away. "What's going on between you two? What's his game plan now that he's no longer playing basketball? I adore Jay, but my first concern is your well-being and protecting your interest."

Blue placed her purse on the console, planted both hands palms down, and stood there pondering the best possible answer to get her mother off of her back.

"Mom." She slowly turned around to face Jean. "I have it all under control. I'm doing fine, and my money is safe."

"I'm not convinced," Jean said, rising to her feet. She took a deep breath and then hung her head sideways. The pitiful look she cast angered Blue even more. "You think I can't see what's going on?" She waved her hand, presenting the room. "You think I can't tell Jay's no longer here? You may not want to talk about this right now, and I understand, but I know men…very well. I know the type of man he is." She paused, approaching Blue with a slow gait. "I already know what he'll try to do, and frankly, my dear daughter, I'm not sure if you're up for the challenge," she stated, staring directly into Blue's eyes.

Blue shifted on her feet, determined not to fidget under the weight of her mother's intent stare. She didn't appreciate the hint at potential weakness. After a few moments, Jean's demeanor shifted.

"Call me if you need me," she said, then turned on her heels and sauntered out of the door.

As much as Blue hated to admit it, her mother was right, but this time she was ready for the fight.

CHAPTER 17

Gavin

Gavin stepped out of the steamy shower and dried his body as he grooved to his favorite selection of Alfonzo Blackwell's latest jazz CD. Every now and then he'd press his lips together and finger air notes as he played an imaginary saxophone to the crisp melodies floating through the house from his Bose speaker system. He was grateful to have the house to himself. Jay had been gone for a few days, and Gavin hoped he'd stay gone.

Gavin tracked moist footprints from the bath to where his iPod played in the connecting bedroom and switched genres from Jazz to R&B. The sexually-charged but soulful tunes always placed him in a good mood just before a date.

The beige button-down shirt he slipped on was starched to perfection. Monogram cufflinks finished the sleeves. Gavin slipped his well-oiled legs into dark blue jeans, and then slipped on espresso-colored shoes and a matching sports jacket. When he looked in the mirror, he jerked his collar and winked while mouthing the words to an old party song by Montell Jordan. Kenneth Cole's Black for Men flavored the air as Gavin sprayed it over his body. He sniffed. One last squirt added the final touch.

Gavin checked his watch and confirmed he was good on time. It was just after seven, and he had until eight p.m. to get over to Lisa's place.

The phone rang. It was Gavin's doorman letting him know his female guest had arrived.

"Thanks. Send her up," he instructed the doorman.

For a moment, Gavin wondered why Lisa hadn't waited for him to come to her, but then he figured there was nothing wrong with getting the night started early. They could enjoy a cocktail before heading out. Gavin grabbed two glasses and had filled them with Merlot by the time the elevator doors opened.

Blue walked in and took a glass from his hand.

"Thanks!"

"Hey…you're …uh…welcome," Gavin fumbled, surprised to see Blue.

Blue took a long sip and closed her eyes. The moan she let out after she swallowed was a testament to how much she enjoyed the taste. She finished off the glass and handed it back to Gavin, who still hadn't moved.

"Hey, that's my song," Blue said, swaying to 112's *Anywhere.* "What's up with the mood you're setting here? Wine and 112. That's a sexy combination. It's just me, Gavin. Are you trying to tell me something?" Blue teased and snickered.

"Not at all! I thought you were my friend Lisa."

"Oh." A veil of embarrassment draped her. "I thought you were expecting me. I don't mean…with the wine and all. Anyway, I called you."

"Oh, yes! You're right," Gavin said, scrunching his face and sucking air through his teeth. "Ah, damn. Sorry, I forgot. There was something you wanted to talk about, right?"

"Yeah." Blue's eyes bounced around the room, avoiding Gavin's.

"Hold on a minute," he said, holding the glasses up.

He ran to the bedroom, turned off the music, and put the wine glasses in the kitchen. His glass was still full.

"Okay. Now, what's up? What happened?"

"Um…well. You know what?" Blue took a breath. "This can wait. I didn't realize you were going out. We can talk another time."

"You sure? It's not a problem. I can call and let her know I'll be a few minutes late."

Gavin didn't want to let her down, but he also didn't want to keep Lisa waiting.

There he was, putting Lisa aside for Blue. His priorities confused him. Gavin convinced himself that he was just being a good and loyal friend—again.

"No, don't worry. Let me know when it will be a good time. I don't want to interrupt. It looks like you're all geared up for a hot date. Don't let me mess that up for you." Blue let out a nervous chuckle.

Gavin walked over to her.

"If you need to talk to me now, then let's talk," he said.

"No, I insist. It can wait. Go out and have fun," Blue said and turned to walk to the elevator. She turned back to Gavin with her head hung down, but her eyes lifted slowly to meet his. They stood face to face for moments without speaking.

"Are you sure?" he asked again.

"Yes, I'm sure," she said.

"Call me if you need me," he offered one last time.

"I will. Thanks…as always," she responded, avoiding his eyes.

They stood at that place again with weighted silence between them. Gavin didn't trust himself with her nor did he want to take advantage of her emotional frailty. This *was* his "best friend's" wife. He'd blown his chance back in college. He pitied her, but cared for her more.

"Okay," Blue said and sighed. "I'm going. I don't want to hold you up." She didn't move and neither did he. "Thanks again. Call me tomorrow so I can fill you in. I need some advice, okay?"

"Okay."

Blue leaned in and kissed his lips. Gavin bit down on his teeth and kept his lips tight. She leaned in again. He closed his eyes and wished her away, though his attempt failed to douse the sparks that flickered between them. He could almost hear them crackle. Blue ran her tongue across his lips and kissed him once more. Gavin responded and quickly pulled away, leaving a slight distance.

"I'll call you tomorrow," he said, looking past her. "I've got to get uptown quick."

After pressing the call button for the elevator, he busied himself checking his watch as he walked to the kitchen, leaving Blue standing by the elevator door. He refused to turn back until just before the elevator doors closed. When he did, he could see a glistening trail of tears sliding down Blue's cheeks.

Gavin took a deep breath. He'd never told Blue that Jay was staying with him. And he'd never told Jay that he was still in touch with Blue. He tried his best to shake off the shift in atmosphere that Blue's visit created with her presence. He hoped Lisa wouldn't sense his discomfort. When she pressed her lips against his at the end of the night, surely the soft, fresh touch of Blue's lips would be on his mind.

Grabbing his keys, he headed for the elevator door. Instead of boarding right away, he stood at the entrance tossing the keys in the air as he tried to ready his heart and mind for Lisa. Blue was in his system, fastening herself to his emotions, squeezing Lisa out.

CHAPTER 18
Blue

Blue rushed home, burst through the door and into her bedroom where she threw herself across the bed. Her encounter with Gavin left her embarrassed. Within minutes, her pillow was soaked. She punched it a few times, then buried her face to muffle her cries. Jay was to blame for everything. She wanted revenge, but a clear plan had yet to form in her convoluted mind. Vengeance would give her temporary gratification. More than anything, she just wanted the pain and anger to go away.

Blue got up and ran to Jay's closet, where some of his clothes were still hanging. She ripped his expensive suits and other garments from the hangers, marched to the guest room, and threw them on the floor.

"You bastard! Why did you do this to me?" she cried.

Her breathing was ragged as she made several trips back and forth until Jay's closet was empty. Blue trudged around the rest of the house schlepping anything she could find that belonged to Jay. High piles of clothing, sports paraphernalia, footwear, pictures, and keepsake basketballs littered the room until Blue could barely close the door. She thought about throwing a match into the heap.

"I hate you!" she screamed, then crumbled into her hands. "God. My best friend and my husband."

Pictures and balls crashed into the walls as she tossed them across the room. Her breathing was reduced to spurts of air. She stopped and took several deep breaths to avoid hyperventilating. That pain in the pit of her belly burned again. Blue cradled her stomach and fell to her knees.

"Why me?"

Washed down in sweat and exhaustion, the heaviness gave way to fatigue, and she lay on top of the clothes sniffling until she fell asleep.

She dreamed that Jay was back and things were like they used to be, until he announced to her that he and Mia were getting married. He even invited Blue to the wedding with a magnificent smile. Blue's confusion lingered until she was fully awake.

She looked around the room, squinting, trying to decipher her reality. Then the phone rang. Slowly, she pulled herself up and dragged her body back to the bedroom. The muffled ringing stopped and started again from inside her purse. She dug inside and studied the missed calls. One from her brother Richard, one from her cousin Fran, and most shockingly, the last one was from Jay. Blue tossed the phone on the bed and turned away, catching a glimpse of herself in the mirror. She stepped in closer to examine her bulging red eyes.

The phone rang again. The neon blue numbers on the clock told her it was past three in the morning. She let it ring.

Going to work the next morning was out of the question. She'd have to call in or work from home. She couldn't show up with swollen eyes for everyone to surreptitiously query the origin of her worn appearance.

When the phone rang again, Blue snatched it off of the bed and answered. "What?"

"Are you okay?" Gavin asked.

"It's late, Gavin."

"I know, but I just got back in and wanted to check up on you.

You looked really upset when you left earlier."

Blue wiped her face. "How was your date?" she asked, trying to sound normal.

"It was cool. I wanted to say sorry." Gavin paused. "Would you like to meet me for lunch so we can talk?"

Blue thought about how her face would look and decided she could hide her puffy eyes behind designer shades.

"That's cool. Where do you want to go?"

"I don't care. You pick the place."

"Okay, I'll think about it."

"All right. Let's make it for two o'clock after the rush. Cool?"

"Cool."

"Oh, and Blue?"

"Yeah?"

"Stop crying. It's going to be all right. It just takes a little time."

"I'm not crying. I'm sleepy. It's after three in the morning, remember?" Blue said, upset that she was still unable to hide the agony in her voice.

She ended the call, and while walking to the mirror, she knew she would probably stand Gavin up. She was far too raw for a public appearance, even if it was with Gavin. Though she had plans for him, she'd have to wait a day or two before she began putting them into action.

Instead of going back to bed, Blue went to the kitchen, put on water for tea, and headed to her home office. She pulled the files containing all of her financial records. Studying the statements and trust documents, she confirmed Jay wasn't entitled to her trust, but could have access to her monthly disbursements, which she'd pooled into an investment account that was in her name only. Now she needed to find a way to protect those investments because she wasn't about to let Jay get his hands on that money. Her mother was right. She needed to get on the ball.

By the time Blue finished going through all of her statements, the sun had made its way through the creases in her wood blinds, casting radiant stripes across the room. She called her mother and told her that she'd meet her for breakfast.

Blue showered and plundered through the junk drawer in the kitchen in search of her car keys. It had been weeks since she'd driven anywhere. Living in the city, it was easier to jump in a taxi as opposed to pulling her car from the garage and dealing with the erratic traffic just to park in another garage or spend countless minutes circling overcrowded Manhattan neighborhoods for a parking space.

When the attendant pulled her white convertible Mercedes from her designated spot, it was covered with an opaque layer of dust. Blue twisted her nose at the dirty car. She'd surely have to run it through the car wash before taking the quick ride over the bridge into Queens to meet her mother. Rolling up in that filthy vehicle would definitely give her mother something to fuss about.

***

Blue pulled up in front of her mother's sprawling home in Jamaica Estates and tooted the horn lightly.

Jean sprung down her front steps almost immediately, looking elegant in a sweeping, ankle-length sundress, her usual ponytail, brilliant red lips, and sandals with dazzling stones.

Blue looked at her mother and smiled. People believed they were sisters despite the twenty-five year difference between their ages.

Jean gracefully entered the car, filling the air with the sweet fragrance of her signature perfume. For as long as Blue could remember, her mother had always wore Jessica McClintock. Its distinct feminine aroma always garnered the attention of the men, who fell over themselves to offer up compliments.

"That was quick," Jean said as she gently pulled the door close. "It's been a long time since we've broken bread together. I figured it would be nice to go over to the diner on the corner of Francis Lewis and Horace Harding. You remember that one, don't you? It's the same one that Bill Clinton came to when he first got into office years ago. I love it over there."

"Yes," Blue replied as she shifted the car into gear and cruised away.

"Why don't you put the top down," Jean suggested, looking up at the ceiling of the car. "It's such a nice day. I'm not worried about my hair. Are you? With the kind of hair you have, who could tell if it gets a little ruffled from the wind?" she said, lifting a lock of Blue's coils between her index finger and thumb.

Without looking in her mother's direction, Blue envisioned the scowl Jean wore as she commented on her hair. She bit her lip to keep from responding flippantly. Snide remarks fell from her mother's lips with such ease that Blue assumed she was oblivious to her own thought process. Pushing the offhandedness aside, Blue called her office to tell them she wouldn't be in. Jean continued to talk despite seeing her on the phone.

Once inside the diner, they were seated quickly. Before the

hostess could walk away from the table, Jean ordered her to bring her a cup of green tea and lightly buttered wheat toast. Blue rolled her eyes and waited for their rightful waiter to approach the table before giving her order.

"Okay, so spill it. What's up? There's only one reason why you would have called and invited me to breakfast. Besides showing up at your house the other day, I haven't seen you in months." Jean shuffled in her seat and sat proud. "You've decided to listen to my advice from the other day, huh?"

"Actually, yes! You were right. Things aren't going so well with Jay and me. I want to be certain that I protect my interests like you said." Blue fed her mother's ego. "I need to transfer some funds, and I need your help."

A brilliant smile eased across Jean's face as she shimmied in her seat. "Of course I'll help."

Jean's excitement concerned Blue, but she understood where it came from. Winning was personal for Jean, and Blue's request for her assistance was win number one. Helping to keep Jay's hands off of her daughter's money would be win number two. Right now, Jay represented all the men who had done Jean wrong or tried to get their greedy hands on her money, including Blue's father. Jean was Blue's ace in the hole, but she still couldn't reveal the truth about everything that had happened.

After breakfast, they headed to the banks and transferred Blue's investment accounts into Jean's name. Now that the money was safe, Blue wondered what her mother's assistance would cost her.

CHAPTER 19

Mia

Mia swung a hard right off of Linden Boulevard, sped through three stop signs, made a quick left, and pulled up in front of her childhood home in St. Albans, Queens. She questioned whether or not she should actually get out of the car. The only reason she'd decided to stop by was because Myra knew she was in town. After her mother's call, it was obvious Mrs. Reynolds knew, also.

Myra's late model Altima was in the driveway. Wishful thinking made Mia hope her sister wasn't inside. A few familiar faces walked past, and Mia wondered if anyone noticed her. The cheap Dodge rental wouldn't give her away because it wasn't a car she would be expected to drive. She watched more people pass by as she pondered her reservations about going inside. Plus, Myra's car was still in the driveway.

The urgent tapping on the driver's side window startled Mia. She looked up and scowled when she saw Myra standing outside the car with her arms folded. Mia sucked her teeth, paused, and then eased down the window.

"You coming inside or what? Everyone is waiting," Myra demanded.

Before Mia could conjure up an indignant answer, Myra had already headed up the walkway. The front door was open, and their tightfisted stepfather was standing in the opening in his old transit uniform, decked out with a cheerful smile. That man hadn't worked on Saturday in years, but his cheap ass wore uniforms seven days a week to keep from spending money on clothes. It was evident that much hadn't changed around the Reynolds' household. Mia braced for the visit and lugged herself out of the car.

"Hey, baby girl! It's good to see you," Clarence said, grabbing Mia into his arms. Mia didn't return his enthusiasm. "Your mother's been in here cooking all day just for you. Got all your favorite foods. Should have seen the grocery bill. I thought your mama lost her mind," he said, chuckling. "But she's a good cook, so I can't complain." He laughed from somewhere deep in his belly.

Stepping into her mother's home was like falling into a neatly packaged 1980s time warp. Every wall was painted dull beige, with heavy oak furniture taking up too much space in each room—a complete contrast to the crisp, feminine, but contemporary, palette in Mia's place.

Mia forced a smile as Clarence took her by the hand and led the way to the kitchen.

"She's here, baby," he said, presenting Mia to her mother.

A cozy smile enveloped Eve Reynolds' face. She put down the dishtowel and held her arms out for her daughter. Mia stepped into her mother's loving embrace. Eve pulled back and held Mia at arm's distance, examining her daughter before pulling her in for a second hug.

"Looking good, girl," Eve said, smiling her approval.

As Eve looked her over, Mia almost felt exposed, hoping her mother-sense didn't pick up on the fact that she was pregnant. She wanted to save that bit of information for another time.

"A little skinny for my taste, but still looking good," Eve continued. "I like your haircut. I've been seeing that look around the city lately." Eve stopped and smiled. "You've always been on top of the trends ever since you were a little girl." Eve's hand guided Mia towards a seat in the small eat-in kitchen. "Sit down and talk to me some. I wish your brother could be here to see you. Have you seen Myra?" she asked before turning her attention to the soulful cuisine cooking on the stove.

Mia discreetly rolled her eyes at the mention of Myra's name.

"Yes, when I pulled up. I don't know where she went," Mia said.

"Well, I hope she plans on staying for dinner. I made some of your favorites, like turnips and dumplings, macaroni and cheese, honey BBQ chicken, cornbread, and for dessert, Dad ran over to Junior's and picked up a cheesecake. You can't get that in Atlanta." Eve puffed her chest and smiled. "I didn't put pork in the greens because I know you don't eat it anymore."

Mia's mouth watered from the flavorful medley of aromas wafting throughout the home and the litany of goodies her mother named. It had been a long time since she'd had her mother's home cooking. Mia would come home more often if she weren't so disgusted by her mother's submissiveness to her paltry husband.

Eve was full of life and she still had a nice figure. Those high cheekbones and straight black hair made her beautiful. Mia felt she could have had so much more out of life, but had settled for a meager existence with Clarence. Mia didn't know what Clarence had over her mother, but it was sickening.

Myra bore down on Mia's private thoughts with the heavy tension she carried into the room.

"Ma, it smells so good in this kitchen. All this for her?" Myra asked, referencing Mia with a flip of her head. "I'm here all the time, and I don't get all my favorites," she teased, then gave her mother a kiss on the cheek.

"Where's Kenny?" Mia asked about her baby brother.

"He's away this weekend with his new girlfriend," Myra answered without looking directly at Mia.

"Oh," Mia said.

"Well, dinner is ready. Let's get the table together so we can all eat," Eve directed.

Getting up, Mia helped Myra set the table in the adjoining dining area. She grimaced in response to Myra's demeaning gaze.

Mia stopped placing the plates and commanded of Myra, "What?" She whispered hard, trying to keep their mother from overhearing the impending fight.

Myra followed Mia's lead, matching her hard whisper. "You know what! How could you? Blue is your best friend!" Myra shook her head. "I can't believe you."

"We aren't friends anymore," Mia said, flipping her hand dismissively.

"So that gives you the right to screw her husband? Nothing, and I mean nothing, justifies that." Myra tossed her hands in the air. "I can't believe you," she repeated.

"Mind your business!" Mia said somewhat loud and then pulled her voice in. She looked around before continuing. "You don't know the entire story, so don't judge me." She paused, placing her hands on her hips. "And since when did you work as a security guard for the W anyway?"

"For your information, I'm the head of security, and as far as you and Jay are concerned, I know all I need to know after seeing the two of you practically screwing." Myra recoiled as if remembering the sight made her nauseous. "I don't care what happens between friends. Boyfriends, husbands, and ex-husbands," she said, counting on her fingers, "are always off limits." Myra then narrowed her eyes at Mia. "You have always been selfish and ungrateful!"

Mia put her hands on her hip, cocked her head to the side, and glared back at Myra.

"What are you trying to say, Myra? You're no role model for the sweet and innocent. I know some of the things you've done, too."

"I never said I was innocent, but I've never slept with my best friend's husband either." Myra stepped to Mia, her eyes brandishing her suspicions. "Are you getting money from him, too?"

"I take damn good care of myself," Mia said, raising the volume on their conversation. "I've never asked you, Ma, or that cheap-ass Clarence for anything."

Myra's mouth fell agape. Mia took a step back as Myra closed in on her.

"That's your problem," Myra said, lowering back to a whisper. She huffed. "Talk about taking care of yourself. Tell me this, when is the last time you worked?"

"That's none of your damn business!" Mia screamed, stepping all the way into Myra's space.

Myra didn't back down. "Oh yeah?" she screamed back. "It will be when your gold-digging ass gets into a situation that you can't finagle your way out of. Who are you going to call then, huh? Me! Just like the other times. And where do you think the money comes from?" Myra stopped like she was waiting for Mia to answer. "Cheap-ass Clarence!"

Clarence and Eve rushed into the dining room with puzzled

faces. Clarence's expression fell with the mention of him being cheap. He and Eve exchanged questionable looks.

"What the hell is going on in here? What are you two fussing about, and what the hell is this talk about Clarence being cheap?" Eve asked.

Mia grunted. "I'm leaving, Ma. Thanks for dinner," she said and started to walk off.

Eve hopped over to Mia and grabbed her arm. "What? You just got here. What's this all about?" Eve inquired, looking back and forth between Mia and Myra.

"Ask your daughter!" Myra snapped. "You know what, Mia? You don't have to leave. I will. Besides, I get to see a lot more of Mom and *Dad* than you do," Myra said, then stomped out, slamming the door behind her.

Clarence and Eve watched Myra's exit and then looked back at Mia.

"Ma, I'm sorry," Mia said with both hands in the air. "I've got to go. I'll call you when I get back to Atlanta."

Mia gave both her parents a quick kiss on the cheek and walked out, leaving them baffled. Eve called after her several times, but Mia just walked faster.

By the time Mia got behind the steering wheel, she was winded. She jammed the keys into the ignition, slapped the car into drive, and sped off. The car jerked forward, then caught the gear. After a few blocks, Mia pulled over and caught her breath.

Her mother didn't deserve that treatment, but she couldn't spend another minute stifled in that environment. Myra's words penetrated, pissing her off. She knew sleeping with Jay was wrong, but now that Blue had written her off as a friend and evicted her from their house, there was nothing left to lose. She was free to be with him if she wanted. Besides, he was going to be the father of her child. The more she thought about it, the more comfortable she became with the idea. All she had to do was help him sustain regular funds. Then they would be perfect together.

CHAPTER 20

Blue

Jay was waiting in the lobby when Blue arrived home from work. She quickly spun around to make a hasty exit, but it was too late. Jay was on her heels, calling her name, by the time she made it to the door.

Blue felt Jay at her back but refused to turn around. She closed her eyes and took a deep breath, hoping his presence was a figment of her imagination.

"Hey, babe. Can we talk?" Jay asked, gently touching her shoulder. "It won't take long," he continued, talking to her back.

Blue turned slowly and walked towards the elevator, replaying the way Jay said 'babe' over and over in her head. The soft cadence took Blue back to the way things used to be. Back then, those words had soothed her spirit. Now the expression grated at her nerves. She wanted to slap him for his audacity.

"I'm not your babe," Blue said, but kept walking. She smiled at Tony, the doorman, who returned a look that said, *Call me if you need me.* With a wink and a smile, Blue acknowledged her compliance as she stepped into the elevator with Jay still on her heels. The last thing she wanted was a scene in the lobby of her building, so she quickly relented and allowed Jay to come up.

Neither of them spoke during the ride up to the home they'd once shared. Blue walked into the apartment, stepped out of her shoes, dropped her bag on the console near the entrance, and motioned for Jay to have a seat in the living room. Words still had not been exchanged.

Jay sat quietly while looking around the apartment. Blue excused herself before he could begin. His belongings were still on the floor in the guestroom. Blue closed the door, then returned to the living room and sat down on the opposite side.

After a long breath, Blue asked, "What do you want?"

"Us," Jay said. "I want us back. I'll admit I messed up, but we can get past this. It isn't like you don't know the lifestyle of athletes, and you've never seemed to be concerned about other women before. Let's go back to what we were."

Blue cut her eyes before staring up at the ceiling. She then stood to her feet and crossed her arms in front of her. With the anger and energy that suddenly began coursing through her body, sitting made her feel like she would explode.

"First of all, there is no 'us'!" Blue glared as she spoke, waving her finger back and forth. "Second, I can't believe…no, I do believe your nerve, because you've always thought everyone was supposed to overlook your offenses. Well, like your former coach..." Blue paused for effect when she noticed the disapproval in Jay's eyes at the mention of his coach. "I'm done with you. Never again will there be an 'us'."

Jay stood and began pacing, then walked to the massive windows overlooking Manhattan's East Side.

"Do you still love me?" he asked, looking over the city.

Blue didn't know if she wanted to cry or push him through the massive windows he was peering through.

"This conversation is over," she said, throwing her hands up. "How about you see yourself out?" Blue turned to walk off towards the kitchen.

"Do you still love me?" Jay asked again. His tone was stoic and purposeful.

"Why?" Blue asked, rubbing her temples.

"I need to know. I need to know if there is still a chance for us."

Blue raised a brow and stared at him in disbelief. Suddenly, conflicting feelings flooded her. The part that still loved Jay wanted to reach out and touch him. The angry part wanted to slap him hard and relish in the after sting. The part harboring the pain simply wanted to know why. None of these parts would have their say because she kept quiet.

Jay went to her. "Babe," he said, taking her hands in his, "I still love you, too." Obviously, he took her silence for granted. "I don't know what happened to me that night. I never meant to cause you any pain. I was wrong, and I'm sorry. I just need for you to tell me if you can find it in your heart to forgive me."

As tears fell reluctantly, Blue became angrier for letting Jay get inside her emotions. He apparently took the tears and her silence as a license to continue.

"I can make this up to you. I know I can," he almost pleaded before attempting to embrace her.

Blue pushed him back with all the force she could conjure up in both hands. Jay stumbled back, then looked at her in disbelief.

"Did you forget the fact that you fucked my best friend and got her pregnant?" Blue's voice elevated with each word. The curse fell out with unusual ease. She felt her breathing become ragged.

Jay shrugged her off. "I don't even think the baby is mine. You know how Mia is. She's *your* friend."

"Get the hell out of my house!" Blue screamed.

Jay looked away for a moment, and Blue started pushing him in the direction of the door.

"Blue!" Jay kept calling her name, but she wouldn't respond. "Babe!"

Blue stopped. "I told you to stop calling me that. Now get the hell out of my house," she squeezed through tight teeth.

Jay turned and walked the rest of the way to the door on his own. He turned back to Blue and cast a calculating gaze.

"Fine. If this is how you want it, then I want the townhouse in Atlanta. You can keep this shit here. And I want every dime I'm entitled to as your husband."

Instead of leaving, he walked back to her, closing in so tightly she could feel his breath on her face.

"You know how I am when I don't get what I want. Trust me, you don't want this fight!" Jay threatened as he backed away with a snide leer. He turned and quickened his pace, then slammed the door shut as he left.

Blue watched him leave, feeling the nip from his brisk emotional shift. She quickly shook off the uncomfortable feeling and allowed her anger to spearhead her thoughts. She was ready for him and was almost happy he'd already begun to underestimate her.

CHAPTER 21

Gavin

Jay stormed into the penthouse and walked straight to the guestroom without acknowledging Gavin's presence. Obscenities littered the air as he stomped around ranting about his encounter with Blue.

Gavin decided to give Jay a few minutes to vent until he heard things hitting the walls. That's when he flung the remote on the couch and darted toward the room Jay temporarily occupied.

"What's going on, man?" Gavin asked, swinging the bedroom door open.

Inside the room, Jay was washed down in frustration, pacing and taking aimless shots at the air. Gavin took a chance and stepped into the room. At first, Jay didn't notice he was there.

"Jay...Jay!" Gavin had to call his name louder the second time.

Jay stopped. He turned to Gavin heaving.

"What's wrong with you, man?"

Jay shook his head and continued pacing.

"People live under me," Gavin said, bringing attention to Jay's thunderous stomping. "What's wrong with you?" he asked again.

"I just came from my apartment." Jay stood still again and put his hand on his hip.

"And?" Gavin asked.

"Blue said there's no chance of us getting back together." Jay started pacing again, looked at Gavin's face, and stopped. "If it wasn't for Mia, I know she would take me back. What the hell am I supposed to do now? I have no job—no money!" Jay grunted hard.

Gavin raised his brows, wondering if Jay really understood the extent of his actions. Then his eyebrows creased in question.

"What does Mia have to do with this?"

Jay sighed. "She's pregnant," he said and dropped his head.

"So what does that have to do with…no…don't tell me." Realization hit Gavin like a medicine ball to the abdomen, and his eyes grew wide. "Don't tell me it's yours!"

Jay turned away from Gavin's astounded gaze. "Possibly." He waved Gavin off.

"What don't you understand?" Gavin asked.

"I guess it's over then." Jay threw his hands up.

"Yes! Accept it."

Just then, Gavin's phone rang; it was Blue. Leaving Jay to himself, Gavin walked into his bedroom and answered.

"Hey, what's up? Are you all right?"

"No," Blue said, her voice soggy. "That bastard just left here!"

"I know," Gavin said.

Blue sucked her teeth and sniffled. "I'm sorry about standing you up the other day for lunch. I just wasn't feeling up to it."

"No need to explain. I understand," he told her.

"You are the only person I can talk to."

"I know…." Gavin almost said her name aloud.

After a long pause, Blue asked, "Can I come over?"

Gavin looked toward Jay's room. "I was on my way out. I'll stop by there. Is that okay?"

"That's fine. Thank you," Blue replied.

Gavin looked in on Jay, who was still seated on the edge of the bed with his head buried in his hands.

"I'll see you in a minute," he said to Blue and hung up.

Gavin walked back to the room and asked Jay, "When are you leaving?"

"Soon," Jay responded, then got up and closed the door blocking the space between them.

Gavin pushed the door back open. Normally, he would have cared about the fact that Jay was upset, but Jay's behavior lately had made him extremely difficult to deal with. The only thing Gavin cared about right now was getting Jay out of his life for good.

Jay also had a tendency to destroy things when angry. Gavin had no intentions of leaving him in the house alone while he went to check on Blue. Wherever Jay had been for the past few days, Gavin figured he could go back there.

When Gavin reopened the door, Jay glared at him. Gavin wasn't moved by his fury and pushed the door open more to show him. Jay huffed.

"What!" Jay said, throwing his hands up. "Can't a man get a minute to himself?"

"I need you to find a place to go for the night," Gavin said, ignoring Jay's comment.

"Are you kidding? Can't you take that chick out instead of bringing her here?" Jay looked at Gavin in disbelief and then shook his head.

"I'm going to act like you didn't say that! I don't know where you've been for the past few days, but perhaps you can chill there for just one more night."

Gavin wouldn't confirm or deny whether he was asking Jay to leave because of a date. He just wanted Jay out, and the reason behind it wasn't any of his business.

Jay stared at him for a few seconds longer before relenting. "Damn! Just give me a few minutes," he said, then began stuffing more clothes into the bag he had just emptied on the bed.

Gavin closed the door, finally giving Jay his privacy, and went to handle his next order of business. He dialed Lisa, who picked up right away.

"Hey there!" Lisa purred into the phone.

"Are you going to be ready for me later this evening?" he asked.

"Hmmm. I'm ready for you now!" she said.

Gavin could hear the sultry coating in her voice.

"That sounds good to me. I'll come straight to you when I get back from Queens," he replied.

"Queens?" Lisa said, surprised.

"Yeah. I need to take something to my dad. I won't be long. Just be ready for me, okay?" Gavin lied, buying himself time to meet up with Blue first.

CHAPTER 22

Mia

Mia stuffed three more saltine crackers into her mouth and pushed the dry clump down with bottled water. Another wave of dizziness washed over her as she lifted herself from the bed. The light of day had begun to give way to the amber glow of the evening sun. Mia couldn't believe she'd spent the entire day lying around battling nausea. After a deep breath, she trudged about slowly to prepare for a night out with Princeton Manning. After three cancellations, she had to make tonight work, nauseous or not. It was only fair since it was Princeton's money that paid for her new place. She could have paid for the condo on her own, but why spend her money when she could spend someone else's instead?

Mia stepped over the unpacked boxes she'd been meaning to go through the past few days. The room looked like a Lego City made of cardboard. Boxes were stacked two and three high, leaning against sterile beige walls. The only visible part of the floor was a narrow path that led from the bed to the bath. The master bedroom in Blue's townhouse was much larger, and Mia longed for the extra space. Sliding boxes out of her way with the side of her leg, she created a new path to the colossal walk-in closet and thumbed through her clothes, the only items she'd taken the time to unpack.

When Mia finally made it to the shower, she stood motionless, allowing the hot stream to knead away the kinks she'd acquired from lying around all day. She held her belly. At nearly five months, she still only had a small pouch. She caressed her belly and wondered if she was really ready for motherhood.

"Snap out of it, girl," Mia said to herself as she dried her body and dressed with a sense of determination.

The doorbell rang just as she zipped the side of her dress. Finally feeling refreshed, Mia dabbed on a light scent of fragrance and headed for the door.

Princeton's eyes roamed her body from head to toe. He licked his lips.

"Spin around," he said, leading her with his hand.

Mia obliged. Her chest was swollen with pride as she spun like a ballerina on the tips of her stilettos. The ivory strapless number effectively hid her stomach and caressed her curves in all the right places, but her usual high heels were getting to be too much for her. Lately— with resistance—she'd began opting for lower ones.

"Damn!" Princeton approved, wetting his lips again before sliding them into a lustful lopsided smile.

"Is that all you can say?" Mia teased. Princeton simply arched his brows and Mia laughed. "Have a seat. I'll be back down in a minute. I need to add my finishing touches."

"You look fine to me." Princeton leaned in to kiss Mia, but she pulled back.

"Not yet," she said, placing her index finger against his mouth. "You don't look half bad yourself," she added, taking note of his tailor-made suit.

"Hurry up. I can't wait to get you out tonight. You look fine as hell. Plus, I have some things I want to talk to you about," Princeton said.

***

The pair dined at an upscale steakhouse in the heart of downtown Atlanta. Mia was surprised to find a fancy restaurant she hadn't known about and wondered how Princeton knew of the place. The mature, distinguished-looking waiters kept the daily specials and the orders in their heads. Prices weren't listed on the menus. Mia was both impressed and disappointed because she couldn't confirm whether or not she ordered the most expensive thing. It took a slight measure of enjoyment out of spending Princeton's money. She finally decided on the lobster and filet mignon combination, assuming it would be one of the most expensive dishes on the menu. She seductively whispered her drink request into the waiter's ear, giving the impression she was asking for an interesting cocktail, when she was actually ordering a cranberry and orange juice, with a hint of tonic and topped with a slice of lime. She winked at Princeton when she was done, and the glow of anticipation made his eyes sparkle like moonlight.

After placing their orders, Princeton took Mia by both hands and looked into her eyes. He smiled and she smiled back, hoping he wasn't going to tell her that he was in love. She sure didn't love him.

"I want to take care of you," Princeton said without breaking his gaze.

"Oh, that's sweet! But I think you know I can take care of myself."

Mia liked the sound of what Princeton was saying. It always meant perks—more money, gifts, and surprises. She would have to enjoy it while she could, because once the wives got wind of the excessive spending, the cash flow always came to a screeching halt.

"Of course, you can. You've got spunk. More than I've seen in a long time. That's why I'm so attracted to you," Princeton said, rubbing his thumbs across the back of her hands.

"Oh…well, thanks," she said, letting her vanity show.

"How do you like the new place?" he asked.

Mia's smug smile fell away. She pulled her hand back and fingered the rim of her juice mix the waiter had just set on the table.

"It's fine," she said and took a sip. She'd already thanked him in several ways and wondered why he had to keep asking.

"Good. I knew you'd like it," he said.

Mia snickered. His arrogance matched hers. Most of her suitors had monstrous egos, but Princeton's was especially colossal. His record-breaking, million-dollar plus contract probably had a lot to do with it.

"I can make life really good for you," he continued.

"Oh yeah?" Mia said sarcastically, then raised a brow and took another sip.

"I want to set you up. I'll give you a few days to think about it, but here's what I propose." Princeton paused. "The place will be yours. I'll pay for it outright if you like it enough and put your name on it. Whatever you need, I can provide—money, cars, clothes, anything. But, there are conditions." Princeton raised a brow along with his snifter and sipped his cognac.

Mia sat back in her chair fighting the urge to suck her teeth. "What are these conditions?" she asked, straightening her back.

"Make yourself available to me whenever I'm in town." Princeton smiled. "No male visitors in the house, especially athletes. In fact, I don't want you dating any athletes at all."

Mia's brows knit closely. His offer sounded like all the others, even the proposed ban on dating other athletes. They all wanted to believe they were the only ones. She continued to half listen to the rest of the demands that she didn't plan to honor. It wasn't until he made his last statement that he seized her attention.

"And most of all, no babies. I don't do children," he said, shaking his head adamantly.

Mia emptied her glass.

CHAPTER 23

Blue

"Thanks for coming by. I promise I won't bother you much more," Blue said as she opened the door for Gavin. Following his eyes, Blue nudged him in. "Pay no mind to the place. It's not as tidy as it usually is. I haven't been around enough to let the housekeeper in," she ended with a chuckle.

"No, that's not it. It just seems different in here. Feels empty." Gavin shrugged.

"Oh. All of Jay's stuff is gone or packed up in the guestroom." She gestured for Gavin to sit. "Want a drink?"

"Yeah! So what's up?" he asked to her back as she walked toward the open kitchen to retrieve two glasses.

Blue filled two snifters halfway with Louis Royer X.O. and handed one to Gavin. He sniffed the expensive cognac and held his eyes closed for a moment, savoring the fine aroma. Blue plopped down beside him, purposefully breaking his concentration, and took a big gulp.

"Hey, take it easy. You're supposed to sip this nice and easy," he said.

Blue rolled her eyes at Gavin playfully.

"You're lucky I didn't pour this down the sink. It's Jay's favorite." She took another big gulp and set the glass down, meeting the table with a loud clank. She flinched, sinking her head into her shoulders, and then lifted her glass slightly to make sure nothing had cracked.

Gavin shook his head, took a sophisticated sip, and placed his glass on the table before turning to Blue.

"Are you okay now?" he asked.

"Somewhat," she said quietly.

Blue looked around the room. She wanted to control her emotions, but still hadn't mastered them. Blue lifted her face to the ceiling and tried to blink away tears. Resigning on her will, she dropped her head and let them fall.

"What makes him think we can work this out?" She brought the glass back to her lips, held it there for a moment, then sat it back down more cautiously than the time before. "There's been too much damage." Blue picked up the glass again, wiped her tears with the back of her hand, and sipped. "It still hurts, but now I'm angrier. I want to make them pay."

"Blue…" Gavin's tone carried pity. "Don't worry about getting them back. That's not your style. Just focus on moving on."

"Please," Blue snorted. "Both of them deserve a little payback. They've earned it."

Gavin squeezed her shoulder. Blue felt like she was sinking. She grew tired of dancing with her tangled emotions. Finally, her vulnerability lost ground to her fury. Gavin was the only person who had witnessed her raw. In his presence, she felt free enough to give in to whatever emotion took precedence at the time. Gavin held her closer as she cried in his arms. She wasn't crying wounded tears. These stung with frustration.

"You know what?" she asked, while wiping her wet face and looking up at Gavin. "I keep asking myself, what did I do wrong?"

"You didn't do anything wrong. Stop trying to take the blame," he said.

"I know that now, which is why I'm so mad. I didn't bring this on myself."

Blue gulped down her last sip of cognac and poured another glass. Each burn from the amber liquid sliding down her throat made her burden feel a little lighter. She sat back and smiled.

"That's why I need to do things differently. I want both of them to think twice before they mess over someone else like this." Blue chuckled. "You know what he said to me before he walked out today?"

"What?" Gavin asked.

"He wants the house in Atlanta," Blue said dryly. "We haven't even discussed divorce, and he's already dividing up our stuff.' She shook her head. "He had the audacity to tell me that he wants everything he's entitled to as a husband. Then that bastard looked me in the eye and tried to intimidate me." Blue hesitated, going over the words in her head before she said them to Gavin. "He told me, 'You don't want this fight', but I'm ready."

Two more glasses of cognac dulled her senses and emotions, but ignited small sparks in areas that had gone untouched for weeks now. Gavin hadn't said much, and Blue found herself wondering what he was thinking. She turned to study his face. She found him to be undeniably good looking, but he didn't possess Jay's fire.

Even though he was unruly, Jay had always been popular. Being attractive got him lots of attention, and his edge made him desirable. Gavin was the sidekick. Despite his good looks, Jay had always overshadowed him.

Lightly touching his chin with her forefinger, Blue turned Gavin's face toward hers and studied him, taking notice of his creamy brown complexion, the slight angling of his eyes, and the keenness of his nose, the sharpness of the lines framing his hairline, his neatly carved mustache, and the fullness of his lips. She ignored his inquisitive brows and continued her examination in silence. Why hadn't she noticed him first?

Despite his good looks and professional success, no woman had been able to pin him down. The mystery intrigued her.

Gavin held her gaze as she continued to take him in. At first, Blue had wanted to sleep with Gavin to upset Jay, but now she felt something stronger and wondered if sleeping with him to get back at Jay would be enough. She knew it would make Jay mad simply because of his ferocious possessiveness. Whether they were together or not, he wouldn't want anyone else to have her—especially his best friend.

Blue leaned forward and kissed Gavin's lips softly. When she pulled back, his eyes were closed. She leaned in again and parted his lips with her tongue. At first, Gavin showed no resistance, but then he suddenly pulled away. Refusing to let him go, Blue held him by the back of his head until he relented. Passion found its way into their embrace, causing both his tension and reservations to diminish enough to continue their kiss. Time passed before they finished off their zealous exchange with a light peck. In all the years she had been with Jay, he had never kissed her with the kind of passion she just felt with Gavin.

Blue opened her eyes and found his closed. She wanted to experience that passion again, but resisted the urge. It was foreign to her, and she wanted to make sure it was real. Gavin finally opened his eyes and just stared at her.

"I'm sorry," she said, just to pacify him.

Gavin put his finger to her lips. "Don't apologize. I've always wanted to do that."

His admission caught Blue by surprise.

"I've got to go," Gavin said, but failed to move.

"Don't!" Blue wished she could have hid the desperation in her voice. Her intentions weren't completely pure, but the unadulterated lust she felt set fire to her core.

Gavin lifted himself from the couch and lugged his legs toward the door as if they were made of lead. Blue could tell he didn't want to go. She felt like her insides were swaying in a billowy blaze. She didn't want him to leave either, but wasn't sure if she was ready to lure him into her folds. She had specific plans for him when the time was right. Yet, she needed to douse the fire they'd just sparked. His kiss lingered on her lips. She touched the spot with her finger as she watched him trudge to the door.

He put his hands on the knob and looked back at Blue. She swallowed hard, locked into his gaze. She couldn't tame her desires, but she was willing to let him go if he could. She really wanted it to be right. And she wanted him now.

I'll let you make this decision.

Gavin loitered at the door until it appeared he was able to contain his will. In one swift movement, he opened and walked through the door like he was throwing himself out. When the door slammed, Blue realized she hadn't been breathing.

CHAPTER 24

Mia

Once again, Mia stood before her mirrored closet doors examining her body and rubbing her belly. Princeton's offer was attractive, but what was she to do about her pregnancy? Men like him came a dime a dozen, and she wasn't ready to pawn off her unborn child for a nice set up. How long would it be before she got tired of dealing with him and his rigid rules? This baby would help her live comfortably for years to come with or without a nice set up.

"I guess I've made my decision," Mia said to her reflection, then turned to the side. She tried to imagine what she would eventually look like once her stomach grew much larger.

"Hey, beautiful," Princeton called from downstairs.

Mia quickly dropped her tank top and stepped away from the mirror. She plundered through her drawers for a loose-fitting t-shirt. She was annoyed by the fact that Princeton had a copy of the keys to the house. The thought of him coming to town and walking through her doors anytime he pleased helped to confirm her decision.

"What's up?" she called down to him.

"Come here! I have something for you," he shouted up the stairs.

The sweet aroma of cane syrup and waffles greeted her as she descended. Her mouth watered, and her stomach lurched in anticipation. Mia had recently developed an appreciative relationship with food. Putting a little pep in her step, she carefully trotted down the remaining steps and quickly made her way to the kitchen. The sound of her happy sigh filled the kitchen. Princeton looked up at her and laughed.

"Mmm, it smells so good in here. What did you get?" She forgot about asking him why he was there.

"A little something for my lady," he replied.

Mia's mouth watered. A wide smile spread across her face as she visually feasted on the delectable spread of chicken, waffles, creamy white butter, strawberry compote, and organic orange juice.

"Let me get the plates," she said and headed for the cabinets.

The sight and scents of the food made her put off declining his offer until later. She'd worry about that after she ate.

Princeton patted his lap. Mia sat there, and they ate breakfast together.

"Damn, baby. You can eat as much as me. How do you stay so trim?"

If only he knew. Mia laughed. "I work out," she said with her mouth full.

Princeton laughed, too. Then he stepped behind her and gently squeezed her waist.

"Yes, you do," he said, smiling seductively.

With his large hands, he lifted Mia, sitting her on top of the granite peninsula facing him.

"Um. The food was great, but here's the real treat," Princeton said, rubbing his thumbs across her small breasts.

As her nipples stood at attention in response to Princeton's touch, Mia decided to wait another hour or so to tell him that she was declining his offer. When she felt his tongue circle her petite mounds, she figured she'd just tell him later. Once he started kissing her from her breasts down to the crease between her thighs, she forgot all about declining his offer. Mia moved the leftover food and half empty container of juice out of her way and lay back, savoring the skillful assault.

"Damn, baby. You are amazing. That's why I need you in my life," Princeton told her.

As the offer popped into her mind, she rolled her eyes and then looked at Princeton to make sure he hadn't caught her. All of a sudden, Princeton jumped off of the counter and yanked at his sweats. Mia slid off the counter and side-stepped to get out of his way.

"I'm sorry, beautiful. Didn't mean to startle you. I've got something else for you, and I want to get it right now," he said.

Princeton quickly disappeared. When he returned, he had a huge grin on his face and one hand behind his back. Mia wondered what he was hiding and hoped it was her spare key so he couldn't walk in on her anymore.

"What's that?" she asked, not interested in playing games.

"You have to wait. Now let's talk," he responded, sitting on the kitchen stool. With one hand, he lifted Mia back on top of the counter in front of him. "You know I want to take care of you. It's been a few days since I made my proposal, but I wanted to get you a little something to help you decide."

The gifts were always nice, but Mia needed to tell him that she wasn't willing. The time had finally come.

"Prince—" she started.

He covered her mouth with his large hand, interrupting her protest.

"Wait. Don't feel pressured. I just want to help encourage you to accept my offer," he said.

Princeton placed a small, neatly wrapped box in her hands. She looked up at him surprised.

"Open it," he said as a smile swelled across the lower half of his face. "Come on! Open it!" he chanted.

"Okay," Mia said, stretching out the end of the word.

She took a deep breath and opened the small package. Inside, she found a set of keys to an Aston Martin, and her mouth dropped open. She looked at Princeton, stunned. Her eyes blinked repeatedly. Past suitors had showered her with jewelry, shopping sprees, and money, but none of them came close to matching Princeton's level of generosity.

"Princeton, are you serious?"

"There's something else." He pointed to the box.

Mia pulled a small velvet sachet from the bottom of the box with what appeared to be a card inside. As she peeled the legendary black American Express card from the sachet, her eyes grew wider in amazement. The well-known Centurion Card, more informally known as 'the black card', had her name imprinted across the bottom—not his! She couldn't believe it. Immediately, she thought about all the cash she could pull off of the card and stash away. Princeton had outdone himself. His smile beamed as she looked at him and then to the card and keys.

"I can't believe this," she said, her mouth unhinged by surprise.

"Come on. Let's go for a ride," he suggested and scooped her off of the countertop.

Mia couldn't help but laugh as he carried her to the garage where the shiny silver hunk of luxury machinery was perched, gleaming like the sun.

"Princeton, wait! I'm not dressed," she said, referring to her t-shirt and lounge pants.

"We're just going to cruise around the block. No one will ever notice."

After delicately placing her in the driver's seat, he dashed around to the passenger side and jumped in. Mia was fascinated by the fine leather seats and luxurious interior. She fingered the steering wheel. Suddenly, the car started, but the keys were still in her hand. Mia threw her head back and laughed. Princeton had pressed the automatic start button. Daylight oozed through the garage as the door lifted.

"Take your baby for a ride," Princeton said and bellowed a thick laugh.

Mia put the car in gear and stepped on the gas. The car lurched forward. Mia hit the brakes.

"Easy, baby. Be gentle," Princeton cautioned.

Mia slid her foot off of the brakes and tapped the gas lightly. The car moved easily. She gauged the car's momentum until she found the right balance. Then they cruised around the neighborhood, getting to know the ride.

Mia was on a high as she glided through the streets in her development. Maybe she could wait until the next day to tell him that she couldn't accept his offer. After all, she needed to do some shopping first.

CHAPTER 25

Gavin

The soft touch of Blue's kiss stayed with Gavin for days. Lisa's number flashed across the screen of his cell phone. Again, he ignored the call. Gavin used anything he could think of to avoid her, like work, Jay, travel, and family. His respect for Lisa made him want to be fair. Blue had his heart and mind in a state of flux.

The kiss had also refueled Gavin's desire to close the gap on his friendship with Jay. He had given him enough patience and time. Gavin had wanted Blue from the first day he set eyes on her back in college at St. John's University. When he told Jay that he was planning to ask her out, Jay—being selfish—made a game out of winning her over. Gavin sat back and watched as Jay snatched Blue out of his grasp. That was the last time Gavin had confided in Jay about his feelings for any woman. He wondered if Blue knew the real reason Jay had pursued her.

On the day they wed, Gavin stood next to Jay as his best man, forcing back his feelings for the bride. He'd have to settle for being friends for the rest of his life, knowing he would have been the better man. Gavin was at a crossroads.

You can't fall in love with your friend's vulnerable wife, he thought to himself.

"I'm not in love," he said aloud. He wanted to be convincing.

Focus escaped him all day at work and as he made his way home. As the elevator doors to his penthouse opened, he hoped the house was empty. Jay had worn out his welcome.

Gavin marched towards the guestroom that Jay occupied,

knocked once, and pushed the door open. Jay turned around with fury engrained in the lines of his face. Gavin dismissed his anger and walked further into the room. Wild, red eyes revealed that Jay was high. Gavin looked around the room.

"What's all of this?" he asked, referring to the bundles of money Jay had scattered on the bed.

Jay stopped counting the money in his hand and sat on the bed.

"I had to do what I had to do," Jay responded.

"Did you take every dime you own out of the bank?" Gavin asked with his face twisted in confusion, while Jay just glared at him. "Does Blue know about this?"

The expression on Jay's face answered his question.

"Jay." When he didn't respond, Gavin threw his hands up.

Jay went back to counting his money and stuffing it in a duffle bag.

Gavin walked over to the window that faced the building across the street. People scurried around on the sidewalks like mice. Gavin watched them as he thought of what he had to say next.

"Listen…I can give you 'til the end of the week."

"I'll be out of here tomorrow. I'm leaving New York," Jay said without bothering to look up at Gavin as he spoke.

As happy as Gavin was to hear that Jay was leaving, he wondered where he planned to go.

"Where are you going?" he asked anyway. "Let me guess. Atlanta?"

"Yeah," Jay said dismissively, and finished counting his money.

Gavin stood for a few more minutes. Jay's cell phone was on the dresser near Gavin. The display lit up, catching Gavin's attention. Seconds later, the phone rang and Mia's name came up on the display. Gavin wondered what they had to talk about. As Jay continued counting and stashing away his money, Gavin shook his head and walked out.

"I don't have a choice!" Gavin heard Jay yell from inside the room after he finally decided to pick up the phone.

About a half hour later, Jay emerged with his suitcase in hand, holding tightly to the duffle containing his life savings. Gavin stood up from the couch and stepped over to him.
"You're leaving now?" he asked. "What happened to you leaving tomorrow?"

"Change of plans. Thanks for letting me rest my head here for the past few weeks. I'll get that money back to you."

Without another word, Gavin watched as Jay called the elevator and boarded. They didn't even bother to make eye contact as the doors closed between them. Invisible weights fell from Gavin's shoulders. Then his mind carried him back to the kiss.

CHAPTER 26

Mia

"This is such a beautiful home. It must be so hard to leave it," the real estate agent said. "Will you need me to help you find another home in the area?"

Mia put on a show for the real estate agent, acting like the happily married wife. She had done her homework finding an agent who didn't regularly serve the athletes and celebrities throughout Atlanta.

Mia fell right into character. "No. My husband's job is taking us to the west coast." She looked at Jay and smiled.

Jay returned a half smile, not appearing to be as convincing as Mia. When the agent's back was turned, she widened her eyes at Jay.

"I love the west. Good luck with the move," the agent said, making small talk. "So, we are all done here. You do want to go with our multiple-listing service, correct?"

"Actually, no! I'd like for this listing to remain exclusive," Mia requested. "I don't want any "For Sale" signs outside or anything like that, either. We need for this sale to happen as quickly and quietly as possible. Time is of the essence, and we need to get to the west coast as soon as we can."

"Okay, no problem. Shall I set up an open house? That's one way we can move the process along quickly, especially with an exclusive listing. The more customers we can get in, the faster we can try to get this lovely home sold."

"That would be perfect. When would you suggest we do the open house?"

"We can do it next weekend, if you like."

"Oh, I'll be out of town." Mia pretended to think for a moment, while Jay remained silent. "Actually, you don't need us here, do you?"

"We can show the house without you being present," the agent offered.

"Great. Let's do that. I don't want to hold up the process with all of our traveling back and forth for this move."

"Good choice. And don't worry, I'll take care of everything." The agent smiled. "All I need now is your signature here and here, Mr. and Mrs. Mack," she said, marking on the contract where the signatures were required.

Jay and Mia signed the papers to sell Blue and Jay's Atlanta home. Thanks to an old friend of Jay's, they were able to get their hands on a fake license that placed Mia's face beside Blue's credentials.

CHAPTER 27

Blue

"Oh! Let's go to H&M and look around," Francois said, pulling Blue into the flagship Fifth Avenue store.

Just like any woman, shopping therapy was like a ray of sunshine on a dark and gloomy day, and Blue's gloomy days were adding up to a season of overcast. This particular shopping trip didn't seem to help her feel any better, though. Normally, Blue would talk with Mia while strolling through the stores checking out the latest fashions.

Blue wished she had never answered the phone. She'd spent weeks avoiding her family and trying to keep her prying mother's questions at bay. She'd finally told her cousin Francois that she and Jay were no longer together, but spared her the details leading to the divide. The information prompted Fran to ask thousands of question about what happened, but Blue remained lean on her responses. After that, Fran invited Blue out for a day of shopping to ease her mind.

"Look at this dress, Blue. This would look great on you. This turquoise is amazing. Think about how good you would look in it with your curves. Plus, it would bring out your eyes. Try it on," Fran said, tossing the dress to Blue.

"I don't feel like it."

"Come on, Blue. We've been from store to store and haven't bought anything. You love to shop. Just try the dress on. Maybe it will get you in the shopping mood."

She knew Fran meant well, so she trudged to the fitting room.

"Blue, which one are you in?" Fran yelled as she entered the fitting room area.

"I'm over here," Blue called out.

The next thing Blue knew, Fran was tugging at the door and telling her to open it.

"I've got more stuff for you. These will fit your shape better than mine," Fran said, handing Blue a load of clothes.

"I'm not trying on all of this stuff. We'll be here all afternoon," Blue told her, while shielding her half-naked body with the dress she was about to try on. She looked around Fran to make sure no one else saw her.

"So what! We don't have anything else to do today. Hurry so we can go somewhere and have lunch. I'm starving."

Blue sighed and took hold of the clothes. She had to admit, the selections were right on target. Fran knew what looked good on Blue, even though their styles were miles apart. Fran possessed a more daring style, preferring to mix colors and sport bold looks. Blue's jeans, white button-down shirt, and riding boots looked rather subdued against Fran's textured leggings, long fitted tee, bushy brown boots, and fire-orange leather jacket. Blue kept her bushy coils restrained in ponytails, while Fran allowed her wild coils to hang loose and free.

"Come out and let me see."

Blue emerged wearing the first dress.

"Wow! That looks so good on you. I know you're buying that. Jay will wish he never left," Fran said and laughed loud. "Plus, it's perfect for the fall now that summer's almost over."

Blue looked around, offering a shy smile at the folks who appeared to be startled by Fran's outburst. The mention of Jay's name gave her pause.

"Try on the other stuff. I'm going to be in the room next to you trying on my things. Maybe we should hang out tonight. I've got a friend over at the 21 Club. We could go for a few drinks over there. Get your mind on happier thoughts, like martinis and cute dudes!" Fran's booming laugh filtered through the fitting room. Her mouth ran nonstop.

Feeling genuinely lighter, Blue laughed and willingly tried on the rest of the clothes Fran had picked out. She decided to buy everything.

"You should wear the blue dress tonight. Let's go downtown and find some shoes to wear with it," Fran suggested as she galloped to the register alongside Blue. "Let's hop in a taxi, grab a bite to eat, and then shop for some fabulous footwear."

Fran chuckled. Blue shook her head and laughed with her.

"Ma'am, would you like to use another form of payment?" the clerk asked.

Blue's brows creased. "Why?"

"Because your card was declined," the clerk informed her.

"Declined!" Blue yelled at first, then repeated a little softer.

"Yes, ma'am," the clerk said as if she wasn't buying Blue's astonishment.

Confused, Blue took her check card back and gave the clerk another from a different bank. That card was declined, also.

"Here," Fran said, handing her card to the cashier. "Put it on this one."

Blue stepped back bewildered. She couldn't fathom why her cards declined when she had thousands of dollars in both accounts. She didn't always carry her credit cards around, but kept plenty of money in both accounts to cover her daily and occasional spending.

Fran paid for both of their purchases, and they quickly headed out of the store.

"Wait!" Blue grabbed Fran by the arm. "I have to go to the bank and check my accounts."

"Okay," Fran said, looking concerned. "Maybe it was a computer glitch."

"On both accounts? I don't think so. My banks are right here on Fifth Avenue." Blue looked at her watch. "If we hurry, I can catch them before they close."

Anger rose in Blue like steam as the first bank representative showed her the recent withdraws on their joint account. The second bank revealed the same fate. Jay had cleaned them out, leaving less than one hundred dollars in each one. When Blue examined her statements further, she saw that an airline ticket had also been purchased. She thanked the last representative and stormed out of the bank with fire in her eyes. She wanted to cry, but refused to break down in front of her cousin.

Fran followed fast on her heels. "OMG! Blue, I can't believe that bastard. I can give you something to carry you for a little while," Fran offered.

"I'll be fine. I have money. I just need to get to it," Blue told her.

"That son of a…oh man! I can't believe him," Fran said, stomping her feet.

"I can." Blue's response was simple—calm.

"You still want to finish shopping or grab something to eat?" Fran asked.

"I'll still hang out with you later tonight. I have some cash and credit cards at the house," she told her.

"Good. Well, let's go somewhere and have lunch now. I'm starving. My treat!"

"Obviously," Blue said, and they both laughed.

Even though her appetite was doused by the fact Jay had cleaned out their joint accounts, she still went to the restaurant and enjoyed the time she spent with her cousin before they went their separate ways.

During the taxi ride back to her house, Blue called Gavin to vent.

"Your buddy is at it again. Can you believe he cleaned out both of our accounts?" Blue started speaking the moment Gavin answered. She realized she hadn't given him a chance to say hello. "I'm sorry, Gavin. How are you? Do you have a minute?" she said, laughing at her rambling.

"I'm fine, and yes," Gavin said casually, "I can believe that."

"I should fly down to Atlanta," Blue said.

"Why Atlanta?" Gavin inquired.

Blue shrugged. "Where else would he go? He's either there already or on his way. At least in Atlanta, he would have a place to stay. And I wouldn't be surprised if he were heading to Mia's. He paid for his ticket from our account. I saw the transaction when I was at the bank," she said.

"I wouldn't do that if I were you," he told her.

"I'm going!" Blue huffed and fell silent.

After a few moments, Gavin asked, "Do you need anything? Any money?"

"No, I'll be fine." Then Blue thought out loud, "The fight has begun."

She hung up before Gavin could say another word.

The mailman had just locked the mailboxes when Blue arrived

back at her house. She grabbed her mail on her way up to the apartment. Once inside, she headed to her home office. As she passed by the guestroom, she turned her nose up at the mess she had left in there. What happened to her today was a wake-up call that prompted her to take action. She started with Jay's things in the guestroom. She called The Salvation Army and arranged for them to pick up all the junk in there— although she preferred to burn it like the jilted wife in Terry McMillan's book, *Waiting to Exhale*. Her way was more satisfying and safe, though.

Blue pulled all of their bills from the file drawers, ripping open any notices from creditors on both individual and joint accounts. Jay hadn't changed his address yet, so all of his mail still came to the house. Blue logged on to the computer and arranged for funds from the small investment accounts left in her name to be distributed to her by mail. Pretending to be Jay, she began placing calls to cancel all the accounts with Jay's name attached to them.

On one call, the representative insisted the account holder was a male. Blue pretended to be insulted by her oversight, arguing that Jaylin was a unisex name. When Blue asked to speak with her manager, the rep apologized and relented since Blue was able to provide her with all of Jay's credentials, including PIN and social security number. Since they'd been together, Blue had handled all the bills. She was glad for that arrangement now.

By the time Blue finished, she had closed every account with either his or both of their names on them. She moved the emergency money they kept at home to a shoebox in the back of her closet until she decided where to put it. Now the only money Jay could get his hands on was what he had already taken out of their bank account. Blue wished she could see his face when he tried to use any of his credit cards. The last thing she did was call the property management office and had the locks changed immediately.

Blue was ready for whatever came her way. She knew she would catch Jay off guard by simply staying in the game. This time, Jay wouldn't be playing alone.

CHAPTER 28
Gavin

Gavin opened his eyes and stared into Lisa's face for a few moments, trying to regain his composure. As much as he enjoyed being intimate with her, he couldn't help thinking about Blue. He rolled off of Lisa and stared at the ceiling.

Lisa, who was still reveling in the afterglow of their lovemaking session, moaned and closed her eyes. Gavin watched her tongue slide over her lips as if she could taste the remnants of their lovemaking. She pressed her legs together and squirmed. After attempting to quench her fire numerous times, Gavin was spent, but Lisa looked like she still wanted more. Gavin set his gaze back on the ceiling and thought about how unfair their exchange had been. His motivation was not of pure desire, but a need to release. Lisa had obviously mistaken his feverish lovemaking for pure passion. She could never know he was only able to reach his climax by envisioning himself with Blue instead of her.

Gavin's cell phone rang. Without looking at the display, he knew it was Blue.

Lisa reached towards the phone and blindly fumbled with the buttons to make it stop ringing, as she climbed back on top of him for another round. Ready to protest, the clench of her warm, moist walls on his manhood urged him to hold his tongue.

"My goodness, Gavin. You're amazing. I can't...mmm...get enough of you."

Though he didn't think he had any more to give, Gavin felt himself swell, filling her warm walls. Lisa dipped her hips in a sensual gyrating dance while pulling him in deeper, tugging at him, causing the swell of him to grow larger and broader. As he filled her up, a slow groaning rose from her core.

Lisa began to move faster and bounce harder as she rode him to an urgent peak. This time, she howled as she reached pivotal heights.

Gavin held her waist and moved with her, meeting every thrust with equal force. The warm wetness that slathered over him made him grunt repeatedly. As he closed his eyes and pictured Blue's beautiful body on top of him, his muscles clenched, drawing his body into a rigid ball. He pulled himself away and released, feeling the tension rush from him like a waterfall as he met Lisa at the height of ecstasy. Gavin's groan was staccato until his release was complete. Both of them fell back to their own side of the bed, spent—again. Gavin felt as though his vitality was being sucked from him, absorbing into the sheets. He prayed she was sated, because he didn't have anything left for her.

He got up from the bed and headed to the adjoining master bath. The custom shower was large enough for three people. After turning on the water, he stood in the center letting it hit him from several angles.

He could hear the cell phone ringing from the room. Blue was calling back. He was sure of it. Guilt taunted at him for not answering. He hoped there wasn't any kind of emergency. Lifting his face to the spray of the shower, he let the warm water wash over him, cleansing his body and clearing his thoughts. Blue wouldn't leave him alone, and the frustration returned. As Gavin massaged a masculine-scented body wash into his skin, lingering around his manliness, Blue invaded his thoughts again, and he soothed himself with the images in his mind. Her lips. The sway of her hips. The roundness of her ass.

A pair of hands joined him, massaging him from behind. He pretended the soft breasts pressed against his back belonged to Blue as Lisa's hands continued to rove all over his body.

"Did I tell you that you were unbelievable?"

Gavin turned to face Lisa and allowed his tongue to tease her lips. He hoped his kisses would suffice, because he couldn't drum up any excitement. His maleness hung lifelessly. After they washed one another off, the phone rang again. Gavin felt it once more. Blue needed to speak with him but he didn't want Lisa to grow suspicious. Half dry, he trotted to the room to catch the call.

"Hi. Are you busy?" Blue asked.

"Uh…yeah. I…," Gavin looked to see if Lisa was within listening distance, "…have company."

"Oh. Okay."

He glanced back towards the bathroom one more time. "Is there something you need? Is everything all right?"

"Everything's fine. I was having a moment and needed to talk. Just call me later." Blue hung up.

He held the phone a second before disconnecting the call.

"That was her again, wasn't it?"

Lisa's question startled him since he hadn't realized she'd entered the room.

"She's been calling a lot. I hope everything's okay."

Lisa acted as though she wasn't bothered by Blue's calls, but Gavin could tell she was affected and wanted him to know she noticed all the calls.

"Everything seems to be fine." His answer was short and

indifferent.

Lisa walked around the room fumbling with the clothes they had thrown around before hopping in the bed. Gavin could feel the tension beginning to build.

"She's your best friend's wife, right?" Lisa asked, eyeing him suspiciously.

He felt the sting of her disingenuous tone.

"Yep." Gavin busied himself pulling out a pair of sweats and a tank top.

"Oh."

Minutes passed as both of them dressed in silence. There was an uncomfortable shift in the atmosphere. When Lisa finished dressing, she sat on the edge of the bed, while Gavin continued to stir around the room "tidying up". He needed to move through the tension that had descended on the room like dense black smoke, threatening to constrict his breath.

"Gavin."

Here it comes. He straightened his back and took a deep breath. "What's up?"

"Where are we going with this, with us?" Lisa asked as she sat at the end of the bed toying with the strap of her sandals.

The smoke in the room grew thicker. Gavin felt the thickness in his throat and swore he could now smell the impending fire. He didn't feel like answering her question. He wondered why that question always seemed to come up at the most inappropriate time.

CHAPTER 29

Blue

Large empty spaces where Jay's belongings once adorned the walls and filled corners now seemed to loom over each room. Even his absence was obnoxious.

Blue poured a glass of wine to sip while getting dressed. With no idea where she would go, Blue took a quick shower, then threw on a pair of skinny jeans, an embroidered tank, a leather jacket, and boots. Taking her last gulp of wine, she grabbed her bag and keys before heading for the door. If she had to, she would enjoy her own company.

Lost in her thoughts, Blue paced the hall as she awaited the elevator. When the doors opened, she bumped into her neighbor from a few doors down.

"Oh, I'm so sorry. I wasn't paying attention," Blue said after bumping into him. Still digging in her purse in search of her cell phone, she apologized again. "Sorry."

"Ms. Holiday. No problem at all," he said in that peculiar accent. "It was my pleasure," he teased with a friendly smile. "Going out?"

Blue hesitated, wondering why he would care. "Not exactly."

"Oh, okay. Well, maybe you wouldn't mind joining me for a cup of tea?"

"Now?"

"Yes!"

Blue thought for a moment before she replied, "Okay..." She surprised herself by accepting his invitation.

"Kalisto," he said, finishing her sentence. "My name is Kalisto, remember?"

"Of course, I remember," she lied.

Kalisto pushed the call button for the elevator again and motioned for her to step on when the doors opened. So far, he was the perfect gentleman.

On the ride down, Blue looked him over, sneaking peeks at his olive skin, jet-black hair, and steel gray eyes. She had never spent personal time with a man outside of her race before. Kalisto was striking, almost fake looking. He belonged in Hollywood. Blue knew they would garner attention while they were out.

As they walked two blocks to the nearest coffeehouse, people ogled them as they passed by. Blue could read the curiosity in their expressions. Being the perfect gentleman, Kalisto led the way into the cozy establishment. She settled into one of the comfy chairs near the window while he placed their orders.

Blue smiled and shook her head. What am I doing out with my beautiful neighbor? Blue let her smile fade as Kalisto returned to the table with their orders and took the seat next to her. Conversation came easily, and she entertained the idea of getting to know him better. Kalisto was different for her, but she welcomed the distraction. At least they could be friends.

From her peripheral, Blue noticed a man charge toward the coffeehouse, pushing people out of his way. Initially, she paid him no mind, until he ambushed her table. Jay was huffing, his chest rising and collapsing violently as his breath rushed through his nostrils. His mouth curled upwards.

"What are you doing here with him?" Jay yelled into Blue's face.

Blue noticed the slackness in his bottom lip as he spoke, and then the twitch. The bloodshot eyes revealed that he had been drinking along with snorting coke. Her mind flashed back to that night.

For a moment, Kalisto looked confused, but then took a protective stance in front of her.

"Oh, so you want to step to me," Jay said to Kalisto, spit flying out of his mouth.

"Excuse me?" Kalisto asked calmly.

"Jay, leave this man alone. This is our...*my* neighbor. We were just leaving."

Kalisto looked at Blue. The expression in her eyes said, *I'll explain later.* Kalisto shrugged and began to follow Blue's lead, keeping his place between her and Jay.

"Oh, so now you're screwing the neighbors?" Jay yelled, staring Kalisto down.

"Are you serious, Jay?" Blue stopped there. Arguing with him in his current state would be futile. "Let's get out of here, Kalisto."

"You're just trying to get back at me. You want to make me jealous." Jay jabbed his fingers at Blue as he yelled.

Kalisto held his hands up, blocking Jay from touching Blue as she tried to walk away.

"Calm down, sir," Kalisto said.

"Who are you talking to, man? Get away from my wife!"

"Your wife!" Blue yelled from behind Kalisto's back. "You sent me divorce papers, remember?" Blue shook her head again and said to Kalisto, "Let's go."

"You made me do it. You should have taken me back."

She hastened her steps, trying to make it to the door and away
from Jay. She pitied him, but not enough to underestimate him in his
inebriated state. Glancing back, she stole a quick look to see how close he
was. Kalisto was immediately behind her, but Jay was fast on his heels.
For a fleeting moment, Jay looked like he would break down and cry.

"I'm so sorry about this," Blue said, looking back at Kalisto.

"It's no problem."

Suddenly, Jay reached around Kalisto and grabbed Blue's arm.

"Get off of me!" she screamed.

"The lady said to get off of her," Kalisto said.

When Jay didn't release his hold on Blue's arm, Kalisto pried her
arm from his grasp and puffed himself up to Jay.

Jay narrowed his eyes at Kalisto. "Don't touch me. Don't you
ever touch me!" he yelled, and then he pushed Kalisto with such force it
knocked him into Blue.

She fell to the floor, and both men rushed to her aid. Kalisto
grabbed her hand to pull her up. When Jay reached for her, she slapped
his hand away.

Jay looked at Kalisto with fury etched in his brows. He narrowed
his dark eyes and swung his fist hard. The hit connected with Kalisto's
mouth, which bloodied on contact. Kalisto was stunned by the
unexpected punch. He tapped his lip, and upon seeing blood on his hand,
he drew back and swiftly caught Jay with a right hook. The two men
tussled, knocking over tables and moving chairs under their weight.
Patrons scampered to get out of their way.

Blue tried to separate them without getting hit. By the time she
managed to pull them apart, both men had busted lips and blood was

streaming from Kalisto's nose. He wiped the blood away with the back of his sleeve and then drove a left hook into the side of Jay's head. Jay went crashing into the table and chairs beside him.

Blue gasped, then grabbed Kalisto by the hand and ran out of the coffee shop before Jay could make it back to his feet.

"This isn't over, Blue!" Jay yelled.

She paused, casting her eyes back at Jay as he staggered to his feet. She waited for him to make eye contact as he finally caught his footing. He narrowed his angry eyes into slits and glared at her. If he were this bothered by seeing her with a neighbor, what would he think if he saw her with someone he knew well? Blue smiled at the thought, making sure Jay witnessed her smile, and then trotted to catch up with Kalisto, who was walking ahead while tapping at his new injuries.

CHAPTER 30

Mia

Mia drove through the twirling two-lane streets of Atlanta at top speed. She was running late for her appointment with the Realtor. One of the couples that attended the open house for Blue and Jay's townhouse was really interested in buying the home, but they wanted to see it one more time. Jay had returned to New York, so he wouldn't be able to meet with the agent.

Why did he go back? Mia asked herself again. There was no need for him to return to New York. Blue wasn't interested in him. If he would listen to her, she could coach him and secure the money they both needed to live off of.

Mia pressed her palm into the center of the steering wheel, causing the horn to blare at the inattentive driver in front of her.

"Move it, stupid! The light changed hours ago!"

She could see his head snap up, and then he sped off seconds before the light changed to red again. Mia cursed him again before her mind drifted back to Jay.

Princeton was pressing her for an answer to his offer, while still drowning her in lavish gifts to nudge her to a definitive response. Besides his ridiculous demands for exclusivity, the baby issue, and the hints of possessiveness, the only other thing keeping her from saying yes was Jay. Princeton's offer was attractive, but she wanted her baby. The more she thought about it, she wanted Jay, too. At this point, there was nothing to hide.

Jay was her type of man, full of arrogance and testosterone. With him, she could actually have a real family as opposed to floating from one prospect to the next. She found herself wanting that more now that she was pregnant. Mia blamed it on the hormones.

The real estate agent and a young black couple were standing in front of the townhouse, chatting, when Mia pulled up. She tossed the car into an uneven park.

"Good afternoon. Sorry for my tardiness!" Mia greeted each with a smile. "I hope I didn't have you waiting too long." Mia tried to sound sincere as she quickly surveyed the good-looking man and his wife. She was cute, but no big deal.

Mia wondered what he did for a living for him to even be able to afford Blue and Jay's townhouse in trendy Buckhead. From the look of the Wilma Flintstone-sized rock on the woman's tiny hand, this guy had to make a pretty decent piece of change.

Mia held out her hand to greet them. They all offered their hands and polite smiles, but no one responded verbally. Being more than a half hour late, she could sense the annoyance behind their cordial smiles.

"Here are the keys. You can go ahead and show them around. I need to call my husband, so I'll wait out here," she said, handing the agent the spare set of keys that Jay left with her.

"Are you sure?" the agent asked.

"Sure, no problem at all. You already know the layout."

"Okay," the agent said, smiling as she took the keys from Mia. "Let's go have that second look," she said to the couple.

Mia heard the agent rattling off many of the great amenities the home had to offer. Once they were past the threshold, she dialed Jay's number.

"It's me, Jay."

"Me who?" he responded in a sleepy voice.

"Jay, stop playing games. It's Mia. I'm at the house. That couple came back to look at the house again. I think they're going to make an offer today. You need to come back down here so we can finish this up ASAP. Plus, we need to open the account."

"I don't have any money to come back down there now."

"Jay! What the heck happened to all that money you took out of the bank? Why don't you have any money?"

"I had to handle a few things."

Mia suddenly wanted to toss the cell phone. Her ears grew hot. "Jay…I…" She grunted. "What the hell do you mean you had to handle a few things? How'd you spend all that money?"

"What difference does it make? It wasn't yours."

"Jay, I can't do this alone. You need to be here if these people buy this house. Find a way to get down here." She shook her head.

"Alright, let me see what I can work out. I'll call you back later."

"Come on, Jay. Don't mess this up." She ran her hand through her short crop. "Have you spoken with the lawyer?"

"Where am I going to stay if I come down there? Your place?" He asked in a husky tone.

"Don't change the subject, Jay."

With a smile in his voice, he teased, "You want me there or not?"

Mia smiled herself. "I'm being serious. This is not a joke."

"I wasn't joking."

"Just stay focused and work on getting to Atlanta ASAP. Call me back with your flight details." Mia tapped the end button on her

Blackberry.

Mia joined the others inside the house. When she entered, she found the couple engaged in a low discussion, while the agent appeared to make herself busy.

"This is looking really good, Mrs. Holiday. I have a feeling they will be making an offer today."

"Oh, that's great!" Mia feigned excitement. "My husband and I are really looking forward to moving on. We're expecting our first baby. All of these life changing events are happening all at once," she said, offering an endearing smile to the agent.

"Well, congratulations! That's wonderful news. I wish you all the best. I'll do whatever I can to make this a smooth and speedy process."

As Mia looked toward the couple approaching them in the living room, she felt a slight pang in her gut at the sight of their happy, anxious faces and hand holding.

"What's next?" the husband asked, rubbing the palms of his hands together in anticipation. "We'd like to get started on the paperwork ASAP." His wife set her adoring eyes on him as he spoke. "My wife loves this place, and I just want to see her happy, so I don't have to hear her mouth!" he teased, and his wife playfully slapped his arm.

"*Both* of us love the place," she said, rolling her eyes at him. "When can we come into the office to place the offer?"

The agent looked at Mia and flashed a proud smile. "Can you meet me back at the office this evening? I have another home to show and can meet you there around seven. Does that work for you?"

The couple looked at each other in agreement.

"That works just fine. We'll see you at seven," he said, then shook the agent and Mia's hand. "It was a pleasure meeting you, Mrs. Holiday."

"Pleasure meeting you and your wife, as well. I know you will love the home. My husband and I sure did."

"Great. We will see you later," the gentleman said to the agent, before gently ushering his wife out with a soft touch to her back.

Mia walked out of the home behind everyone and locked the door. Just as she joined the others at the curb, a slowing car caught her attention. Mia turned in time to see Peyton King's eyes shift from the real estate sign on the side of agent's car to the group standing at the curb, before locking eyes with Mia. Peyton narrowed her eyes at Mia, and Mia narrowed her eyes right back. She held her defiant stare until Peyton's car was out of sight.

Once the agent said her final goodbyes and promised to call Mia the moment the offer was on the table, Mia pulled out her cell phone. Jay answered after three rings.

"We might have a problem," she said the second he picked up.

CHAPTER 31

Blue

Blue pushed past Gavin as he greeted her at the elevator door. Appearing startled by Blue's hasty entry, Gavin looked at her with confusion settled in his brows.

"I don't know what's going on, but I promise you I will find out. I need to get to Atlanta ASAP. I just don't want to go alone," Blue spoke in a rush.

Gavin followed her with his eyes, looking as though he was having trouble keeping up.

"Oh my goodness. I'm so sorry," she said.

"Just slow down and start from the beginning. I missed something!" he replied, laughing.

Blue stopped pacing and chuckled, too.

"I'm sorry, Gavin. Let me start again." Blue straightened her back. "Hey, Gavin! What's up? My life is a wreck. How's yours?" she said, then leaned over to give him a kiss on the cheek.

Gavin kissed her cheek in return, hugged her, and stepped back with raised brows. Blue laughed again, acknowledging just how bizarre her entry had been. Running her hand through her hair, she sighed and shook her head while smiling.

"I swear I don't know what to do these days. Every time I turn around it's something new." Blue threw her hands up. "Are you busy? Can we go for a cup of coffee?" she asked, but then thought about running into Jay again. "You know what? Scratch that! Do you have coffee or tea here?"

"Which do you prefer? Coffee or tea?"

Blue looked at her watch. "With all the drama in my life, I'm wound up plenty. I'll take herbal tea. No extra caffeine needed here," she said and walked to the oversized window to take in the view of Central Park.

"Did you eat breakfast yet?" Gavin called out from the kitchen.

"Actually, no. You know what? I can't recall the last time I ate."

"Okay," Gavin said as he returned to the living room. "Sit down and tell me what's up. Then we can go for breakfast."

Blue turned to him, but didn't move. The view was so peaceful she didn't want to leave the window. She closed her eyes and tried to imagine feeling the serenity of that peace fall all over her. She felt Gavin approach behind her.

"It kind of does something to you, doesn't it?"

Blue opened her eyes. "Yes, it does. If I lived here, I wouldn't leave this spot," she said, absorbing the serene sway of the treetops in the cool breeze.

She took a long, deep breath and closed her eyes again as if she were outside taking in the fullness of the air. After opening her eyes, she walked to the couch and sat. Gavin followed closely behind and joined her on the opposite couch.

"You ready for all of this?" she asked.

"Drop it on me."

"Okay! The other day, I was having tea with my neighbor Kalisto, and Jay burst into the coffee shop on a rampage."

"Who is Kalisto?"

"This guy that lives down the hall from us...from me? It's not like we were out on a date or anything." Blue felt a need to explain. "We went to the coffee shop down the block from the building." Blue paused to allow Gavin to confirm.

He didn't respond, but his expression encouraged Blue to continue. She fed him every detail about the fight between Kalisto and Jay.

The kettle screamed just as she finished her story. Gavin got up, and moments later, he quickly returned with the hot water and all the fixings for tea to Blue's liking. She fixed her tea while filling him in on all the other details he'd missed since they last spoke.

"Now here's the kicker. Are you ready for this?" She asked as she sat back on the couch, taking a cautious sip from the steaming cup of tea. "I got a call last night from Peyton King."

Gavin looked confused.

"Exactly," Blue said in response to his bewildered look. "Peyton asked me how much was I selling the house in Atlanta for, and I told her I wasn't selling my house."

"What?" Gavin asked with his brows stretched upwards.

"I need to go down there next week and see for myself. Will you come with me?"

Gavin sat still and chewed his bottom lip.

CHAPTER 32

Gavin

Gavin pulled his black Range Rover Sport into his father's blacktop driveway in Cambria Heights, Queens. The hot smell of rubber rose from the bottom of the car as he exited. According to the calendar, summer had come to an end, but it was apparent the sun hadn't received the memo. The blazing heat had caused the asphalt to soften, and it felt sticky against the bottom of Gavin's shoes even in early evening. Using his key, Gavin let himself into the home he grew up in and whistled two quick piercing blows. His father whistled back in the same fashion. A signal they shared dating back to Gavin's childhood.

Immediately, Gavin felt his mother's absence. Since her death a few years back, her lack of presence shrouded him whenever he entered their home.

"I'm in the den," Mr. Gray yelled.

Gavin looked around and marveled at the cleanliness of the house. He knew his dad to be tidy, but today the place was spotless, making the outdated furniture sparkle with a sense of newness. The usual dimness that beheld the space was gone. Without the shine, the house looked like something out of an eighties sitcom, with worn floral couches, chunky wood furniture, and boring beige walls that were covered with mass produced artwork.

"What's up, old man?" Gavin asked as he entered the room.

His father stood, shook Gavin's hand, and hugged him.

"Who cleaned up for you?"

Mr. Gray looked over at him and smiled. "A friend," was the

only response he offered.

Gavin was an exact replica of his father, tall in stature with smooth, nut-brown skin. Only Mr. Gray's salt and pepper mix gave him a distinguished air.

"I see," Gavin said and let the issue hang in the air. "I haven't seen the place this clean since Mom used to clean up around here."

"I know. I miss that," his father replied without taking his eyes off of the TV.

Both men fell silent for a moment as the evening news reported the latest on the political campaigns and the upcoming election.

Mr. Gray clicked off the TV and turned to his son sitting on the couch. "Let's go sit outside. I've got some beers in the cooler."

Mr. Gray lifted his strong, large frame out of his favorite chair with the built-in cup holder and led the way to the back porch. He popped open two beers and handed one to his son.

"The Jets didn't start off strong, but I think they can make it this year."

"What! Dad, you must be getting old. I'm convinced the Cowboys are going to make a comeback."

"The Cowboys! Boy, you must be crazy. Listen here, let's go ahead and bet on those old, tired boys. I could use your money," Mr. Gray said and chuckled.

"You're funny, Pops." Gavin joined him in laughter.

"So what's going on, son?"

"Besides Jay and Blue?"

"Oh, those two again. What's he done this time? I read about him getting cut from the team. That boy has always been hardheaded. I never understood what Blue saw in him."

"They're getting divorced," Gavin told him.

His father's eyes stretched open, and Gavin gave up a few general details.

"That's a shame," he said, shaking his head.

"I know." Gavin paused, trying to figure out how to get the rest of what he had on his chest out in the open. "Here's my problem," he said and looked at his father, who nodded for him to continue. "Jay and I have finally fallen out since all this stuff started to happen, and Blue…well, she's been coming to me to talk and all because she says she has no one else to talk to. She's too embarrassed to talk about this stuff with her family. They don't even know about half of what's been happening. And…"

"You're falling for her, right?"

Gavin just looked at his father and wondered how he always knew.

"What are you going to do about it?" he asked.

Gavin was looking for answers, not for the ball to be thrown right back at him. He looked for his father to say something like, "Leave that girl alone" or "Don't get caught up."

"What I want to do and what I think I should do are two different things. That's why I'm here."

"What do you want to do?"

"Pop!" Gavin stood up and paced the porch. "This is not helping."

Mr. Gray took another swig of beer and repeated his question.

"What I want to do is save her," Gavin finally said, surprised by his own words.

"So you think she needs to be rescued?"

"I think she deserves sincerity. She needs it right now, and I know I can give it to her. I want to give it to her, but Jay is…was my friend."

"You've always cared about her, haven't you?"

Gavin couldn't believe his father's insight. He started pacing the porch again before sitting back down. Neither of them spoke for minutes.

"Pop, what would you do?"

"I saved your mom from my brother."

CHAPTER 33

Mia

The ringing of the phone woke Mia with a start. The neon blue numbers on the alarm clock read 12:33. She squinted, adjusting her eyes to the darkness in the room before grabbing her cell phone. Princeton was calling. Mia shook Jay and pushed him over on his side to try and silence his obscene snoring. When that didn't work, she jumped out of bed and tipped downstairs, answering the phone as she descended.

"Hello," Mia said, trying to sound extra sleepy.

"Did I wake you?" Princeton asked in his baritone voice.

"Yes. I've got to get out early tomorrow morning. I have a lot of business to take care of. How about I give you a call in the morning?"

"Fortunately, that won't be necessary. I just got off the plane, and I'll be there in fifteen minutes."

Mia's eyes stretched wide and anger burned inside.

"Princeton, I told you I have a lot of things to take care of in the morning. Tonight is not good for me. I really need my rest." Mia held her tongue as she tried suppressing her anger.

"Don't worry, I won't bother you. I'll just join you in bed after I take a shower."

"No!" Mia practically shouted. "I really need to get out of here early. I didn't plan on having any company, so the house is not...this is just not a good time. I'm really tired, and I need to be well rested tomorrow so I can focus. Besides, you didn't tell me you were coming here."

"I figured I would surprise you. Now, come on. Open the door.

I'll be there in ten minutes. I promise I won't disturb you. I'll even sleep on the couch. See you in a few. Okay, babe?"

Mia disconnected the call, raced up to the master bedroom, and swiped the light on.

"Get up! Jay! Get up! You've got to get out of here!" Mia yelled while pulling the covers off him.

She shook him until his eyes opened. Jay stared past her.

"Come on. You've got to get up and get out of here. You've got five minutes." She raced to her bag and pulled out her keys. "Here, take my car. I'll come by your house in the morning. Right now, you've got to go."

Jay watched Mia dash around the room. She sprayed the room with a sweet smelling freshener to mask the scent of sex that clung to the air.

"What are you doing? What's going on?" Jay asked as he swung his legs alongside the bed, rubbing the sleep from his eyes.

"Jay, you have to leave now! Here, put your clothes on." Mia threw his pants and shirt at him. She moved feverishly, tossing Jay's stuff in his bag. She cursed Princeton for this surprise visit. "You've got to get out of here. Princeton will be pulling up any minute, and he can't find you here."

"What? Princeton who?"

"Princeton Manning." Mia stood still waiting for Jay to comment.

"Are you serious? You're messing around with that punk?" Jay chuckled. "Oh, so he must have set you up, too?" Jay sighed and shook his head.

Mia expected the name calling, but she didn't expect the comment about Princeton setting her up.

"What's that supposed to mean?"

"That's how Princeton works. He's got his chicks set up all across the game states so he can have a dedicated piece in each location. If you ask me, he's stupid. Women throw themselves at men for free. Why waste all that money setting one up? He must have come to you with an offer you couldn't refuse," Jay commented, while pulling his shirt and pants on.

"Whatever, Jay. If you know how this works, then just get the hell out!" Mia tossed his bag into the hallway, traipsed into the bathroom, and slammed the door behind her. She felt like crying but fought the urge.

Jay pushed the bathroom door open, stared into Mia's heated eyes, and asked for the car keys. Turning her face away from him, she folded her arms over her breasts as though she just realized she was naked.

"They're on the bed. Just hurry up and leave," she said with her back to him.

From the mirror, Mia watched Jay shake his head before walking out. Tears stung her eyes but didn't fall.

She stayed in the bathroom until she heard the engine rev. That's when she finally came out, climbed in her bed, and pulled the covers up to her neck.

No more than five minutes passed before she heard the dense thud of Princeton's feet as he climbed the carpeted steps. Quickly, she swiped at the tears that were still spilling and pretended to be asleep. She could hear Princeton tip around the room, peel his clothes off, then shower before climbing into the bed behind her. His hand found its way around her bare waist, and he spooned her from behind. Within minutes, the rhythm of Princeton's breathing steadied, and he settled into a light snore, while sleep evaded her as she wrestled with anger and shame.

She would be sure to officially decline Princeton's offer in the morning. Sleep never came, but tears did.

CHAPTER 34

Blue

Shock held Blue impassively at the door of her Atlanta townhouse. Finally, she stepped in but stopped in her tracks, causing Gavin to bump into her back. Her bags fell to the floor with a clunk. Blue could see clear to the kitchen at the back of the house. Gavin's mouth dropped as he twisted his head, taking in a panoramic view of his own. The entire place was empty. Not a single piece of furniture decorated the space nor did a piece of art adorn the walls.

"Where is all of my furniture?" She said, stepping further into the townhouse. "What happened?" she asked and rubbed her temples.

She stood unmoving as her mind raced. She hadn't realized she had begun to cry until salted tears curled around her upper lip and dripped into her open mouth. Her heart felt as though it had plunged into the center of her stomach. She couldn't bring herself to walk inside any further. Gavin placed a supportive hand on the small of her back.

"That bastard!" Blue yelled, and Gavin pulled her sodden face to his chest and held her tight. "I hate him! I swear I hate him!" she screamed into his shirt, punctuating her words by slamming her fists on his shoulders.

Gavin held her firm, spooning her into his frame. He ran his hand over the back of Blue's head. Finally, she pulled from his embrace. He allowed her to pull away, but never let go. She wiped the wetness from her face with both palms and the backs of her hands. He wiped her cheeks with his thumbs.

"Blue."

She held her eyes closed, settling into the warmth of Gavin's tone. His touch and words were just what she needed, but she willed herself to tame her feelings for him.

"Blue," he called again.

"Blue," he said one last time, then lifted her face toward him by her chin. "Don't worry," he told her and gently kissed her forehead.

Slowly, he pulled away. Blue opened her eyes and watched him pick up her bags and take them back to the rental car. He returned for her, taking her by the hand and leading her to the passenger seat. He then locked the house with her keys, and they drove in silence to the hotel where Gavin had booked a room for himself.

Blue set her swollen red eyes toward the window, though she saw nothing on the other side as they rode to the hotel. The landscape was like a collection of smeared watercolor images.

When they arrived at the hotel, Blue sat alone in the car while Gavin checked in and summoned a bellhop to retrieve their bags and take them to their room. Then he appeared at the door, opened it slowly, and held his hand out to Blue. She dropped her head and took his hand, allowing him to pull her to a standing position. As Blue stood, she felt the life drain from her limbs. She remained still for a moment trying to reclaim herself. Then, while leaning on Gavin's strength, they entered the hotel hand-in-hand.

The modest quarters appeared stale in comparison to her formerly swanky townhouse. Blue appreciated the diffidence of the cozy room. After he led her to the couch to sit, Gavin moved about calling up room service, finding a place for their bags, and making phone calls. Blue couldn't even make out his words as he conversed with several different people. Not even the waiter's presence was able to shift Blue's directionless focus. She remained deep in thought until Gavin placed himself before her with a steaming cup of tea.

Blue returned from the depths of her thoughts as she sipped her tea. She sniffed long and hard and wiped the tears with the backs of her hands. She was tired of crying. *This will be the last of my tears,* she told herself. The moment she owned that conviction, she felt an emotional shift, and some of her energy returned to her.

She picked up the phone and called Victor Malloy, the family attorney. It was time to play the game on Jay's level.

After pouring out every finite detail of what she'd gone through over the past few weeks, Blue felt lighter. Other than Gavin, she hadn't shared the details of her recent life with anyone. The next call she made was to her mother. Despite their stressed relationship, Jean Holiday would never approve of anyone messing with her family's money. After speaking with Jean, Blue would call her brother Richard. She was gathering her mercenaries in the battle against Jay.

"WHAT?" Jean yelled into the phone.

She said it so loud that Blue held the mouthpiece and looked around for Gavin.

"Yes, Ma. He took all the money from our accounts, sold the furniture from the Atlanta house, and he's trying to sell the house from under me and run off with the money."

"My God! What about your trust fund? Did he get his greasy hands on that?"

"No, Ma."

"Thank goodness. I gave him way too much credit. I'm

extremely disappointed in him. But, he has crossed the line. How dare
he?" Jean added as an afterthought. "We need to get Victor on the line."

"I've already done that, Ma. He's checking things out to make
sure he's not trying to pull any other underhanded tricks. He's got a plan
in action to protect my other assets, and he's handling my divorce."

"Great. That covers him legally. Now what do you plan to do?"
Jean asked.

Blue knew exactly where Jean was going with that comment and
had already asked herself the same question. Blue was more like Jean
than she was willing to admit. *How am I going to get back at Jay?*

The rest of their conversation flowed with ease. Scandal was the
band-aid that temporarily soothed Blue's broken relationship with her
mother. Bitterness, reprisal, and scandal had always been Jean's strong
suit.

Blue made a few more calls before Gavin returned to the room.
She ended her last call as he walked through the door.

"I picked up some fresh fruit," he said, placing the food down on
the table. "How are you doing?"

"Better," Blue responded with a smirk. "I'm going to jump in the
shower now."

"Okay, cool. I'll hang out here," Gavin said, referring to the
small kitchenette and sitting area leading to the bedroom.

Blue showered quickly but thoroughly before anointing herself
with the sweet scents she'd packed for her trip. Tonight they would serve
a completely different purpose. Blue slipped her silk robe over her moist
shimmering skin, leaving it hanging open, fluffed her hair, and sauntered
out to the sitting area.

At first, Gavin didn't seem to notice her as he busied himself flipping channels. Once his attention caught sight of her, he rose, appearing to be moved to his feet by a force. He stared at her. She could tell he was pleasantly stunned. She stepped up, pressed her naked body against his, and kissed him, pushing his mouth open with her lips. Gavin found the small of her back and pulled her in. His touch generated warmth that spiraled to the center of her loins.

Blue wrapped one leg around Gavin's back. As he held her lifted leg, they waltzed toward the bed. He laid Blue on her back and took his time getting to know her body from head to toe. Her temperature rose under the heat of his exploration.

Gavin entered her carefully, allowing Blue to get to know every inch personally until her center tugged at him, pulling him in deeper. Once he filled her to capacity, she tensed and then relaxed, both surprised and delighted by his fullness. Gavin entered but retreated with a questioning look until Blue planted her hand on his behind and pulled him back in. Then she rose to greet his next stride. That license appeared to give him the confidence he needed to give Blue his all. Each new stroke intensified her longing for Gavin and her need to feel loved. She rocked with him until they both glistened with sweat.

Then he flipped her over, stretched her out on her stomach, pulled her legs together, and entered her from behind. He filled his palms with her soft breasts and drove long, steady strokes, causing Blue to grasp at the cotton sheets before biting into a clump, attempting to stifle her screams.

Feeling her body spasm, she screamed into the fluffy pile and tightened around Gavin's firmness. Blue felt the tension ease from her body along with her juices. She could tell by his ragged panting that he tried to resist the inevitable, but ecstasy had stolen his resolve. His grunt extended into a series of guttural moans just before he collapsed on top of her back. The two lay drenched in sweat and other erotic fluids.

A sated smile spread across Blue's face. This particular act of revenge felt amazing. She couldn't wait to tell Jay about how much she'd enjoyed screwing his friend. Suddenly, a quick shroud of guilt covered her, but she shook it off. She had to admit she had feelings for Gavin. He was definitely a skillful lover, but this moment was all about revenge. This news was sure to make Jay extremely irate, while delivering a dreadful blow to his ego.

CHAPTER 35

Gavin

Gavin hummed around the hotel room as he brewed a complimentary pot of coffee. He had the TV and radio playing as he sang to himself just low enough to avoid disturbing Blue's sleep. A cool shower had refreshed him, and the strong coffee revived his senses. He two-stepped to the beat while ironing his crisp dress shirt, almost losing the towel he had wrapped around his waist.

The door to the bedroom creaked as Gavin slowly pushed it open to peek in on Blue. She hadn't budged, and he didn't want to wake her. A satisfied one-sided smile curled into his right cheek as he thought about the night before. Until then, he had only imagined what it would be like to make love to her. It was an experience he would always remember while looking forward to the next time.

Gavin looked at the large-numbered alarm clock and eased the door shut. Then he tiptoed to the couch where his clothes were laid out. He needed to be downtown within twenty minutes to have breakfast with one of his clients. What sense did it make to come to Atlanta and not handle any of his own business?

Gavin sang while getting dressed, as he waited for the valet to bring him the rental, and during the entire ride to the restaurant downtown.

After spotting his client, star baseball player Darren Lewis, Gavin eased next to the curb, threw the car in park, and jumped out to greet the tall, lanky athlete. Darren had the build of a basketball player, but being a kid from the Bronx, baseball was in his heart. His stature made him infamous for all the RBIs he claimed due to his endless, lightning-fast legs. Fans had nicknamed him Jumping Jack Flash.

"Top of the morning to you, my brother!" Gavin said in a mock British accent with a bright smile wrapped across his face. He extended his hand to Darren.

"Top of the morning to you, too, Gavin. You're rather happy this morning," Darren joked along with him.

"Really!" Gavin stopped and thought a moment, then chuckled.

"Must have had a good night."

"A real man never tells," Gavin said and chortled. "Shall we?" He gestured for Darren to step into the restaurant before him.

Darren reared his head back and looked at Gavin with his brows raised, then shook his head and smiled before walking into the bustling eatery. Minnie's Café offered some of the best breakfast in downtown Atlanta, with large servings and cheap prices. It was no wonder why they'd been around for more than twenty-five years, and there was hardly ever an empty table in the place.

The men found their seats, and Gavin followed Darren's eyes, which were plastered on a curvy, big-boned waitress with smooth brown skin. The loud clanging of utensils, dishes, and lively conversation caused them to raise their voices so the pretty waitress could hear their orders. She confirmed their requests in her Southern-born lilt before sauntering away through the thick crowd of patrons and other workers. Watching Darren absorb every sway of her well-rounded hips, Gavin laughed.

When Darren finally pulled his gaze away from the waitress's outstanding bottom, he licked his lips and said, "I just love country women. That woman reminds me of rich, thick, pure cane syrup."

Gavin burst out laughing.

"Hey," Darren said. "Am I lying?"

"Whatever!" Gavin laughed again at the silly metaphor. "Let's get down to business!"

Their food arrived quickly. While they ate, Darren continued to steal glances at the waitress. As Gavin poured a generous sum of cane syrup over his pancakes, he immediately understood Darren's earlier point. The rich dark hue of the syrup reminded him of Blue's supple, glistening skin. Rich sweetness detonated his taste buds, reminding him of Blue's syrupy nectar. Suddenly, he wanted to hurry up and finish with Darren so he could get back to the hotel.

"Oh, yeah! I knew I had something to ask you," Darren blurted, bursting through Gavin's thoughts.

All the sensual images of Blue fell from Gavin's mind.

"Yeah? What's up?"

"What's the deal with your boy Jay?"

Gavin raised his head and eased his fork down. "Why do you ask?"

"Some of the guys were talking about how crazy he's been acting since he got cut from the team."

"Really? How would they know?"

"He's been doing a lot of hanging out, and you know most of us hang in the same places," he said, referring to athletes. "I've been hearing about him acting wild up in New York, but I got to see it for myself last night over at the *spot*."

"And?" Gavin's interest was piqued.

"Yeah. He was buzzed out of his mind, being rough with the

dancers. The club owner gave him a few warnings until Jay eventually lost it. They screamed at each other for a few minutes, but then suddenly, Jay grabbed the dude by his neck and tried to choke the sound out of him." Darren mimicked the act with his hands. "Two huge bouncers, looking like Refrigerator Perry, came barreling over, pried Jay's hands from around the man's neck, and tossed him out of the club." Darren shook his head as he continued.

"A few of us ran outside to make sure he was okay. He cursed at all of us, jumped into a white drop-top Infinity, and peeled off like a madman. I don't think they'll ever get those tire marks off of that pavement," he said, reflecting. "So then, we jumped in our cars and followed him to make sure he got home safely. He was speeding and swerving all over the road."

"And this was late last night?" Gavin asked with his brows planted high on his forehead.

"Yeah. It had to be around two in the morning. That dude is reckless." Darren shoved a forkful of thick cheesy grits in his mouth. "Whatever happened to his wife?" he asked, pausing long enough to wipe a string of cheese from his chin. "Did she leave him when she found out he got cut from the team? You know how these women are, and some of them can really make a man crazy."

"Who? Blue? No. She's not that kind of woman. She...she has her own money. A trust fund baby." Gavin paused and pushed the rest of his pancakes around the plate. He was no longer hungry. "She didn't marry Jay for his money or because he was an athlete." Gavin decided to stop there. "So how's the coach treating you? Do you still think there's a possibility of a trade next season?"

Gavin changed the subject before quickly bringing the discussion to a sharp close. He called the waitress over, paid the bill, shook hands with Darren, and promised to call him when he returned to New York. After learning about Jay's unruly behavior and the fact that he was here in Atlanta, Gavin needed to hurry back to the hotel to warn Blue. He only hoped she would still be in the room when he returned.

CHAPTER 36
Mia

"Mia? Babe? Are you here?"

Mia heard Princeton but didn't answer. She had managed to get fully dressed without waking him. He called after her again, but Mia quickly slipped through the kitchen to the garage, fired up the Jaguar, and backed out swiftly. Jay still had her car from the night before. A quick tap to the remote opener hopefully shut the garage door. She never looked back to confirm.

She snaked around the curvy road and pulled to the right near the stop sign at the end of the street. Her destination was still undecided. Getting out of the house was her primary focus, and she had successfully managed that.

Mia placed her hand on her stomach. It seemed like overnight she went from having an inconspicuous pouch that she could easily hide to having a small rounded belly that required creative styling to keep under wraps.

Her mind flipped from Jay to Princeton as if some impatient viewer were frantically switching channels with a remote. A horn blared behind her, snapping her from the vivid succession of male images. Mia cursed the driver and tossed him the middle finger before shouting, "Go around, stupid!"

"Where the hell am I going?" Mia questioned with her hands in the air. She banged her hands against the steering wheel, grunted, and then dialed Jay's number. After several attempts, she still didn't get him, so she headed toward the townhouse in Buckhead, hoping he'd be there anyway.

Mia smiled as she drove up to the house. At least the sale was going smoothly. Getting the house sold and impersonating Blue was easier than she had anticipated.

Pulling up, she noticed her car stretched recklessly across the lawn. Mia ran to the car, inspecting it for damage. She found a long black scratch etched into the passenger side door.

"Jay!" she screamed. "Damn you!" She charged to the front door.

Mia banged and shouted for a solid five minutes. Neighbors peeked through conspicuous cracks in their blinds. The man next door boldly came out to his front porch. Mia scowled at him. A woman jogging with her toy Maltese looked Mia's way, and Mia glared at her, too. The woman picked up her pace.

"Jay! Open this damn door now!" she hollered, then dialed his cell number again.

Finally, Jay opened the door and walked away, leaving Mia at the threshold. Jay wore sleep like a cloak. She stepped in behind him. He shuffled to the stairs and plopped down. The wood creaked under his weight, and he released a wide-mouthed exaggerated yawn. Stale liquor mixed in with the rank air. Mia felt bile rise and tightened her throat.

"What the hell happened to you? What did you do to my car?" Mia shouted from the door, while holding her forefinger under her nose. She held her other hand to her stomach and swallowed hard. "Give me my damn car keys," she yelled, looking around the empty house. "Where are my keys, Jay?" she asked, stomping into the kitchen. She checked the cabinets and drawers, all while holding her breath.

Jay croaked out his reply. "Upstairs."

"How did my car get scratched like that?"

Jay shielded his eyes from the sunlight meandering through the front window.

"What scratch?"

"You smell awful. Please don't tell me you were driving my car drunk." Mia huffed and kicked at the clothes that littered the floor. She looked around in disgust. "I gave you my keys so you could come here, not to gallivant around the city." She stomped back towards the stairs where Jay sat. "You're going to fix it."

"Could you please keep it down?" Jay scrunched his face and squinted in Mia's direction.

"Give me my keys!" She shoved past Jay, who rested his head against the wall.

"Oh my goodness! It reeks up here!" Mia pinched her nose between her thumb and forefinger.

The click of her heels bellowed through the empty house as she tried to locate the source of the stench. Her stomach lurched again, and she felt the bile rising fast. Again, Mia tightened her jaw, forcing back the gags. She finally found the keys sitting near a chunky pile of vomit near the door of the master bath. Mia gagged and turned her head. She tipped towards the keys, but as she bent over to retrieve them, the putrid stench of the vomit ascended into her nostrils. Mia gagged again and stood stark straight. Her stomach churned, and she covered her mouth with one hand while the other squeezed her stomach. She tightened her throat to control her insides. She gagged a number of times before turning on her heels and running downstairs. The keys would have to wait.

Jay hadn't moved from his perch on the steps. Mia passed him, ran to the front door, yanked it open, stuck her face outside, and sucked in air. Once she caught her breath, she turned to him and turned her lip up. He looked pitiful slumped all along the wall. Mia sighed and admonished herself for feeling pity instead of anger. As pathetic as he was, she still wanted him.

"Jay! Jay!" she yelled.

"What?" he grunted, half asleep.

"You need to clean yourself up." When he didn't move, she called his name louder. "Jay!" she called again, but he didn't move. "Ugh!"

Mia groaned and slammed the door shut behind her. She jumped in the Jag and started the ignition. When she looked in her rear view mirror, she could have sworn she saw Blue pull up in a taxi. Mia threw the car in gear and floored the gas pedal.

CHAPTER 37

Blue

Blue paid the taxi driver, thanked him, and gave him a generous tip. The slanted car in her driveway made her house seem unbefitting against the neat, structured appearances of the other homes. She took a deep breath and charged towards the door in search of Mia.

Blue jammed the key into the lock and swung the door open.

"Mia! Mia!" She yelled, then halted.

Jay sucked his teeth and squinted in Blue's direction. Blue's jaw dropped and so did his.

Blue was the first to speak. "What are you doing here? And where's all my furniture?" she asked. She started towards where he sat on the steps, but the odor made her stop short. She paused and held her forearm to her nose. She looked around. "What the hell is that smell?"

"Listen!"

"No, you listen to me, Jay. Where's all my money? If you think you're going to take my money and sell this house from under me, then you have another thing coming."

"Ah! Would you please be quiet?" Jay yelled, holding his head. "Listen." He struggled to his feet and teetered before gaining steady footing. He walked towards Blue. "I told you that I wanted this house. I just came here to get my head together. I didn't want the furniture that was in here, so I sold it."

"You're a liar, Jay!"

"You don't know shit!" he yelled, then put his hands on his temples. "Blue...baby, I'm sorry."

Blue straightened her neck. "Baby?"

"Blue! Listen, I'm tired. My head hurts. Can we talk about this another time?" Jay shuffled his feet towards the kitchen, turned on the tap, and drank water from his hands.

"I'm warning you. If you try and sell this house from under me, I will sue you for anything and everything you have!"

Jay slammed his hands on the sink. The loud bang echoed through the steel, and Blue jumped. He gripped the sink with both hands and then slowly turned around. She stared at him. Jay slowly walked back toward Blue in the living room.

"It doesn't have to be like this." Jay dropped his shoulders. "Just let me fix it."

"Are you kidding me?"

"Damn it, Blue! People make mistakes."

"Cut the bullshit!"

He sucked his teeth, went to the cabinet, pulled out a half empty bottle of whiskey, and took a long swig.

"You never did know when to quit," Blue commented while shaking her head. "I'm out of here,' she said, then turned to walk out. She paused again. "Don't mess with me, because I will fight you to the end."

Jay took another gulp from the bottle and began to walk towards Blue. She backed up until her rear end hit the doorframe.

"You made me do this."

Blue's head snapped in his direction. "This is my fault?"

"The money in that account belonged to both of us," Jay added.

"Really?" Blue folded her arms in front of her. "When was the last time you put a drop of money in there, huh?"

Jay launched the bottle against the wall. Amber streams of whiskey trickled down. Shards of glass flew in various directions. Blue ducked. Her mouth dropped and then closed quickly.

"Damn it, Blue! I got cut. They cut off my money. What was I supposed to do? You have money. You always did. You don't know what it's like to be broke." Jay bit his lip. "I don't have any family. My grandfather isn't rich. My mother was the other woman, and my dad wanted nothing to do with me until he realized I played for his favorite team. You left me. What was I supposed to do?" Jay slid down the wall and sat on the floor.

At first, Blue didn't respond. She refused to pity him. He wasn't the victim this time.

"That gave you no right to take my money!" Blue sucked her teeth and grunted. "I'm not going to sit here and listen to your sob story. Neither one of us came from a perfect situation." She turned to walk out, but stopped to face Jay again. "I want my money back, and I want my share for the furniture."

Jay waved her off. "I don't have anything to give you."

"Well, get it from your baby's mother. I'm sure she's got something stashed."

Jay threw his hands up. "That baby isn't mine."

"Do you know that for sure?"

Jay looked away.

"And you can't deny that you slept with her," Blue snapped, then changed her attitude. A treacherous grin spread across her lips.

Jay narrowed his eyes at her.

"I just hope you enjoyed sleeping with her as much as I enjoyed

Gavin!"

"What?" Jay's eyes grew wide right before he charged at her.

"You touch me and I will have you arrested!"

Jay halted. Rage lit his eyes like embers. His chest heaved up and down. Then he calmed down, put his hands on his hips, and chuckled.

"You're just saying that. Just trying to piss me off." He snickered. "And it almost worked. Gavin wouldn't do that. And you…you wouldn't stoop to that level. You were never a whore." Jay's slight laugh faded into a half smile and then turned into a scowl. He looked dead into Blue's eyes. "Don't play with me, because I'll have his ass taken out."

Blue kept her eye on Jay, knowing he would pounce like a lion. Then she heard the squeal of brakes. She looked back and saw it was Gavin. She turned her focus back to Jay.

"Really!" Blue taunted. "Well, call me what you want. I wonder, did you ever tell Gavin anything about my special spot, because he had me howling like a wolf last night. I guess I should thank you," she said with a wily smile and backed out.

Jay charged forward, meeting her at the door, but paused when he saw Gavin at her back. The men glared each other down with their chests puffed high. Gavin backed towards the car while holding firmly onto Blue's arm. Jay glared at them even as they pulled away. Blue had finally taken this fight to a whole new level.

CHAPTER 38

Gavin

"Gavin! Why are you driving so fast?" Blue asked, gripping the door handle with one hand and her seat with the other.

At first, Gavin just looked at her, shook his head, and then set his focus back on the road.

"Can you please slow down just a little? What's wrong with you?" Blue asked, even though she already knew. Never before had she witnessed him act this way. He'd always been in smooth control of his emotions.

Gavin slammed on the brakes, and the car heaved forward, tossing both of them towards the dashboard. Fiercely, he pulled the car to the side of the road and threw the gear in park. He looked over at Blue once again before pushing the door open and jumping out. Gavin paced from the front of the car to the back. After a while, she stepped out and stopped him in his tracks.

"Gavin." Blue called his name gently and stood before him with pleading eyes.

Gavin wasn't buying it.

"That's why you did it?"

Blue sighed. "What difference does it make? Jay and I are no longer together, and the two of you are no longer friends."

Gavin looked at her and shook his head. "That's the only reason you had sex with me?"

His accusation and intense gaze made Blue uneasy. He narrowed his eyes when she didn't respond.

"To make Jay jealous, huh? I was your pawn!" Gavin yelled, jabbing his finger into his chest. His anger outpaced his self-control. "That's not how this was supposed to go down, Blue. That shit wasn't right." He threw his hands in the air and walked away.

Blue ran behind him and turned him by his shoulder.

"Gavin, you don't understand. You don't know what it's like. The pain, the unanswered questions. I wanted him to be angry like I was and feel what I felt for just a moment."

"So you used me to accomplish that?"

"Gavin, I didn't mean to hurt you. I'm sorry," she said, touching his arm.

"Whatever, Blue!" Gavin shrugged her hand off of him. He walked down the narrow two-lane road away from the car.

"Gavin, wait!" Blue trotted to catch up with him. "I'm sorry," she said to his back. "Please! Listen to me. I wasn't thinking clearly. I didn't believe he really cared. So, I did what I knew would get to him. Whether he cares about me or not, I knew he would get upset. Now I realize I hurt you in the process, and I'm sorry for that."

Gavin turn and looked at her, but didn't speak.

"It's obvious I didn't think this whole thing through. I never meant to upset you," she continued, hoping he would see her sincerity.

"Well, now you brought a real problem to my doorstep." Gavin stepped past Blue and headed back to the car.

"Wait! I'm not in this alone," she said, shuffling quickly to keep up with him. "My intentions may have been a little misguided, but I don't remember having to force you to have sex with me."

Gavin turned fast. Blue flinched from the sudden move.

"Exactly. I had sex...made love to you because I wanted to. I came to Atlanta with you because I wanted to, but not for this bullshit. So, how about we hurry up and handle your business so I can get back home and handle mine."

Gavin swiftly walked back to the car and jumped in. As soon as Blue pulled her door closed, he sped off and she held on tight. Words didn't pass between them until they reached the hotel room. The only time Blue opened her mouth was to thank Gavin for holding the door open.

Blue went straight to the bedroom and closed the door behind her, while Gavin stayed in the living area looking out the window at the parking lot and greenery on the hotel's grounds. He felt his cell phone vibrate again. Someone had been calling repeatedly since they'd left the house. Again, he pressed ignore, sending the call to voicemail.

Gavin waited for the indicator to flash, then he pressed the number one on his phone to dial his voicemail. The electronic voice told him that he had three messages, all of which were from Jay, and all were filled with violent threats. Until then, he'd thought Jay didn't care about Blue either, but it was obvious from the way Jay shouted, cursed, and cried that he still loved her.

The phone rang again. This time, Gavin took a deep breath and answered.

"Yeah."

"You finally got your chance, huh? How does it feel to have my sloppy seconds? Are you happy now? You couldn't wait to take my place, could you?" Jay went on without giving Gavin the space to infuse a single word. "Don't let me catch you out in the street."

"Do what you feel you have to do," Gavin said and hung up.

Feelings welled up inside him that were hard for any man to handle. Both he and his former best friend were clearly in love with the same woman.

CHAPTER 39

Mia

Mia pulled into her garage and remained behind the wheel. After a long, hard, deep breath, she climbed out of the car and quietly entered the house. Peeking through the first floor, she searched for any signs that Princeton was still around before heading up to the bedroom.

The running shower revealed Princeton's whereabouts. She sat on the edge of the bed waiting for him to emerge from the master bath. The tips of her ears had grown hot like they usually did when she was either under tremendous pressure or angry. This time, she was a little of both. The cheery melodies that emanated from the shower annoyed her. Princeton's light mood was in sharp contrast to her edgy state. She looked over at her alarm clock, down to her expensive wristwatch, and then back to the bold, bright numbers on the clock. She sat for a few more moments before checking the time again. She sucked her teeth. When she got tired of sitting, she stood, tapping her feet.

When the water stopped, Mia sat back down and glanced at her watch yet again. She stood just as Princeton stepped through the door.

"Hey!" he smiled. "How's my—"

"I can't do this anymore," Mia blurted with her arms crossed.

"You can't do what?" Princeton asked, looking confused.

"This!" Mia said, dramatically waving her arms around the room. "I can't do *you* anymore. I don't want to deal with the surprise visits or your ridiculous rules. I can't be controlled like this."

"Really!" Princeton said and stared at her for a few moments. "What's wrong, baby? Is there something you need?" he asked, walking toward the bed, planting moist footprints on the carpet. "Just tell Daddy what it is and I've got it covered."

Princeton smiled proudly, then stepped towards Mia. Drops of water rolled down his naked body like rain clinging to a window. He held his hands out to her.

"I'm serious," Mia responded, moving out of his reach. "This won't work, and I need you to leave now."

Princeton looked confused again. "You're serious?" His brows clenched.

"You don't want to be with me?"

Mia sucked her teeth at his arrogance.

"What's the problem?" he asked.

"I'm not interested in being a well-kept side chick that's obligated to be at your beck and call anytime you decide you want to fly through town. That's not how I work. I can't sit around waiting for someone to call the shots for me. I'm my own woman, and I call my own shots."

"Oh, so you don't like some of my rules?" Princeton opened his arms to her again. Mia turned her head. "Well, baby, we can make some adjustments." He stepped over to the bed and pulled on his boxers and jeans. "Just tell me what you want. But, let me warn you. There are some things I'm not willing to negotiate." Princeton smiled again before slipping his shirt over his head.

She wanted to punch the grin right off of his face.

"Negotiate!" Mia shook her head. "This is over. When you're finished getting dressed, do me a favor and leave. I'm not interested in being your Atlanta piece!"

Princeton stopped dressing, looked at Mia, and tightened his lips.

"I see," he said, sliding his foot into a sock. "You didn't tell me you weren't interested when I gave you the keys to the Jag. You didn't seem to be so uninterested when I handed you that black card." Princeton pushed his heel into his sneaker and stood. "I'll tell you what. You can be finished with all of this, but I'm not finished with you. I've spent a lot of money on you, and I plan to get my money's worth."

"Excuse me! You can have all of that shit back—the car, the card, and even this house. It means nothing to me."

"All of you tricks are the same!" he spat, shaking his head.

"What? Who are you calling a trick?" She shouted.

"You know what you are," he said with disgust.

Mia's jaw dropped as he closed in on her.

"Don't act like you didn't know what you were getting into when you took this place. I wasn't going to marry you."

"I didn't ask you to marry me," Mia yelled after finally shutting her gaped mouth. "I didn't ask you for anything."

"And you had no problem taking it from me, either. What happened?" Princeton paused and cocked his head sideways. "Did you grow some morals while I was away? You know how this goes. I give you the money, fine cars, and jewels, and you give me what I want whenever I'm in town. That's it. You don't make demands. I'll be done when I'm ready, and until then, you just do as I say," he ordered, and then turned his back, dismissing her.

Mia took the keys to the house and car out of her bag and threw them at Princeton, hitting him in his chest and face. She snarled at him, then turned on her heels and headed for the door.

As she turned, Mia felt Princeton's large presence loom closely. When she looked back, he was immediately behind her. He snatched her by the back of her shirt and tossed her to the other side of the room. Mia's head met the wall with force, and the room moved in waves. She grabbed the back of her head and let out a wounded cry. Princeton was approaching fast. Mia scampered to her feet and grabbed a vase from the wooden shelf. As he neared, she swung with all her might, missing him. Easily, Princeton grabbed the vase from her grip and tossed it like a child's toy. The crystal shattered into tiny pieces as it hit the window frame across the room.

Mia started swinging, landing several ineffective punches to Princeton's face and chest. He swatted at her fighting hands like he was shooing at flies. Then she opened her hands and began slapping at his face. She tried to pierce him, but her perfectly manicured tips failed to break his skin. Growing weary and worrying about her baby, Mia dropped her hands from exhaustion. She caught sight of Princeton as he pulled his fist back.

"Princeton, no! I'm pregnant!" she shouted, placing her hand over her stomach, leaving her face open for the impending abuse.

His wrath continued despite her cries. She cowered just in time to miss getting slammed by his hefty hands. Princeton's blow went through the wall. The time Princeton took trying to pry his fist from the hole he created gave Mia time to react. She drew her leg back and drove her knee deep into his groin. He grunted and doubled over. Mia ducked under his arm and jetted out of the room, but not before grabbing her bag and the keys to the Jag. Princeton continued to moan as he hurled threats at her retreating back. By the time she reached the first landing, Princeton had freed himself and was coming up behind her.

Fear kicked her adrenaline into high gear, and Mia raced to the garage, making it to the car just as Princeton reached the first floor. Her hands were shaking so badly, she didn't think she would be able to get the car started. Just as it cranked, Princeton pulled the door leading from the house to the garage off the hinges and barreled through the doorway. Mia jammed her foot down on the gas, jerking the car into reverse. He kept coming. When the car was clear of the garage, she shoved the gear in drive and pushed the gas pedal to the floor. The car skipped and flew forward in time to escape Princeton's reach.

Mia drove away from the complex at top speed. It wasn't until her tears rolled back into her ears that she realized she was crying. She cut a hard right at the entrance to the complex, causing the car to go into a partial tailspin. Instinctively, she cut the wheel, straightened out the car, and zoomed onto the main road.

Her heart rate was in sync with her odometer—both reaching dangerous limits. With trembling hands and a racing pulse, Mia drove away as fast as the sleek car could carry her.

CHAPTER 40

Gavin

Gavin heard Blue at the door of the hotel room as he sat in the living area nursing a rocks glass half-filled with scotch. She entered and paused when she saw Gavin seated near the door.

"Hey," she greeted cautiously.

"Hey," he replied without turning.

With her eyes averted, Blue walked past Gavin into the bedroom and closed the door.

He tightened his lips, shook his head, and downed the last of the amber inferno in his glass. The spiced liquid slithered down his throat, heating his chest like lava.

Gavin fought the urge to toss the glass across the room. The shattered shards could have relieved the pressure from the frustration choking him. Jay and Blue tossed across his mind. He poured another drink and sat back down.

The room door creaked, but he acted unfazed. He could feel Blue's gaze settling on him.

"Gavin," Blue called softly.

A raised brow was his only acknowledgment. Blue sighed.

"You don't have to talk to me. Just listen," she said.

Gavin raised his glass, signaling for her to continue.

"I don't really know what else to say. I've said sorry a hundred times since yesterday. I've realized how this whole thing must look to you, but you have to know that hurting you wasn't my intention. Again...I'm sorry. I really am. I don't want to lose you as a friend."

Gavin tightened his lips, took another sip, and nodded his head. A large, quick swallow consumed the remnants of the firewater. Without a word, he put the glass down, picked up his keys, and walked out the door.

After the valet pulled his car from the hotel lot, Gavin cruised through the streets of Atlanta from College Park to Downtown, through Buckhead and all the way out to Stone Mountain. Gavin drove until he could no longer ignore the emptiness in his stomach. Lunchtime had come and gone, and so had the scotch he consumed earlier. His insides felt desolate, and his strength started to wither. Jumping on 85, he drove back downtown and treated himself to the hefty servings at one of his many favorite soul food restaurants. He stayed long enough for the thin late-afternoon crowd to grow thick with evening professionals dealing business, networking, and gathering for after-work cocktails and conversation.

Gavin drove around some more, making a few quick calls to local clients until the doors to the sinful pastures of Magic City were opened. He found a seat at the bar with a clear line of sight to the stage and opened up a tab. The crowd at the club gradually grew into a thunderous enclave of animated, frisky, and brassy male and female celebrities, athletes, and locals. Gavin absorbed the mixed tapestry of playmakers and wannabes, shaking his head at the few overzealous characters who were brusquely ejected from the club by super-sized bouncers the moment they got carried away.

It was the last of the unruly drunks that caught Gavin's attention. His eyes met Jay's hollowed glare as he was being dragged to the door. When Jay caught sight of Gavin, he fought in vain to free himself from the clutches of the Goliath-sized chaps in charge of securing the premises. Gavin swallowed the last of his cognac, closed his tab, and headed for the door. He knew that no matter what time he walked out, Jay would be outside waiting.

The second he set foot over the threshold, Jay was in his face.

"Why did you do it?" Jay shouted. Spit flew into the air.

"It wasn't even like that, man," Gavin said, remaining calm.

Gavin's only out was to show him that he was willing to face him like a man. Reasonable conversation or any kind of explanation would prove pointless in Jay's state.

"Yeah, right. You didn't have to do it, man. Blue was mine. All the women in the world, and you had to go after mine. You already got it all," Jay said, his word sloshing past his slack lips.

"Just get your hands out of my face." Gavin remained calm.

"You're lucky I don't pummel your ass right here...telling me to get my hands outta your face," Jay grumbled and puffed his chest up at Gavin. "I should beat you down right here, right now. That'll teach you to run after another man's woman," Jay snarled.

"No need, dude. We can see each other back in New York...handle this like a man...sober." Gavin stepped back from Jay, but his eyes stayed on him. "We'll deal with this when the time is right."

"I want to deal with this right now, coward," Jay said before taking a step back and charging at him.

Gavin sidestepped, removing himself from Jay's path.

Jay stumbled, turned around, and charged at him again. Gavin moved one more time, and Jay's stagger landed him on the ground. Jay rolled around on the asphalt clutching his shoulder in pain.

Gavin stepped closer to make sure Jay wasn't hurt badly before heading to his car.

"I'll see you in New York," Jay shouted, still rolling and grappling with the pain in his shoulder.

"I'll be ready when you are," Gavin said, then got in his car and pulled off.

CHAPTER 41

Mia

Mia was finally able to get Jay on the phone.

"What's up?" he answered.

"Where the hell have you been? I've been trying to call you for at least twenty-four hours. I need my car," she said as she scampered around the hotel room, peeping out of the window every few minutes.

"All right, all right. I'll bring it to the house. Let me get myself together first."

"No! Don't bring it to the house. Princeton's there." The simple mention of Princeton's name propelled her to the window one more time. She didn't think he knew where she was, but anxiety coaxed her paranoia to the surface. "Um…meet me…" She thought for a moment. "Meet me down here at the hotel. I need a favor."

"Ah, what now?" Jay grumbled.

"Don't forget that's my car you're driving around in," she huffed.

Jay delayed his response for a moment. "All right! Damn!"

"Jay!"

"What?" he tossed back.

"Ugh! Just meet me at my hotel. I'm at the Hilton on Peachtree Industrial in Gwinnett. I need you to be here within the hour. You'll have to follow me in my car so I can drop off this car. Then I'll need for you to bring me back to the hotel to get the rest of my stuff."

Mia had a strong feeling she needed to get rid of the Jag fast. As possessive as Princeton was, she suspected he might track her via the anti-theft system or GPS. She wouldn't put it past him to equip the car with some type of high-tech tracking device so he could trace her every move. What had she gotten herself into with him?

Jay remained silent.

"Just come on," she said and ended the call.

Mia crept to the window, peering through the side of the heavy floral-print drapery like a Russian spy. Her mouth dropped as she watched the source of her paranoia play out before her eyes. A black Hummer pulled to a stop right behind the Jag. Princeton leapt from the passenger seat, jogged around the car, and looked over the Jag before raking his eyes along the hotel from window to window. Mia jerked back, hoping she hadn't been spotted. She eased the curtain back into place with her trembling hand and backed away. Her suspicions were confirmed.

Dashing for her cell phone, she retrieved it and grappled at the buttons to pull up Jay's number.

"Jay!" Mia's voice was filled with desperation. "You have to come now. Please."

"What's the problem?"

"I need you. I need you right now. Please." Her voice was worn. "Please come now," she said, on the verge of tears.

"Okay, I'll be right there. Are you by yourself? Are you okay?"

"I just need you to get here as soon as you can…and don't come to the front. Pull in to the service entrance. I'll come out from there."

"What?"

"I'll explain everything when you get here. Just come as fast as you can."

"I'm coming now. Give me a few minutes."

Jay's final words gave temporary ease to the thumping in Mia's chest and the thrashing in her belly.

She returned to the window and spied through the sheers, careful not to move the draperies. The Hummer and Jag were still in place, but there was no sign of Princeton. Mia gasped, grabbed her purse and cell phone, and ran for the door. She looked back at the shopping bags she had spent the morning acquiring.

The bags filled the perimeter of the room, her just reprieve and parting gift for Princeton's aggressive behavior. *It's not worth it right now.* Paranoia shrouded her while she tried her best to spend as much of his money as she could. Throughout her quick shopping spree, she had spent much of her time looking over her shoulder, figuring he'd try to catch up to her at some point. There were only so many places that people with abundance shopped, lived, dined, and rested their heads in Atlanta. She knew he'd come upon her sooner or later.

The thousands of dollars she'd siphoned from his cards through cash advances weren't enough after his violence the day before. This last-ditch effort to make a dent in his pockets made her feel like she'd gotten some kind of revenge. It was worth the risk. Now she was looking at the possibility of having to leave her expensive jewels and new digs right there in the hotel room.

Mia swung the door open and raced through the hallway, leaving the bags but holding her pregnant belly. The ding alerting the arrival of the elevator gave her pause. Urgent footsteps followed the pinging. Princeton's subterranean voice boomed through the halls, bouncing off of the walls. Mia turned on her heels to head toward the stairwell. She'd paid for the room in cash, but knew it wouldn't take much for a star like Princeton to get what he wanted from the hotel staff. Apparently, someone had given her up.

The stairs were too far down the other end of the hall. She looked left and right, then dipped into an open room that was being serviced. The frail, foreign worker froze in her place when she saw Mia rush into the room. Mia gave a quick frantic smile and gestured towards the bathroom as if nature was calling her with vehemence. The woman nodded and smiled, ushering Mia towards the bathroom with her small, weathered hands.

Once inside, Mia pressed her ear against the door panel. Princeton's baritone voice still permeated the air, muddying it with profanity. Mia was every kind of bitch Princeton could think of. She jumped at the loud banging as if he was pounding on the door she hid behind.

"Open this door, Mia! I know you're in there! Come on, open the door!" he yelled in sync with his insistent banging.

Mia squeezed her eyes shut and pressed her ear against the door even harder. The churning in her stomach threatened to make her heave. When her cell phone rang, she almost dropped it. The phone bounced in the air a few times before she garnered a solid grasp on it and answered the call.

"Hello," she whispered, pushing the phone into her free ear.

"I'm almost there. Why are you whispering?" Jay asked.

"He's here," she said, this time completely unable to suppress the tremor in her voice.

"Who's there?" he asked.

"Princeton. He's after me. He flipped out on me yesterday when I told him that I couldn't be with him." Mia quickly gave Jay a few more details to paint a clearer picture of the situation.

"Okay. Where are you now?" he asked.

"I'm in a room across from mine…room 304. He's banging on my door like a maniac. I can't go out there right now."

"Just give me a few more minutes."

"Be careful, Jay. He's not alone." Mia heard Jay disconnect the call.

Mia pressed her ear against the bathroom door. She could hear the little woman yelling at the men in another language. She didn't know exactly what she was saying, but it wasn't hard to figure out. The woman ran back to the room and picked up the phone. She spoke fast, half in her native tongue. All Mia could make out in accented English was the word 'security'. Mia heard the woman's padded steps as she traipsed back past the bathroom chanting, "I call security on you."

Mia dialed Jay again.

"Where are you?" she whispered loudly while pacing the bathroom.

Pounding from the men's heavy steps resumed. Mia reoccupied her position at the bathroom door, holding the side of her face against the wood to listen. It sounded like the men were walking back towards the elevator. The ping resonated again, and Mia could hear their voices fade behind the closing doors. She heard a second ping and then silence. She pulled away from the door one last time and waited a few minutes before emerging from the restroom.

Mia exited slowly, looking in all directions. As she came out, the small woman stared at her with critical eyes and her hands on her hips. Mia dismissed her suspicions with a wave of her hand and crept towards the door. She peeked out and ran back to her room. She walked circles in the carpet, pacing and wringing her hands.

"Come on, Jay. Hurry up," she said, checking her watch repeatedly.

A few minutes later, there was a tap on the door. Mia's heart pounded. She didn't know whether to answer the door or let the person keep knocking.

"It's me," she heard Jay say. "Open the door."

Mia cracked the door slightly, pressing her eye against the slim opening to make sure it was him.

"Thank God you're here," she said, swinging the door open to let him in.

"Where is he?" Jay asked.

"I hope they left." Mia ushered Jay into the room. Nervously, she snatched up her packages on the floor. "Help me with these bags. Where's the car?"

"Out front."

Mia let the bags fall from her grip. "Jay, why? I told you to pull 'round back. We can go out the service entrance or something."

"I'm not running from any man. I came through the front, and I'm leaving through the front." Jay shook his head. "What would I look like trying to creep out of a back door? Let's go," he said and started grabbing at some of the bags. "Wait a minute." He stood promptly. "What the hell is all of this stuff anyway?"

Mia averted her eyes and grabbed the last bag.

Jay huffed.

"I'm sure he doesn't realize how much of his money you just spent," Jay said and chuckled.

Mia cut her eyes at him but confirmed nothing.

"You're unbelievable," he said, laughing.

The moment the elevator doors opened to the lobby, Mia spotted Princeton and his accomplice. She held tight to Jay's arm and pretended not to see him, hoping they could slip out undetected. Mia knew Jay had spotted Princeton, also, because his gait grew in masculinity. Jay walked taller and harder, his puffed chest leading the way.

Mia caught sight of Princeton through her peripheral vision. She tensed, squeezing her grip on Jay's arm. He stopped and turned as if the heat of Princeton's glare tapped him on the shoulder. Mia thought she would explode when their eyes met. Neither of the men uttered a word, but their eyes dared the other to make a move. To Mia, the lobby felt like the temperature had climbed a few degrees higher. Moments later, Jay nodded and cocked his head to the side. Princeton nodded back and chewed his bottom lip. The fire in his eyes cast sweltering flames across the room and singed Mia's skin. Princeton's glare toggled from Jay to Mia. The one resting on Jay said, *You've got this for now*. The hotter one reserved for Mia said, *This isn't over*.

Slowly, Jay turned away and started towards the hotel's front bay. By the time they made it into the car, Princeton and his henchman were exiting the front door. Jay led Mia to the passenger side while he stuffed all of her bags into the trunk. She filtered through her purse, pulled out the keys to the Jag, and tossed them along with Princeton's limitless credit card out the window as they pulled off.

Jay looked over at her and shook his head.

"Thank you so much. You saved me. I think he'll leave me alone now that he's seen me with you." She laid her head back, feeling lucky Jay had made it to her in time. Slowly, her breathing returned to a more natural pace.

"Jay," Mia called out to him.

"What?" Jay said with a hint of exasperation.

"See what I mean?" She leaned her head towards Jay. "We work well together. We belong together," she added.

Jay looked over at her and then back at the road.

"We're going to be great together," she continued, ignoring his blank stare.

"Why, because we're both fucked-up individuals?" he responded and laughed.

Mia stared at him with her lips curled upwards. Jay smirked.

"No," she said with a light scolding. "Because we have a lot in common." Mia shook her head and huffed. "We can do a lot together. What can stop us?"

Mia sucked in air, turned her back on Jay, and stared out of the window, watching the blur of the construction, homes, and trees as they whizzed by.

"Where am I taking you?" he asked, gazing at her from the side.

Mia grunted. "Your house," she stated confidently.

"No! I need to take you somewhere else," he said.

"Where? I can't go back to my house...I mean, Princeton's place. I can't go back to the hotel. You're going to have to take me back to your house." Mia thought for a moment. "Speaking of which, I need to contact Carol at the real estate office to get an idea of when we can wrap this sale up. We can find a new place together."

Mia dialed Carol's number. She answered on the first ring.

"Oh, Mrs. Holiday. I was just about to call you. The couple has decided not to go forward with the purchase of the townhouse. But, I have another couple from out of town that I think would be interested. I'll give a call to schedule an appointment when they come back."

"Sure. Thanks," Mia said, disappointed.

Between Carol's news and Jay's begrudged body language, Mia's feelings were hurt. She brushed off the pang of rejection and focused on making the best of her time with Jay at his home. By the time she found a new place, they would be moving in together—as a couple. At least that's what she planned.

CHAPTER 42

Blue

Blue drove her rented Sedan around her former Atlanta neighborhood, reminiscing over more tranquil times. She had loved living there when Jay played for the local team. Her eyes misted.

"No more tears. That life is over," she said aloud.

Blue hung a quick left to exit the complex, when Jay and Mia whizzed past her in Mia's car. It was obvious they hadn't spotted her in the rental. She pulled the car over to the side of the two-lane road. She hadn't confronted Mia since she'd arrived in Atlanta a few days ago. There was so much to say, but now she wasn't up to dealing with the confrontation alone. The odds were surely against her with Mia and Jay together.

She hit her turn signal and pulled back onto the road in the opposite direction of the complex. She would have her day with Mia soon. As she mulled over the events of the past few months, her eyes misted over again. This time, she didn't try to stop the tears. Some of the anger and bitterness had subsided, but that burning question nagged at her conscience. *Why would Mia do this to me?*

Blue drove without considering her destination until she reached the hotel. She checked her face in the rear view mirror and pulled herself together before going up to the room. Waiting there was another relationship falling apart at the seams. She'd searched her mind for the right tools to mend this one before it withered into nothing more than irreparable scraps.

Night had fallen, and Blue hoped Gavin was in the room. Since the confrontation with Jay, Gavin spent most of his time out eating and hanging with clients—or so he said.

A sultry melody glided through the doorframe as she approached their room. Pain resonated note by note as the weighted melody writhed through the air. The feelings transmitted from an iPod somehow filled the space, making the air thick. A melancholy tonic note ended the piece, leaving a lingering sliver of sadness in the atmosphere. Blue had to take a deep breath before pushing the door open. The manner of the room seemed dark and heavy.

Gavin sat slack in the living room chair with his head back, eyes shut, and a near empty glass dangling from his hand.

"Hey," she said, cutting through the tension.

"Hey," he replied, lifting his head slowly. She walked into the bedroom to put down her bag and keys, and then joined Gavin in the living area. Another sad song began to add its weight to the atmosphere. She lowered the volume on Gavin's speakers. Her heart couldn't take any more.

Gavin sat up.

"You eat yet?" she asked.

"No," he said, looking at his watch.

"Neither did I. Come on, let me treat you," she offered.

Gavin hesitated, then flipped his hands in the air. "Let's go!"

Blue smiled. "And turn this music off. It's depressing me."

She drove them to one of her favorite Italian spots, Magiano's, at the Perimeter Mall. Their meal began with light conversation until the wine and food put them both at ease.

"I'm leaving in the morning," he told her.

"Gavin! Why!" Blue asked. She was alarmed about being left in Atlanta without him. "We only have one more day. I just have a few more things to handle before I can leave." She dropped her shoulders. "When did you change your flight?"

"Today," he said, staring down at the pasta he pushed around on his plate.

Blue put her fork down and sat back in her chair.

"I've got to get back to work. I came to help you out, but you're doing fine on your own. I need to get back to handle things in my office."

"Gavin, believe me, things are not going as well as you think. The only reason I didn't ask you to come with me yesterday is because I knew you were upset with me. I need you here."

Gavin frowned.

"Please stay one more day," Blue pleaded.

"I can't," he said, holding his hand up in finality.

Blue sighed and rested her head in her hands.

"My leaving early does not have to destroy our dinner. We were finally beginning to enjoy each other's company again."

"You're right. Let's have a nice dinner. I'll try to convince you to change your flight on the way back to the hotel."

Gavin laughed, and the conversation flowed more easily for the rest of the meal. By the time they entered the room, they were laughing loudly, buzzed from the wine. When the banter reached a lull, he walked to the closet and pulled out his suitcase.

"Let me get my bags together." Uneasiness took hold of the space between them again. "I'm on the early flight, and I have to get this rental back before I board my flight."

Blue didn't respond right away. Her shoulders hung. The lighter feelings from earlier were now dashed.

"Gavin…"

He turned around.

Blue shut her eyes and nodded her head. "Please," she continued anyway.

"I'm sorry," he said with a firmness that gave her pause.

Blue walked over to him, standing just inches away for a few moments, then hugged him tight. He wrapped his arms around Blue's body. She lifted her face and their lips met. Blue melted into Gavin. He received her and then pulled away.

She stood there looking puzzled, while Gavin gently moved her hands from around him, turned away, and began tending to his luggage.

"Okay," she said with her hands up in surrender. "Get home safe." She dropped her hands and backed away. "Call me when you land," she added, before slamming the door to the room, severing the space between them.

Inside the room, Blue sat on the side of the bed, pulled out her cell phone, and dialed a number. They answered on the first ring.

"Hey, girl."

"Guess where I am?" Blue teased.

"Woman, don't tell me you're in Atlanta!" Peyton said.

"Yes, I am!" Blue replied, trying to mask the disappointment in her voice.

"Why didn't you tell me you were coming? I would have rolled out the old red carpet. Welcome mats just aren't fancy enough for the likes of us," Peyton said and giggled.

"It's a quick trip. But, I need to see you while I'm here. There's something I want to do, and you're the perfect person to help me do it. Are you in?"

"Oh, this sounds scandalous!" Peyton giggled some more.

"That it is, girl. That it is!" Blue said.

"Well, count me in," Peyton replied in her sugary Southern twang and then roared with laughter.

CHAPTER 43

Mia

Mia woke up next to Jay and smiled. She placed her hand on her bare stomach and giggled. She had Jay right where she wanted him.

"Jay," she crooned. "Wake up, babe."

He grunted.

"Jay," she sang. "Wake up," she continued on the same note.

He grunted again.

Mia rolled him over onto his back, and Jay settled into the new position without opening his eyes. She climbed on top of him, licking his ears and whispering. When she started rubbing him, his body began to respond. A smile crept across his sleepy face. Mia continued moving against him until warmth emanated between them. Jay's hands found her hips and guided her, pulling her closer to him. He released himself from the confines of his boxers and pushed against her before entering. Mia slowly rocked back and forth on top of him.

Jay squeezed her hips into him and hastened the tempo. Lifting his torso, he drove deeper into Mia, intensifying the moment. With one hand, he continued guiding her hips, and with the other, he grabbed her breast and squeezed her nipple. The pain caused Mia to wince, which sent shivers down her spine.

Mia bit her lip to keep from being completely consumed by the pleasure Jay prompted. His even pounding turned into swift ramming, causing her to bounce high over him.

Jay lifted her off of him, positioned her on all fours, and took her from the back. Mia always enjoyed his rough rides. The intense mixture of pain and pleasure was sensually staggering.

"Oh…my…Jay! Oh! I'm…going to…" She completed her sentence with a howl as her peak rippled through her body, leaving her drained.

Jay continued pounding as her juices washed over him. Her walls clenched from the currents that had yet to release their hold on her body. Jay reached the edge and grunted repeatedly as his body writhed during the peak of pleasure until he exploded. Moments later, both of them were lying on their backs with sweat dotting their skin. Lazily, they floated back to reality. Mia rolled on her side and watched as the last few quivers rippled through Jay's core. She loved watching his climax claim control of his body.

"See? If we find a place and move in together, you can have this anytime you want."

Jay opened his eyes. All quaking stopped. He flung his feet over the side of the bed and dragged himself to the master bath.

"Jay!" Mia climbed out of bed, fast on his heels.

He tried to close the door on her, but she caught it before it hit the frame. She stepped in as he emptied his bladder.

"Jay, I'm serious. Do you think I'm doing all of this to help you for nothing? You know we're perfect for one another. By the time we're done, you'll have all the money you need. The baby will be well taken care of."

Jay shook off the last of the urine, washed his hands, and walked past Mia to the bedroom.

"What's the problem?" Mia shrugged. "Blue? She doesn't even want you."

She couldn't understand how Blue continued to be a barrier between them. Mia followed Jay around the room, lecturing at his back.

"Who else is going to deal with you? Admit it, baby. I'm the one. It takes a woman like me to be able to handle a man like you," she said and squeezed his behind.

Jay smiled and climbed back into bed. Mia slid under the covers next to him.

"Hey, have you heard back from the lawyer about what we…you asked for in the divorce?" she asked, fingering his chest. "Hollywood husbands do this kind of thing all the time."

"I don't know about that," Jay said.

"Oh, please. What are you worried about? Trust me. This guy is good at what he does."

"Mia, she saw the place empty when she came over here the other day. She accused me of trying to sell the place from under her."

"Well, what did you say?" Mia sat straight up in the bed.

"I didn't confirm or deny anything. But, I wouldn't underestimate Blue if I were you. She acts like she's got a little fight in her now."

"I'm not worried about Blue." Mia huffed. "I see I'm going to have to put some fire under Carol's ass. We need to get this place sold—fast!"

"We need to be careful."

"Whatever." She rolled her eyes at him. "Whose side are you on anyway? Blue's innocent little behind doesn't have the kind of legal connections that I have. I can make almost anything go my way. Stick with me and you'll be a well-kept man in more ways than one."

CHAPTER 44

Blue

Blue pressed the bell to Peyton's grand home located in a beautiful secluded section of Ashford-Dunwoody. She could smell the essence of the lake just behind the house as she'd approached the door. The doorbell chimed a jingle throughout the house. Within seconds, Peyton's small frame appeared in a silhouette on the other side of the door. She peeked through the glass and smiled.

"Hey, girlfriend!" Peyton pulled Blue into an endearing embrace.

"Hey, Peyton!" Blue smiled. She always enjoyed hearing Peyton's drawl.

"Girl, I'm so excited. I couldn't wait for you to get here. Come on in." Peyton ushered Blue the rest of the way in and pushed the door closed behind her.

It had been a long time since Blue had visited Peyton. The home appeared grander than she remembered. Their heels echoed as they walked through the massive vestibule where several pieces of vibrant artwork lined the walls. They passed a living room, a sitting room with a fireplace, the study, and an elegantly set formal dining room on their way to the kitchen, which was positioned at the back of the house. Each area was cleanly designed with an Asian-inspired flair. An elegant display of sushi and wine decorated the massive kitchen island.

"I know you love sushi, girl. So, I ordered some and pulled out a few bottles of wine from our stash in the cellar. You like white, right? No pun intended." Peyton giggled.

"Right!"

"Let's eat first, and then we'll get down to business. The plates are on the counter. Come on and pull up a stool."

They savored the robust tastes of the Asian delicacies. Peyton turned red after placing a little too much wasabi on her spicy tuna roll.

"Oh my goodness!" She sniffed. "That thing opened my sinuses right up!"

They laughed as Peyton gulped down a half glass of wine in an attempt to douse the fire burning her palate. By the time they were finished, only scraps remained on each plate and one bottle of wine was completely empty.

"Are you ready?" Peyton asked rhetorically while rubbing her hands together.

"As ready as I'll ever be," Blue replied and took a deep breath.

Peyton hopped down from the stool, grabbed their glasses and a second bottle of wine, and then started down the hall.

"Follow me. I have everything set up on the computer in the study."

Once they were in the study, Peyton positioned herself behind a beautifully crafted cherry wood desk and began clicking keys on the computer. Blue pulled up a chair beside her.

"So here's what the guy did. I took all of the DVDs you sent me and told him we wanted a portion of each one placed on a single DVD. He viewed all the footage and strung together what he thought was the best parts into one DVD. Also, he put together some shorter clips of the video on a second DVD."

"Did you look at this yet?"

"Honey, I was too scared to look at this without you. It's

probably a bit much, don't you think?" Peyton admitted.

"I know," Blue agreed.

"Okay. So here goes," Peyton said. She took a deep breath and clicked the triangle on the screen, setting the home movie into action. Then she looked at Blue with lifted brows.

Moments later, the sound of Mia's moans engulfed the room. Peyton fumbled with the mouse to lower the volume. Mia appeared on screen naked and engaged in various sexual positions with several well-known married athletes. Occasionally, Mia would steal glances at the camera with a naughty smirk, full-blown wicked smile, or a wink.

Peyton and Blue kept looking at each other with gaping mouths and wide eyes.

"Okay!" Blue said, shielding her face from the computer screen with her hand. "I've seen enough."

"I'm sure that dude had an interesting time working on this DVD," Peyton commented.

"Peyton, I can't thank you enough for your help with this," Blue said, hugging her.

"It was not a problem at all. I was happy to help. You know how I feel about that woman. Oh! Did I just call her a woman? Shame on me." They laughed together.

Peyton pulled the DVD out of the machine and handed everything to Blue.

"So what are you going to do with all of this?" Peyton asked.

"Right now, I'm just going to hold on to these until the time is right."

"That's some powerful footage. A lot of marriages will be in disrepair because of that DVD."

"I know." Blue thought for a moment about her own ruined marriage. She didn't want to be the catalyst for the other wives. "I plan to be careful how I use it."

The girls were silent for a moment as Blue reflected on what she had just seen.

"Well, Peyton, I have to go. I need to get ready for my flight out in the morning."

"Okay, honey. Keep me posted, and let me know if you need any more of my help," Peyton offered.

"Thanks!" Blue leaned over and gave her girlfriend a friendly kiss on the cheek and another hug.

Peyton walked Blue out. After they reached the car and said their final goodbyes, Blue jumped in the car, but Peyton stood silent. Blue hoped Peyton wouldn't ask.

"Blue?"

"Yes, Peyton?"

Peyton was silent at first, but Blue knew the question behind her lips. She hoped Peyton would lose the nerve to ask.

"Please be honest with me."

Blue held her breath.

"Was Ken on any of those DVDs?"

Blue's heart sank, and she looked at Peyton. Distress glazed her eyes.

"Just tell me, Blue. Was he on there or not?"

Blue dropped her head. "I'm sorry." She looked back up at Peyton. "Yes…he was."

Peyton closed her eyes and gasped, then blinked rapidly. Blue
had purposely held that particular DVD back, along with a few others.
She'd hoped Peyton wouldn't ask about Ken being in the videos. It hurt
to tell her yes, but she couldn't lie. Blue knew Peyton's pain personally.

"I knew it." Her eyes glistened. "I just needed confirmation.
Thank you for being honest with me." Peyton blinked again, starting the
tears strolling down her pink cheeks. "Call me when you touch down so I
know you got home safely, okay?" Peyton spun around and ran into the
house.

Right then, Blue knew the first thing she was going to do with
the DVD once she got home.

CHAPTER 45

Gavin

The moment he touched down, Gavin got right back into the
swing of things, which had included calling Lisa and asking her to meet
him for dinner. He was surprised when she agreed. Now he waited on her
arrival at his favorite African restaurant in Midtown. He relished the
exquisite flavors of the Ivory Coast-inspired cuisine and signature
cocktails. Gavin had just ordered his second snifter of scotch when she
walked in. She wasn't as beautiful as Blue, but she was pretty enough.

"How are you doing?" He stood to greet her with a friendly hug.

"Fine, and how are you?" Lisa asked, her tone flat.

"Busy. Life's been a little crazy," Gavin said, trying to initiate
comfortable small talk.

"Interesting," Lisa said in a tone absent of any indication.

"Shall we eat?" He summoned the hostess, who showed the
couple to their table.

The dimly-lit ethnically designed décor was the perfect setting
for how Gavin intended to end the evening.

As soon as the waiter left to get their drinks, Lisa didn't waste
time getting to the point. "Why did you invite me to dinner?"

"First of all, let me apologize. I got dragged into the middle of a
lot of drama with some very close friends. But now, my focus is back,
and I'd like to know if there's a way we can start over again."

Lisa smiled, showing her first sign of giving in. "I didn't like
being pushed aside. I was offended by the way you treated me, because I
thought we had a solid friendship. Maybe even something that could have

turned into something bigger."

"Maybe we do. How about we start all over again, take it slow, and see what comes?" Gavin said, trying to gauge her emotions.

"I don't know. I think you have some making up to do," she replied as a coy smile spread across her lips.

"I can work with that." Gavin felt his own lips curl into a satisfied smile. This was a start. "So I have some making up to do, huh?"

Blue's number came up on Gavin's phone, but he ignored the call and silenced his ringer. He hadn't answered any of her calls since he'd returned from Atlanta and tried not to feel bad about it. His heart couldn't shake the lingering attachment they'd created when they'd slept together. Gavin still felt her presence during late hours when he was alone.

After dinner, Gavin and Lisa walked around Rockefeller Center holding hands until he escorted her home to Harlem. The taxi waited as they stood outside the door exchanging goodbyes.

"Do you want to come in?" she asked.

"I don't know if that's a good idea when we're trying to start over. Technically, this would be our first date," Gavin joked, secretly hoping she would buy his attempt at sincerity. In reality, he'd wanted to bed her from the moment he saw her toned legs extending from the short sexy dress she wore.

"That would be right. Well, what about if we just picked up where we left off? Would you come in then?" she asked with a sly smile.

"That would mean this isn't our first date, and that opens the door for a lot of possibilities," Gavin said, licking his lips.

"What kind of possibilities?" she nudged.

"I could possibly...show you how much I missed you," Gavin said, closing the space between them. He stood dangerously close and then leaned in a hair's width from her face.

"Yeah, maybe you could...possibly...start making things up to me." She lifted her chin, and her lips brushed his firm chin. She pulled her bottom lip in and ran her tongue across it, cooling the heat generated from his touch.

"That's a possibility." Gavin's voice lowered and his manhood began to respond.

Twin smiles spread across their faces. Gavin paid the taxi, and accompanied Lisa inside. Before Lisa could flick the lights on, they were all over each other.

"How am I doing so far?" Gavin asked, lust weighing down his breath.

"So far, so good," she said between kisses.

Gavin pulled her dress over her head as she tugged at his belt buckle. Seconds later, they were naked, kissing their way to the couch. He lifted her into his arms and carried her. Laying her down gently, he reacquainted himself with her body, touching her in some places that made her giggle and others that caused her to moan.

Lisa massaged him to sturdy lengths and then guided him inside.

Gavin felt her body tense as he entered her. It didn't take long for either of them to enter that place of ecstasy, filling the room with purrs of delight.

Afterwards, Lisa got up to get a glass of water. When she returned, Gavin was still perched in the same spot on the couch.

"How was that for a start?"

"It was a start. Now let's see how you plan to finish," she teased.

Lisa straddled him and fed him the water from her glass.

CHAPTER 46

Mia

"Why don't you want me to come with you, Jay? I don't have to join you in court, but I could be there for you. Make sure everything goes as planned. I know how to work with Scott. I've sent him plenty of clients over the years. He'll do anything for me."

Mia had been trying to nudge Jay into allowing her to accompany him back to New York for the past few days.

"I should be there," she added, and sat wide-legged on the bed, allowing her protruding belly to rest between her legs.

Blue and Jay were scheduled to meet with their lawyers about their impending divorce. After weeks of staying in his home, Mia finally had Jay where she wanted him, and refused to let an unescorted trip to New York cause her efforts to become undone. Now at the end of her second trimester, her pregnancy was obvious. She wanted Blue to see her. Carrying Jay's baby gave her an edge. If she didn't have Jay's complete heart and mind, at least she shared something with him that Blue couldn't.

Blue seemed to have garnered some kind of hold on Jay despite their distance. It was evident in the softening of his eyes whenever her name came up lately. Oddly, he acted like he cared all of a sudden. It would take work to maintain the bit of leverage Mia had gained thus far. Maybe the pregnancy hormones were making her sensitive to the ebb and flow of Jay's emotions. Either way, she needed to protect her interests at all costs.

Jay stared at her as if he didn't like the way that sounded. "What kind of relationship do you have with this lawyer guy?" he asked while stuffing unfolded clothes into an overnight bag. His question brought Mia back to the here and now.

"Nothing like that, Jay." She liked the fact that Jay appeared to be jealous. "He's appreciative of all the business I've given him over the years. I've done a few favors for him, so he owes me. That's all. He'll do whatever's necessary to make a situation work in my best interest. *And* he's a great attorney." Mia pouted. "I want to be there, though," she said, crossing her arms.

"Mia, it's not a good idea. Stay here in Atlanta. I'll see you when I get back next week."

"Next week!" Mia rose to her feet, holding the lower portion of her belly. "Your appointment is tomorrow. Why do you have to stay for the remainder of the week?"

"I have other business to take care of. I still officially live in New York, remember?"

"Ugh! I have my doctor's appointment on Friday and I wanted you to come with me," she told him, and began pacing.

"Why?"

Mia stopped in her tracks and reared her head back. "What do you mean why?"

She hated that he wasn't the least bit enthused about their baby. His suspicions pained her. She knew this baby was his—at least she hoped.

Jay huffed. "Mia, Let's not forget *you're* the one who's excited about this baby. I never wanted children." He turned back and said, "I don't even know if this kid is mine."

"If!" she shouted.

"Yes. *If*…this kid is mine, I'll do what I have to do to take care of it. But, don't look for me to run around like the excited daddy, holding on for every detail about the new baby's arrival."

Jay's words felt like daggers sliding through Mia's skin. The fact that he had the ability to penetrate through to her heart made her uncomfortable, but she still wanted him.

"No problem. I'll never ask your selfish ass to come to an appointment with me again," she sulked.

Jay finished packing his bags and trotted down the steps. Mia followed fast on his heels. She lamented over the fact that he had to go to New York. She had gotten used to playing house with him. Glued to his heels, she trailed him around the house pouting.

"Why are you acting like this?" Jay stopped short, causing Mia to stumble to a halt behind him.

"Whatever, Jay. Have a nice trip!" She waved him off and walked away.

"Are you going to be here to give me some when I get back?" Jay asked.

Mia rolled her eyes and held her tongue for a beat. "Give you some what?" she finally asked, already knowing what he was referring to.

Jay smiled, looked between her thighs, and raised a brow.

"Goodbye, Jay," Mia said, and stomped back up the stairs.

When she was sure Jay was gone, she let the tears fall. He didn't really love her, but she hoped the baby would change things. Mia sat in the center of the same bed she'd made love to him in and cried. Then she pulled herself together and dialed Carol's number, hoping to hear some good news about the sale of the house. Again, her call went unanswered. So, she left another message.

"Hi, Carol. This is Mrs. Holiday. I'm just calling to see about the house. I haven't heard anything lately and wanted to know how things were going. Please call me at your earliest convenience."

Shortly after Mia put the phone down, it rang. Assuming it was the real estate agent, she answered without checking the caller ID.

"Finally, you answered my call." The wonder in Princeton's tone was evident.

Mia picked up on Princeton's voice and hung up. The phone buzzed with a text message from Princeton. *Just want 2 talk 2 u.*

No! She texted back.

Is this baby mine?

Not yours. Don't worry. U don't do babies, remember?

Still need to talk.

Lose my number!

Mia shut her phone off, crawled in the bed, and cried herself to sleep.

When she woke, the house was dim. Evening had arrived, and her stomach growled. After a long refreshing shower, Mia jumped in the car and headed downtown to fill her belly at one of her favorite fine dining establishments.

The soul food menu enticed her. She didn't let her hostess leave the table without first pointing out her waitress. Mia ordered several selections from the list of appetizers as succulent aromas met her nostrils, escalating her hunger. Just as she began to indulge, a shadow loomed over her table. Mia looked up and froze with fear.

"You don't look happy to see me," Princeton said. "Dining alone? Where's your boy, Jay?"

"What do you want?" Mia asked, trying to mask trepidation as annoyance.

Princeton slid the chair back and sat across from Mia at her table.

"I don't remember inviting you to sit down," she snapped.

"The chair was free," Princeton responded, donning a lopsided grin.

Mia sucked her teeth.

"Listen. We need to talk," he said.

"No, we don't. I told you the baby isn't yours." Mia held her firmness, hoping Princeton couldn't detect how frightened she really was.

"Not about the baby…about us," he said.

"There's no *us* to talk about." Mia rolled her eyes again. Her fear was waning, losing its power to irritation.

Princeton banged the table with his fist. The dishes on the table clinked and the water glass tipped over, spilling all over the table, Mia, and the floor. She flinched and her stomach felt weak, threatening to protest the little bit of food she'd just taken in. Princeton leaned over the table and spoke in a low tone.

"You may think you're done with me, but I'm not done with you. How do you suppose you're going to pay me back for all the things you charged on my card that day? The least you could do is thank me," he said, and snarled.

Mia rolled her eyes and turned away, her foot tapping nervously. She was scared again.

Princeton sat back in his chair. "Now, I think it's only fair that you go out to dinner with me one last time. I won't hurt you...if you don't make me. Ha!"

Mia jumped when Princeton let out his version of a cynical laugh.

"Really. No need to be afraid. Just give me my time. I'm in town until Friday," he said as he stood. "Just let me know what night works best for you." He then disappeared into the crowd.

Mia's appetite vanished. She asked for a takeout plate, dropped enough money on the table to cover her meal and a hefty tip, and left. Men usually didn't intimidate her, but this one did. In fact, Princeton downright frightened her. The vulnerability angered her, but Mia would find a way to turn the tables.

CHAPTER 47

Blue

The day had finally come for Blue and Jay to sit before their lawyers. She'd tried to envision what this day would entail. Her erratic thoughts had robbed her of much-needed sleep. She woke lacking the energy she needed to face the day.

Blue checked herself in the mirror for the last time. She finger-fluffed her hair and brushed imaginary lint off the shoulders of her suit jacket. Blue wanted to look professional but feminine. Wearing the caramel-colored suit Jay had always favored was perfect. Blue wasn't interested in enticing Jay, though. She simply wanted to remind him of what he'd lost.

Blue looked around for her phone, purse, keys, and overcoat. The display on her Blackberry shone. She picked up the phone, viewed the number, and answered it before it had a chance to ring.

"Good Morning, Victor," Blue greeted, mustering up as much cheer as she possibly could.

"Good morning, Blue. Are you ready?" Victor's voice was full and strong. Blue was thankful at least he was ready for battle.

"As ready as I'm ever going to be," she said and sighed.

"Don't be nervous. Everything will be fine. I'll meet you in front of the courthouse. This one is in the bag!"

"Okay. See you soon. Bye." Blue disconnected the call, grabbed her purse, and headed out.

The doorman hailed a taxi, and she was en route to yet another life-altering adventure. Despite her ample breakfast, anxiety nestled in her belly. She placed her hand on her stomach, trying to settle the frenzy.

Blue spotted Victor the moment she stepped out of the taxi. A few feet away, Jay stood beside another gentleman, who she assumed was his lawyer. There was something oddly familiar about the man, but she couldn't place him. Victor escorted Blue past the metal detectors and into a receiving area where they would wait until called by the judge. Victor checked in and took a seat next to Blue. Shortly after, Jay entered with his attorney.

The way Jay stared at her made her wish she'd worn a different suit. She no longer wanted to be noticed. Jay donned the same scowl as the day she'd dropped the bomb on him about her sleeping with Gavin. Blue initiated small talk with Victor to keep from focusing on Jay's steady gaze. She kept rubbing her moist palms on her skirt, trying to eliminate the wet, clammy feeling. She coached her anxiety away, recalling the anger of his betrayal.

"Mack/Holiday!" A slight woman with dusty brown hair and a frumpy floral dress commanded the room's attention. Her arms were loaded down with endless manila files. "Mack/Holiday, please follow me!" she said with a voice that exposed a serious cigarette habit.

The four of them entered a small room with a conference table and a third party whom she presumed was an arbitrator. Blue had hoped for a woman who could understand her plight, but instead, it was a man who resembled the most recent bachelor from a reality show.

Their attorneys officially began with their petitions. Victor went first, explaining Blue's petition to file for divorce based on physical and verbal abuse, infidelity, and a laundry list of other charges Blue hadn't realized she could put in her petition.

Blue was interested in selling the Atlanta home and splitting the proceeds, then walking away clean. She asked Jay for nothing more, even though she had proof of his infidelity. Most of all, she simply wanted out of the marriage.

When it was time for Jay's attorney to speak, he advised the court that Jay's petition was filed by reason of abandonment, infidelity, neglect, irreconcilable differences, and a barrage of other ridiculous and unfounded claims. Blue's mouth dropped at the mention of the bogus charges. Scott Cooper went on to explain that Blue had left Jay simply because he lost his job, then turned around and had an affair with his best friend. Scott argued that Jay deserved spousal support to the tune of twenty-five thousand dollars a month. He wanted all property to be sold and the proceeds split in half, including the New York penthouse she had inherited from her grandfather.

Blue's loud gasp garnered the attention of everyone in the room. Her jaw hit the floor, and she felt the air being squeezed from her lungs. When she realized all eyes were on her, she covered her mouth and tried to regain her composure as she willed her eyes not to water. Victor reached down and held her hand. His face showed no sign of defeat, but Blue wasn't convinced. From that point forward, Blue heard nothing else that was said by either attorney. She returned to herself when she and Victor were back outside.

"Let's grab a cup of coffee," he suggested, walking her along.

They walked the short distance to the local coffeehouse where Blue ordered a latte just before plopping into her seat. For the past hour, she had shaken her head every time she thought about Jay's petition.

"Why is he doing this, Victor?" Blue asked.

"Relax, Blue. There's nothing to worry about. I see this kind of stuff all of the time," Victor said, unfazed.

"My grandfather's penthouse! Twenty-five thousand a month! Where am I supposed to get that kind of money? Why should I support him? It's his fault he lost his job. And he slept with my best friend. How dare he tell those lies?"

Victor waved her off. "He was reaching."

"But what if the judge grants him what he wants?" Blue felt her heart plummet. Her grandfather would roll over in his grave if he knew about this.

"Believe me when I say that's not going to happen." Victor never lost his cool.

"How can you be so sure?" Blue wasn't convinced. She stared at her latte, unable to bring it to her mouth again. The previous sips threatened to churn her stomach like a whirlpool.

"Blue, this is new for you, not me. Just trust me." Victor calmly sipped his black coffee.

"He's trying to get his hands on my trust fund. He wants to wipe me out!" Blue rested her head in her hands.

"Don't worry. He can't. There are legal stipulations on it that will not allow him access no matter what he tries."

"He told that lawyer a bunch of lies. I didn't leave him because he lost his job! I can't believe he told them I slept with his best friend. That wasn't until after we separated."

Victor raised his brow, and then held his hand up as if to say, *That's none of my business.*

Blue was embarrassed. "They're not friends anymore. I mean,

they were friends when it happened...forget it."

Victor laughed. "You don't have to explain anything to me." He cupped her hand in his. "Say that you will trust me. Have I ever let your family down?" he asked, lifting his brow.

"No," Blue responded and relaxed her shoulders.

"Why don't you take the rest of the day off and get a massage or something? Treat yourself and relax. I'll be in touch soon so we can meet and talk about our next steps. Be ready for a fight, but don't worry. We're going to win."

"Thanks, Victor," Blue said, slouching back in her chair. Finally, she smiled. She had Victor on her side, so she was going to win this fight.

"One last thing," Victor said just as Blue was about to get up. "I've got some information about your home in Atlanta. You're going to have to take another trip very soon."

Blue sighed. "Is it what I suspected?"

"That's what it looks like," he replied with a frown.

Blue left Victor at Starbucks and took a taxi back home. When she entered her penthouse, she felt like she was having a panic attack. She wanted to call Gavin, but he hadn't answered her calls in weeks. No matter how hard she tried to relax, she couldn't. She was ready for the fight, but like any other struggle, there was a chance she'd have to take a hit. With round one behind her, she was willing to face round two head on, but she felt like she didn't have anyone in her corner. There was only one person whose presence could help her maintain. Somehow she had to get him back into her life.

CHAPTER 48

Mia

Mia waited anxiously for Princeton's arrival. She was ready to get this night behind her so she could close this chapter of her life for good. Her pink strapless dress hugged her curves like race car tires on asphalt. Now that she was close to her third trimester, she wore studded designer flats instead of stilettos.

Princeton pulled up in front of the townhouse in the Jag. Not wanting him to come inside, Mia met him on the walkway.

"Just look at you, baby girl. Beautiful. Simply beautiful." Princeton adored her with his eyes.

"Thanks."

On the way to the restaurant, Princeton did all the talking while Mia half listened and fingered her Blackberry.

When Princeton pulled in front of a renowned grill and lounge, the valet immediately walked over and got into the driver's seat. Princeton trotted to the passenger side and carefully helped Mia out. As she emerged, his smile spread from one ear to the next. All eyes were on them. R&B music blared from hidden speakers throughout the bustling restaurant. He made it a point to smile, nod, and wave hello to every familiar face in the place. She knew just as many people as he did, but didn't make a big deal about it. Mia rolled her eyes at his ostentatious behavior.

Princeton pulled out her chair before taking his seat. Once again, he was the perfect gentleman, but Mia knew better.

"Have you been here before?" Princeton yelled, trying to be

heard above the music.

"What?" Mia yelled back as she leaned into the table, trying to hear.

"Have. You. Ever. Been. Here. Before?" he pronounced louder.

Mia shook her head no. *Let him feel like he's showing me something I've never seen,* she thought. Princeton moved to the music. Soon after, their waitress approached the table.

"Hey, Mia!" a short, curvaceous waitress greeted. She looked down at her stomach and then met her eyes with a wink. "How are *you* doing these days?"

"I'm fine. Thanks."

The girl raised a brow at Mia's dry response, but appeared to have gotten the picture.

"What did she say?" Princeton shouted at Mia.

"She asked me what I would like to have today!"

"Oh!" Princeton shouted back.

Mia and the waitress quickly glanced at one another and smiled.

They placed their orders and then waited patiently for their food. Mia looked around the place and played with her Blackberry while enjoying the music.

Princeton was on the other side of the table, lip-syncing into his spoon.

Her phone vibrated; she had finally received what she was waiting for. Immediately, her mood brightened. The food arrived, and they ate until all that was left to savor were the remnants of sauce on their fingers.

Mia invited Princeton out onto the dance floor to kill a little time.

He danced with a simple smoothness, his languid movements were almost mesmerizing. Mia enjoyed dancing, but after a few songs, she was ready to go home.

"I've had a good time, but I'm getting tired," Mia said, leading Princeton back to the table.

"Ah, baby, so soon!" He frowned.

"Yes! I'm really tired," she said, placing her hand on her stomach.

"Well, if I take you home now, will you invite me in?" he asked.

"Maybe," Mia replied with a smirk before walking away.

Princeton paid the bill and practically dragged Mia outside to the valet.

"That was a nice place, right?" he asked once they were inside the car.

"Yes. The music was a little loud, but the food was tasty."

"Glad you enjoyed it. I just wanted to show you a nice time. Make up for that last time we were together. Maybe I can convince you to stick around for a little while," he said.

Mia turned slightly to cut her eyes. "Oh, how sweet." She pretended to allow his comments to melt her resolve.

"You're finally coming around. I'm sorry about the other week, baby. I just didn't understand why you didn't want to be with me anymore. I wasn't ready to let you go."

Mia turned her head and looked out the window.

"Plus, now I know I can't get you pregnant." Princeton laughed.

Mia mocked his laugh, cut her eyes, and looked back out the window.

"Here we are," he said when they pulled up in front of the townhouse. "Now…" He adjusted himself toward her, gently ran his finger along her jaw, and then caressed her chin. "Are you going to invite me in?"

"Should I?" she asked, wearing a no-nonsense expression.

"Baby, you can trust me. I won't harm you." Princeton crossed his heart and held his right hand in the hair. "I promise," he said.

Mia pretended to think about it for a while, her eyes cast toward the sky.

Princeton held his hand up like a Boy Scout. "I promise!" he said again.

"Okay," She responded as if he were pulling her arm.

Princeton hopped out of the car and followed Mia up the walkway like a jovial puppy.

"No furniture? I can take you shopping, if you want," he said as he stepped inside the townhouse.

"I won't be here long. Besides, I have all the furniture I need."

"Where?" he asked, looking around again.

"In the bedroom."

"That's what I'm talking about," Princeton said, rubbing his hands together.

Mia took to the steps and curled her finger, summoning Princeton to follow her. He trailed behind her gleefully. She laughed at his silly eagerness and wondered what she had done to this man to make him act the way he did. When they hit the bedroom, Princeton's hands groped all over her body, even caressing her belly.

"Wait! Let me get comfortable," she said.

Mia put her keys down and fiddled with a few things on the dresser. After a short trip to the adjoining bathroom, she stood before him and removed her pink dress, exposing her matching lace undergarments.

Princeton sucked his bottom lip as he watched her undress. He took her into his arms and laid her down on the bed.

She scooted back to the center of the king-sized bed and lay sideways. He climbed on top of her and kissed her body from head to toe. Then he quickly removed his clothes and resumed his position, placing moist peck prints from her neck to her center. He kissed around her stomach.

"You look beautiful pregnant," he whispered.

Princeton's tongue found her center again, tasting her longer and slower, darting his tongue in and out of her opening. Mia squirmed. He strummed and she squealed. The smile plastered on his face was like a pat on his own back.

"I got more for you, baby," he said.

Princeton entered her carefully, then gradually increased his vigor.

Mia clamped her walls to clutch his manhood. "Turn over!" she ordered, and he submissively obeyed.

Mia lowered herself on to him and rode him with zeal, pressing herself against him vigorously. Over and over, she rose and fell against his pelvis, switching her pace without warning. She guided him in deeper and then pulled him all the way out. When Princeton's eyes rolled into the back of his head, she got up.

"What...where...come back...baby, don't stop," he stammered.

Mia straddled him and rode until he groaned and his entire body convulsed. She clasped her walls around his manhood as he eased her off of him.

His body tensed like one large muscle. After gently pushing her off, he leaned over the side of the bed to catch his breath. "You see...woman...you make me crazy. That's why I can't get enough of you," he said as he lay back with a smile plastered across his face.

"Yeah, blame it on me," she said and laughed.

Mia rested back against a stack of large fluffy pillows. Princeton joined her at the head of the bed, took a deep breath, and smiled again. She traced his taut chest and abs with her finger.

"What's your wife like?" she asked.

After a long silence, he answered. "She's a nice woman."

"She looks sweet."

Princeton sat up.

"And those two boys are just adorable. Tell me, do they really like living out there in the midst of that expansive forest you have them tucked away in?"

"Don't try to play games with me, Mia." Princeton waved his finger in her face.

Mia took hold of his finger and kissed it with her eyes trained on him.

"No," she said casually, "don't play games with me."

She winked at him. Princeton narrowed his eyes.

"And before you jump on me, smile because you're on streaming video. If you so much as touch a hair on my body, this place will be crawling with huge men ready to beat your ass to a bloody pulp. You will never run a single yard again." Mia paused to let Princeton absorb what she had just said.

"What?" he said, his face scrunched in disbelief.

"Listen to me closely," she said seductively. "As we speak, this nice little video that we just made is being downloaded by my famed attorney, Scott Cooper. You may know him. And if you don't want to upset your happy little home, you'll behave for me."

"You bitch!" Princeton sat straight up in the bed.

"That I am! Now hush because I'm not done. If you cooperate, this will never get to your wife or the commissioner, who happens to be your father-in-law, right? That way, your happy home, your career, and your prized legs will stay intact."

Princeton raised his hand like he wanted to hit Mia.

"Uh, uh, uh. You're being watched, remember?" she sang. "We don't want to add assault to this little party of treachery, now do we? Think, sweetie. Your job…your wife…your children…they're all on the line here." Mia pursed her lips.

Princeton tightened his lips as his hands balled into fists.

"Now, all you have to do is leave me alone. Don't call me, don't visit me, and if you see me on the street, don't even bother saying hello. Now, if you doubt me, feel free to go over to that little laptop on the dresser, hit any key, and click on play. Or you can take a look out the window and you'll see this place is surrounded."

Princeton hit the enter key, and the screen displayed live video of Mia lying across the bed. She walked over to the computer, hit a few keys, and started the video from the beginning. Then she fast-forwarded to scenes of him kissing all over her naked body, burying his face between her legs, and grunting through his pinnacle moment.

Princeton looked at her with disbelief. Mia held up the tiny remote in her hand.

"If you close that window on the screen, you'll see a lovely picture of your wife and the boys in your beautiful home."

Princeton did as she said. When the picture appeared, he stumbled away from the computer.

"Shit!" Princeton stomped his feet, snatched his clothes, threw them on, and dashed down the steps, cursing Mia the entire way.

After minimizing the screen, she followed him down the steps.

"I could beat the shit out of you, but you're not worth it," he said when he reached the bottom.

"I know. I'm trifling, right?" She laughed as she followed him down at a slow, distant pace.

Princeton snarled at her, yanked open the front door, and halted. Two men, who appeared to weigh an excess of three hundred pounds each, and were dressed all in black, were positioned on each end of his Jag. He looked back at Mia.

"Bye! Have a nice life, and tell your wife I said hello." She waved and slammed the door.

CHAPTER 49

Gavin

When Gavin drove his vehicle into his father's driveway, the front door was already opened, anticipating his arrival.

"You ready?" He turned to ask Lisa.

"Of course! I'm excited about meeting your dad! Are *you* ready for this?" she asked.

"Hell yeah, I'm ready. It's been so long since I brought a woman to meet him that he was starting to question my manhood. Now maybe he'll get off my back." Gavin chuckled as Lisa playfully slapped his arm.

"Okay, let's go!" Lisa said, smiling.

Gavin trotted to Lisa's side of the car and opened the door for her. By the time they reached the front door, his father was pushing it open for them to enter.

"Hey, son," Mr. Gray greeted as he held the door open.

"What's up, Pop?" Gavin said, hugging his dad.

Gavin presented Lisa to his father like a gift.

"This is Lisa. Lisa, this is my father George Gray."

Mr. Gray shook Lisa's hand and then kissed the back of it.

"Nice to meet you, young lady," he said, then winked at her.

"Hey, old man. Lay off my woman," Gavin teased. They all laughed.

"Nice to meet you, too, Mr. Gray. I've heard a lot of great things about you."

"Don't believe any of it," he joked. "Come on in, young people. I've got a nice dinner prepared. We're going to eat out on the porch and enjoy the nice weather."

"That sounds good. You got any beer, Pop?"

"Now what kind of question is that?" Mr. Gray turned his attention to Lisa. "And what about the lady? What would you like to drink?"

"Oh, I'm fine. Thanks," Lisa said.

"Fine? You don't want to start out with a nice cocktail?" Mr. Gray knitted his brow and looked at Gavin. "You don't drink?" Before Lisa could respond, Mr. Gray looked back at Gavin and said, "Where did you find her?"

Lisa looked alarmed.

"Stop messing with her, Dad."

Mr. Gray snickered, enjoying the tease.

"Come on in here, girl. You'll get to know me soon enough."

Lisa released the breath she'd been holding and smiled.

"My dad can be a bit of a jokester at times."

Mr. Gray led Lisa and Gavin past the kitchen and onto the back porch.

"Hello!" A pretty, ample-sized woman around his father's age, greeted them as they passed through. She was leaning over the sink preparing what looked like a pitcher of fresh lemonade.

"Hello," Lisa and Gavin responded together.

"Dad, who's that?" Gavin whispered as they stepped onto the back porch.

"Oh." Mr. Gray smiled, then snickered. "That's a friend of mine," he said with a wink.

Lisa chuckled.

"Is she joining us for dinner?" Gavin asked.

"No. She's about to leave. She just stopped by to help me out a little, that's all. She's nice like that. Makes sure I'm well taken care of. You know what I mean?"

"I bet," Gavin replied.

Just then, the woman came out carrying a tray with a potbelly pitcher and matching glasses filled with lemonade. Each rim was garnished with a fresh lemon slice.

"Millie, I want you to meet my son Gavin. Gavin, this is my dear friend Millie."

They traded nods.

"And this here is Lisa," Mr. Gray continued with a grand sweep of his hand. "She's a dear friend of Gavin's."

Millie extended her hand to greet both Gavin and Lisa.

"Very nice to meet the two of you," she said with a slight southern lilt, then turned her attention to Mr. Gray. "Uh, George, I'll be on my way. I'll give you a call in the morning." She directed her attention back towards Gavin and Lisa. "Enjoy the evening, and I hope you also enjoy the food. Have a blessed night."

"Thank you, ma'am," Gavin and Lisa replied together, displaying their manners.

When Gavin was sure that Ms. Millie was out of earshot, he whispered, "Dear friend?" and smiled.

Mr. Gray smiled and raised a single brow.

"Millie offered to help fix a nice dinner for you when I told her that my son was coming to visit with a *friend*." Mr. Gray used both hands to draw air quotes around the word 'friend'.

"Oh, that was very nice," Lisa said.

Gavin rubbed his hands together. "Sounds tasty. What did she cook?"

"Shoot," Mr. Gray sang, "she prepared a little bit of everything. I hope you brought your appetites with you today."

Gavin and Lisa followed Mr. Gray back into the house to check out the food. The stove and countertops were filled with fine smelling, down-home, soul cooking. They filled their plates with collard greens, rice, yams, baked macaroni and cheese, and turkey wings.

"Make sure you leave room for dessert. Millie brought over some of her homemade peach cobbler and red velvet cake," Mr. Gray added.

Minimal words were passed among the three as they indulged. Once Gavin came up for air, he patted his stomach and took a deep breath. He peered over at Lisa who seemed to have settled in comfortably.

"Whew," Lisa said. "I haven't eaten like that since…Thanksgiving!"

"Girl, it looks like you barely touched your food. You didn't have but a little bit anyway. You can't be full," Mr. Gray said.

Lisa smiled. "Believe me, Mr. Gray. I'm stuffed. Now, if you will excuse me, I need to run to the ladies' room." She turned to Gavin. "Could you show me where it is?"

"Sure." Gavin stood and led Lisa to the restroom, then joined his father back on the porch.

Mr. Gray looked past the door before turning to Gavin. "How long have you been dating this girl?

"Why?" Gavin asked.

"What happened to Blue?" he asked.

"That's not going to work out, Dad," Gavin said, dismissing his father's inquiries with a wave of his hand.

"Why not? A few weeks ago, you were here talking about how you wanted to rescue that girl—be her knight in shining armor. Now you have this new girl in here. What happened? I mean, she seems like a nice girl, but are you sure about her or are you trying to distract yourself from Blue?"

"Not now, Dad." Gavin turned away.

"Why not now? That truth won't change if we wait and talk about it later," his father said.

"I know. I just don't want to talk about it right now. I'm trying to make this thing work with Lisa." Gavin stood and started pacing the porch, while he kept looking towards the door in search of Lisa.

"Trying or forcing?" Mr. Gray asked.

"Dad!" Gavin wanted his father to stop.

"What?" Mr. Gray locked eyes with Gavin. "How long do you think it's going to last?" A few minutes passed with no response from Gavin, so he continued. "When's the last time you spoke to Blue?"

"It's been a while," Gavin practically whispered.

"Who's fault?" Mr. Gray asked.

Usually, Gavin appreciated Mr. Gray's no-nonsense manner. Today, it was agitating him. "Mine. Why?"

"You tell *me* why," Mr. Gray replied, tossing the ball back in Gavin's corner.

"I won't...I haven't been...answering her calls," he finally relented.

"Um hmm, just what I figured. That's why you've been single so long. Had me questioning you." Mr. Gray snickered because of the look Gavin gave him. "Relax, boy. I know you're all man. Deal with your feelings, son. That's all I have to say." Mr. Gray stood. "You want some peach cobbler or some of that red velvet?"

Gavin dropped his head into his hands, and then catching his father's signal, he lifted it quickly. He'd changed the subject just in time for Lisa to reappear. Gavin wasn't sure if she'd heard any of what his father had said and wondered if his uneasiness showed.

"Lisa, honey, I'm going to get me a little of that peach cobbler and red velvet cake. Would you like some, too?" Mr. Gray asked as he made his way past her.

"Pop, stop calling my girl, honey!" he teased.

Mr. Gray chuckled. Gavin took a deep breath and joined Lisa and his father as they laughed.

Lisa looked at Gavin and smiled when he said the words 'my girl'.

Gavin noticed she gave pause to those words and hoped he wouldn't end up regretting that statement later—for the second time. His emotions were on a seesaw.

After dessert, the three chatted late into the evening. When it was time to go, Gavin almost regretted the ride back to Manhattan with just him and Lisa in the car. His father had raised ghosts that he'd tried his best to deny when he called him out about Blue. As long as he avoided her, it was easy to move forward. But, Gavin knew he could only avoid Blue for so long. He thought he was making a statement by bringing Lisa to meet his father. Now he questioned the statement and the target it was intended for.

CHAPTER 50

Mia

Jay picked up his pace against the constant flow of people and the winds whipping around the tall downtown buildings. Mia remained right on his heels with her mink coat hanging open. Autumn had arrived in New York with a vengeance, and the weather was seasonably cool. It may not have been fur season yet, but Mia didn't care. She refused to let him out of her sight. Jay looked at her for a moment, then continued down the street towards the courthouse.

"What's the problem, Jay? I didn't come all the way to New York to sit at that damn hotel and wait around! I know you aren't trying to hide me after all this time?"

"You shouldn't be here. Don't think you're coming inside with me when it's time to go before the judge."

"Whatever, Jay. I'm here and that's what matters."

"Don't start your shit. I already know Blue is going to be ready to blow up when she sees you. I told you before we left this wasn't a good idea."

"Well, she's got to know that we're together. Everybody else knows."

Mia made sure of that every chance she got. She was especially proud of the way she and Jay gallivanted around Atlanta in all the athletic and celebrity circles. Paparazzi had captured them at quite a few events. Though they were never a main attraction, she made sure they remained highly visual. After each gathering, she wasted no time putting her pictures up on Facebook and Twitter for all of her "friends" to see. Every now and then, she'd scour the blogs to see if there were any new pictures of them on the internet. If so, she'd quickly post a link on her social networks.

Jay just looked at her, lifted his eyes to the ceiling, and sighed. "Blue doesn't deserve this, Mia." With his shoulders hung in shame, he looked away, standing still for a moment.

Mia felt her skin heat up. A quick pang of guilt surged through her, but she shook it off. Jay was finally hers, she reminded herself. All she had to do was continue to make sure he didn't have the time or energy for anyone else. Once they were back in Atlanta, she wouldn't have to hear about Blue anymore.

"What's so bad about me being here, Jay?" Mia asked, breaking the silence. "Don't you want me to support you?"

"That doesn't mean you have to come to court with me."

Mia pulled his arm, making him face her.

"Having you show up at my divorce proceedings allegedly pregnant with my child is not the kind of support that helps in this situation."

Mia looked away and tapped her feet when he said 'allegedly'. Then she pouted—which had become commonplace in her third trimester.

"Okay," she said. "I'll find something to do. Call me when you're done."

As much as she wanted Blue to see them together, she didn't want to blow things for Jay. Yet, she prayed that seeing Blue wouldn't have any effect on him.

"Thank you!" Jay said, exasperated.

Mia huffed.

"Thank you," he said again, but this time in a more casual tone.

When Jay turned to walk into the courthouse, Mia cleared her throat. He looked back to see what the problem was, and she walked up and kissed him sensually on the lips.

"Good luck in there," she said while thumbing away the pink gloss she'd left on his lips.

"Thanks," he replied and walked away.

"Hey, Scott," Mia said as she spotted the attorney she'd connected Jay with.

"Hey, baby." Scott leaned over her belly and squeezed her in his arms. The hug lingered. "I see you've been busy," he said and rubbed her stomach.

Jay had stopped walking when Scott approached, and he stared when Scott pulled her in for the hug. The change in Jay's demeanor made Mia smile. Jealousy was the only way she could manage to get a rise from Jay—the only indication that they had a connection. She took what she could get.

"You ready?" Jay called out to Scott.

"Yes, sir. Let's go," he said cheerfully.

Jay looked back at Mia, paused, and walked back over to her.

"You and this guy are awfully familiar with one another," he said.

"Jay, babe, don't tell me you're jealous." A full smile spanned her cheeks. She wasn't fazed by his burning gaze.

"I don't see anything funny here."

Jay was clearly agitated, but before Mia could respond, he turned and followed Scott into the courthouse.

Mia busied herself at the shops throughout downtown Manhattan. When she got bored, she made her way back to the courthouse and went inside. After receiving directions from the officer, she perused the courthouse, but found no sign of Blue or Jay.

Minutes later, she heard a door open, and Jay whizzed past with Scott on his heels. His face was twisted in anger as he ranted about something being unfair. Mia jumped to her feet and scurried to Jay.

"Baby, what happened?" Mia asked, trotting alongside of him.

"Let's just get outside, and we can tell you all about it then," Scott said.

"What are you doing in here?" Jay yelled. "I told you to stay outside."

"Don't yell at me like that. I just asked what happened," Mia said, feeling the sting of tears behind her eyes.

"Let's take this outside, guys. I don't want to make a scene. Jay, you have to calm down. The judges make note of these kinds of outbursts. This is a minor setback—par for the course." Scott looked around. "We're getting too much attention. Let's get outside now," he said, referring to the eyes that were trained on them.

"What the hell happened in there?" Mia's question was ignored again. "Just tell me what's wrong."

Jay's anger, mixed with her impatience, made her anxious. She managed to suppress the tears, but her breathing began outpacing her control.

"Everything!" Jay yelled. "This didn't go the way it was supposed to."

Mia flinched under the roar of Jay's thunderous tone. "Why?" she asked, trying to maintain her composure and keep her anger in check.

People were beginning to stare, and this wasn't the type of attention Mia relished.

Jay stopped abruptly, whipped his head in Mia's direction, opened his mouth to speak, and then shut it tight. Mia wanted to lash out, but from the look on his face, she thought again and held her tongue. Just as they started toward the exit again, Blue stepped out and looked directly into Mia's eyes.

"Just keep walking," Scott said, grabbing Mia by the arm and guiding her toward the exit.

Blue picked up her pace, following them. Her attorney trailed close behind. Looking back, Mia saw Blue point her out to the lawyer as she mouthed, "That's her."

For the first time, Mia questioned her decision to come to court with Jay. She quickly pulled herself together. This was supposed to be her moment, and she didn't want Blue to witness any kind of breakdown between her and Jay. They had to at least appear to be a strong, united front. Mia rubbed a comforting circle along Jay's back and then turned back to look at Blue with a slight smile as Scott ushered her and Jay out of the courthouse. Even after they hit the pavement, Scott continued to hasten them away from the building.

"Mia!" Blue called behind them.

When Mia turned around, Blue's lawyer was holding her arm. Blue pulled her arm from his grasp and marched towards Mia, who stopped and waited for Blue with her arms folded.

"Come on, Mia. Let's go," urged Scott.

"Mia!" Jay ordered.

Mia didn't budge. Blue approached her, stopping a hair's width away from her nose.

"How dare you show up here today!"

"Do I need permission from you to go somewhere with my man?" Mia smiled and rubbed her well-rounded belly.

Blue slapped Mia's face so hard, she stumbled backwards a few feet. The slap caught her completely off guard. From the reaction of everyone else in their party and the immediate bystanders, everyone was surprised. Jay ran and stood between the two women.

"Mia, let's go!" he ordered.

"Let's go?" Mia said, still holding her face. "She hits me, and all you have to say is, let's go? You didn't say anything to Blue. *I'm* your woman. *I'm* carrying your baby. You're not supposed to let her get away with that!" Mia shouted.

She pulled her flailing arms in and squirmed out of Jay's reach, but he succeeded in grabbing hold of her arms and held her firm.

Blue hadn't moved.

"Mia!" Jay yelled again, positioning himself in the way, blocking Mia's line of sight to Blue.

"Mia, my ass! I'll deal with you later." Mia swung her head around Jay, trying to see Blue.

Jay refused to move when Mia tried to push him out of the way. Realizing she wasn't getting around Jay, she shouted over him toward Blue.

"You always thought you were better than me with your trust fund, blue eyes, and all your fancy clothes and men. Well, this one doesn't want you anymore. He's mine now."

"Mia, stop." Jay forced his words through clenched teeth.

"I never flaunted anything in your face. I shared everything I ever had with you!" Blue said, looking flustered.

"You were showing off! You could have kept your shit! I didn't need any of it," Mia yelled, still writhing in Jay's hold.

"What?" Blue looked bewildered.

"Now you know how it feels to be the one without the man." Mia turned her back. "Come on, Jay. Let's go." She grabbed him by his hand and marched down the street.

"Mia!" Blue called after her, and Mia turned with her lips perched. "Be careful of what you covet!"

Mia dismissed Blue's comment with a wave of her hand and kept walking.

CHAPTER 51

Blue

Blue hit the send button before she could talk herself out of it. At some point, she would regret it, but right now, it felt so right. She kept thinking Scott Cooper had looked familiar, but she couldn't pinpoint why.

After Mia had lashed out at her, Blue had returned home and went through Mia's sex DVDs. Initially, her intent was to send a few clips to Jay just so he could know exactly what he was dealing with. It was when she recognized Scott in one of the tapes that it all came together. His pasty backside was hiked in the air with his face disappeared between Mia's legs. Blue saw his face full and clear when he spun Mia around to enter her from behind. What shocked her most was when Mia strapped up and entered Scott from behind.

Blue's phone rang, and she picked it up immediately. It was the call she'd been waiting for.

"Blue! What the hell is this?" Jay snapped into the phone.

"That's your baby's mama!" she said and chuckled.

"Where did you get this?" he asked after a long pause.

"Oh, you didn't know she keeps a video log of her escapades? Look at you. You're a star." She threw her head back and laughed.

"This isn't funny, Blue. Did you show this to your lawyer?" He asked. She detected the alarm in his voice.

"Now that's the question of the decade, isn't it?" She snickered. "Oh, and guess what? I've got more. I wanted to make sure you got this before I sent the other one. Trust me, you won't believe your eyes." Blue laughed again. "Oh, and by the way, how did you find that attorney of yours? He's good," she said, elongating the last word.

"Where did this video come from?" he asked again.

"Don't worry about that. Just get ready for the next clip. Hang up so I can send it to you now."

After disconnecting the call, Blue emailed the video of Scott and Mia to Jay. She waited for almost an hour, but never got a call back. She didn't need to hear from Jay to know he got the message.

Blue poured a glass of Merlot to help wash down the lump of guilt rising in her throat. As much as she despised Mia, she wasn't built for revenge. Instead of washing down the guilt, the wine brought other emotions to the surface. Now Blue was buzzed, and all the emotions were mixed together like a knot of yarn. But, she still had one more thing to do.

***

Blue looked up at the sign on the real estate office to make sure the name matched the one given to her by the attorney. Once inside, she admired the pictures of lavish homes that adorned the walls throughout the reception area. A polished young woman was seated behind the circular mahogany reception desk. She wore a neatly sculpted bun nestled at the base of her head. Perfectly placed make-up made her look like the poster child for businesswoman of the year. She acknowledged Blue with a polite smile and nod. The moment Blue turned her eyes away from the last picture, the receptionist was at her side with a warm smile.

"How may I help you today, ma'am?"

Blue was impressed by her cool professionalism.

"I'd like to speak to an agent about a property."

"Sure. Are you looking to sell or purchase?"

"It's for a property you currently have listed." Blue gave the woman the address.

"Oh, yes. Carol Mathews is handling that property. I'll get Ms. Mathews on the line for you," she said.

Blue found herself watching the woman's taut long legs as she walked back to the other side of the desk. She listened as the receptionist summoned the agent through the sophisticated phone system.

"Ms. Mathews is in, and she'll be right down. In the meantime, would you like some coffee, tea, or water?"

"I'll take some water. Thank you," Blue said and sat on the sleek white couch to wait.

She was happy to catch Carol in the office and hoped the meeting would be worth the quick one-day trip to Atlanta.

The woman promptly returned with a bottle of sparkling water and a mug adorned with the company's logo and website.

"The mug is yours to keep, ma'am. Ms. Mathews shouldn't be long."

Blue smiled again. She was thoroughly impressed with the service she'd received thus far. Blue made mental notes about aspects of the chic décor that she'd like to emulate in her own home. The clean lines of the contemporary furniture and the simple muted palate made the place feel like a page out of a swank decorating magazine.

Within minutes, Ms. Mathews was standing before her. She was another well put-together woman, smartly dressed in brown slacks, a pink tapered button-down shirt, and stylish multicolored pumps that matched impeccably. Her brunette locks framed her face in an orderly bob. Even though her make-up was minimal, it didn't stop her deep-set green eyes from sparkling. She reminded Blue of a modish woman from the ultraconservative banking industry.

"Good morning. I'm Carol Mathews," the woman said, extending her hand, delivering a firm but boney handshake.

"Good morning. My name is Blue Holiday."

Confusion etched the lines of Carol's face for a moment, but her cool professional demeanor remained intact.

"I'm sorry. Did you say your name was Blue Holiday?"

"Yes," Blue said and smiled, taking note of Carol's suspicion.

"That's funny. That's also the name of the owner of the home you inquired about. Could this be a coincidence?" Carol asked with a knowing look on her face.

"I'm afraid not. That's why I'm here to speak with you today," Blue said.

Realization flashed in Carol's eyes.

"Please follow me," Carol said, opening the door for Blue. "Marietta," she called to the receptionist, "please hold all my calls."

Blue followed Carol past the reception area into a bustling office with soft green walls framed in beige molding, with desks in the center and small pod-like offices along the sides. Despite the dismal market, the place seemed busy.

"Maria, please pull the Holiday-Mack file and bring it into my office. Thank you," Carol said to the young woman seated at a desk outside of her office. "Please, have a seat, Ms. Holiday."

By the time, Blue took a seat, Maria was handing Carol the files. She thanked her assistant and slid the glass door to her office closed.

With a creased forehead, Carol reviewed the documents in the files and then looked at Blue.

"Do you have any identification, Ms. Holiday?"

"Plenty," Blue said, and pulled out her license, passport, social security card, and several major credit cards."

"I see," Carol acknowledged, and compared Blue's documents with what she had in the file. "Have you reported this to the authorities?"

"Not yet. I wanted to speak with you first."

"No problem. Well, the first thing we do is report these situations to the authorities," Carol informed her.

Blue nodded her confirmation. "I'll take care of that as soon as I leave here."

"Great. In the meantime, I'll remove the listing. It's a great home, but the market has been slow. In a different environment, this house wouldn't have lasted a month." Carol fell quiet, then sighed before handing all of Blue's identification back to her. "Once you have spoken to the police, let me know if there is anything I can do to help."

"Thank you. I appreciate your cooperation," Blue said and stood to shake Carol's hand.

Blue smiled, but Carol's face remained poised and professional. Blue could tell by the look in her eyes that she was troubled.

"Good day to you, Ms. Holiday."

"Good day to you, as well, Ms. Mathews."

As Blue walked out of Carol's office, she wondered what the outcome would be. Maybe she should have dealt with Mia and Jay directly. She paused for a moment, contemplating. Shaking off her reservation, Blue nodded her goodbye to the receptionist on her way out. She needed to shake the guilt. Blue dialed Vic on his cell phone. When he answered, she simply said, "It's done."

CHAPTER 52

Mia

Mia turned her nose up at the other women inside the jail cell. She couldn't believe she was actually sharing a cramped, damp-smelling space with them. Mia rolled her eyes and scanned the dull gray walls, trying to avoid eye contact with the others. One woman reminded her of a football player, with her baggy sweats, oversized white t-shirt, combat boots, and cornrows masking all signs of femininity. Mia wanted to walk over and punch her square in the eye for staring at her so greedily. Instead, she kept cutting her eyes at the woman, who laughed every time.

A loudmouth woman, who wore a matted wig, smelled like fish, and was dressed in too-tight clothing, kept declaring her innocence through the bars. Two "home girls" laughed and spoke openly about the beating they gave some lady, which had landed them in jail. Most of the women kept to themselves, trying to avoid eye contact and conversation. Between the bold lesbian and the petite woman hovering in the corner crying like a baby, Mia felt like she was going to pull her hair out. The merging odors had started to make her nauseous, making the experience worse. She'd been breathing through her mouth since she entered the cell. Her hands covered her stomach the entire time, as if she could shield the baby from the repulsive elements.

Shifting her weight from one foot to the other, her feet were killing her, but she refused to sit on the dirty bench and give them a rest. She'd have to tolerate the environment until Scott showed up and got her out. She felt severely overdressed with her leggings, knee-high, cat-heeled boots, and studded maternity tunic.

"You have the right to remain silent…" Mia heard the detective with the cheap suit say as she replayed the arrest in her mind. Never in a million years did she consider the fact that her actions would have led to her actually serving time.

Mia bit her bottom lip and blinked several times before facing the back wall of the cell. She couldn't dare show any weakness in the presence of these women. She wasn't like them. They belonged in prison, not her. She wondered what Jay was experiencing in his cell and hoped Scott didn't take too long getting them out.

"Ms. Reynolds!" one of the officers yelled in a booming voice. Mia raised her hand to acknowledge him. "Come with me, please." His keys clanked loudly as he opened the cell door.

"My man didn't come yet? I need to get out of here. I told you it wasn't me," said the fishy woman with the bad wig.

The officer completely ignored her as he cuffed Mia and led her down the hall to a small room. Scott stood to his feet when she entered. Pity painted his face, and a lump grew in her throat. She willed to remain whole, but she had never been so happy to see Scott in her life. She fought the urge to run over and hug his neck tight. As Mia breathed a sigh of relief, the officer pulled out a chair for her on the opposite side of the table and stepped back.

She could no longer hold back the tears.

"Scott!" Mia wiped the streaming tears against her shoulder. "You have to get me the hell out of here."

Scott caressed Mia's shoulders. "I'm working on it."

"What are they saying?" Mia asked, wiping more tears on her shoulder.

Scott took a deep breath. "You're being charged with identity theft, which with a conviction carries a sentence of one to seven years in prison…"

"One to seven years! I can't do time!" Mia yelled, slamming both hands down on the metal table. Officers looked in her direction, bracing for conflict.

Scott reached across the table and gently touched her shoulder. "Let me finish."

Mia sniffed, nodded her head, and slumped in her chair.

"The second charge is conspiracy to commit fraud, which offers a similar penalty plus restitution. However, since Jay conspired with you, we can try to get that reduced.

"Oh my God! Scott, what can you do?"

"We can enter a plea and aim for getting you off without jail time. You'll probably end up with probation and you will more than likely have to pay some kind of restitution."

"What's restitution? Will this work? How long will this take? Will I have to stay in here the whole time?" The questions flowed from Mia like water.

Scott tilted his head. "Restitution is a fine. And yes, it can work."

"I don't know what to expect," she said, interrupting him before he could answer the rest of her questions. "I just know I can't go to jail! Not with a baby on the way."

"Don't worry. I'll work it out. But, I must warn you that you will not get off scot-free. You'll most likely end up having to pay the fine and maybe even do a few years of probation, and you won't be allowed to leave the state."

"I'll be fine as long as I don't have to serve any time. What about Jay?"

"I haven't spoken to him yet, but he's being charged with aiding and abetting you with your conspiracy charge. I'm sure I can get him off on probation, and since he's an athlete, they'll probably throw some community service at him or something like that. At least that's what I'm shooting for. Let's just pray we don't end up with a judge who wants to make an example of him."

Mia shook her head. She wanted to see and speak to Jay so badly. Guilt was sucking the lifeblood out of her like a leech. This wasn't how she'd wanted things to turn out. Her eyes narrowed instinctively at the thought of Blue. Even though this whole thing had been Mia's idea, she was furious at Blue for reporting her. She never saw this coming, because she didn't think Blue had it in her to take it to this level.

"Trust me, Mia."

They both fell silent for a moment.

"Well, I have to go now and see about Jay. I'll see you in court tomorrow. You should be able to go home after the arraignment."

"You mean to tell me I have to spend the night in this nasty circus?" Mia said, twisting her lips as if she smelled something bad.

"In central booking, unfortunately."

"Ugh! I can't believe this! How much do they want for bail?" Mia asked, wondering how much this would cut into her stash.

"I'm requesting that the two of you be released on your own recognizance."

Mia closed her eyes, trying to prepare herself for her return to the cell. Scott nodded towards the officer, indicating the meeting was over.

Mia only hoped that she'd get through the night without contracting a disease or having to fight.

***

Mia struggled to keep it together as she entered the courtroom for their arraignment. She knew the puffiness of her eyes would reveal the fact that she had silently cried through most of the night. Sleep was not an option. Not among those women in her cell.

Mia's heart dropped when she laid her eyes on Jay. He looked downtrodden and scruffy, and like her, still dressed in yesterday's clothes. She pressed her lips together and swallowed. Scott came and sat between her and Jay. Across the room she spotted Blue and her lawyer, Victor. Blue never looked in her direction. When the judge knocked his gavel, Mia jumped. Her nerves were frayed. Mia swallowed again as nervousness churned in her belly.

Judge Samuels summoned the attention of the entire courtroom when he banged his gavel again. This time he did it harder than the first. He nodded at the D.A. who began recounting the charges that Scott discussed with Mia yesterday evening. He requested the maximum punishment allowed for each count, which was up to seven years for Mia and up to one year for Jay, along with twenty five thousand dollars in bail for both.

"Your Honor, my clients have no prior charges. We're asking that the charges for Mr. Mack be reduced from the Class D felony to a misdemeanor. We are willing to enter a plea and commit to probation and community service. My clients pose no risk, and we request they be released on their own recognizance."

The D.A. cleared his throat before speaking. "Your Honor, Mr.

Mack has a record of erratic behavior, which is one of the reasons he was recently let go from his professional basketball team. He has demonstrated violent behavior in the past, and I'm afraid he may pose some risk to my client as they are in the midst of a contentious divorce proceeding."

Judge Samuels looked down and shuffled the papers in front of him. He then lifted his eyes over the steel rim of his glasses and gazed at Mia and Jay. "I will release Ms. Reynolds on her own recognizance. However, I'm setting bail for Mr. Mack at twenty-five thousand dollars. I want to see them back here in four weeks." He peered at Jay. "You, sir, be sure to keep your nose clean during that time." The judge slammed his gavel, sealing his directive, and the court began shuffling again.

Victor straightened his papers and placed them into his briefcase before making a swift exit with Blue, who walked straight-backed at his side. She still didn't turn to acknowledge Mia or Jay on her way out.

"Can you cover bail?" Scott asked Jay.

Jay sat back in his chair and cast his gaze on the ceiling. Moments passed before he responded. "Yeah, it's in the house," he said and paused. "In a bag at the back of the garage… inside of a storage bin."

"All cash!" Mia asked.

Jay looked at Mia for a moment. "Yes, all cash."

Mia rolled her eyes. "Don't worry. I'm just trying to get you out of here. I'll be back. Can I go now?" she asked Scott.

"We have a little paperwork to handle and then you'll be free to go. But, remember, you are not allowed to leave the state."

"I'm just happy to be free!" Mia said.

She couldn't wait to finally get out of the courtroom, get home, and take a shower. She'd focus on being mad and making Blue pay for ratting on her later.

CHAPTER 53

Gavin

Lisa squealed with joy as she planted a juicy kiss on Gavin's cheek before jumping out of the bed, leaving him behind.

"I'm excited and nervous about today," she said about their dinner plans.

"Why?" Gavin asked as he lay back with his hands behind his head.

"You know…because of all of…this." Lisa waved her hand around the room. "And you," she added, then walked back and stood at the side of the bed, smiling down at Gavin. "I'm happy," she said and sat beside him. "I really like being with you."

Gavin pulled up on his side, leaning on his elbow. "I like being with you, too," he said before leading her lips to his with the help of his finger on her chin. "Can we be together again?" he teased, licking his lips at her bare breasts.

"Stop playing, Gavin." She swatted at his playful hand as he traced the edge of her nipples. "I'm serious."

She paused, presumably thinking about what she wanted to say next. Gavin hoped she wasn't going to get too deep.

"I'm happy things are going well with us. I wasn't sure if we would make it this far, but when you took me to meet your father…" Lisa looked as if she were miles away and took a reminiscent breath. "I knew then that I was in a good place. Now we're going to have Thanksgiving dinner with my family!"

Gavin smiled. It was all he could do as he second-guessed his motives for the umpteenth time. Taking Lisa to meet his father was one thing. It kept him in control of their level of commitment, but since that day, things had moved fast—at least from his perspective. Meeting her family could be too much too soon—especially with his mind oscillating between Lisa and his concerns for Blue. Just as he anticipated, Lisa brought up the fact that he had referred to her as *his girl* in front of his father. He let her hang with the idea because it kept him distracted. And now it had been at least a week since Blue's last call, which he hadn't answered.

Gavin assumed if he kept ignoring her, she'd go away. However, when she finally stopped calling, he'd found himself wondering about her. Whenever his phone rang, he'd snatch it up to see who was calling. The friend in him wanted to reach out to her just to make sure she was okay. The lover that she'd coaxed out of him was still jaded at being used. He wanted to forget her and Jay. Lisa was helping, but her presence was more like a band-aid fruitlessly covering a gaping wound.

Lisa continued smiling at Gavin. He pulled her in for a long kiss, his way of responding without actually responding. He'd come to using that tactic whenever Lisa took the conversation to a place he didn't want to journey into. Most times it worked, as they would end up making love.

At first, Lisa gave in, but then pulled back. "Gavin," she said, searching his eyes, "you never say much when we start talking about where our relationship is going."

He tried hard to keep his game face on. "What does that mean?" he asked, finding himself at a loss for words. He knew playing dumb wouldn't go over well with Lisa, but he wanted to buy a little time. "What am I supposed to say?"

"Say something. Your actions seem to comply with where I think we are in this relationship, but your words—or lack of—make me question what's really going on between us."

Gavin sat up fully. "Lisa, I'm cool with us. Let's just enjoy this ride without having to put pressure on the situation by trying to identify exactly where we are every step of the way."

Lisa sat quietly, gnawing on her bottom lip. After a while, she huffed. "Okay," she said with a hint of disappointment. "We'd better start getting ready."

"Yeah," Gavin agreed and headed to the bathroom.

He liked Lisa, but couldn't help holding out for something he constantly told himself he didn't want.

The only thing that kept him from picking up the phone or reaching out to Blue after she'd stopped calling was the fact that Lisa was in his life. With her, he was safe—at least until he ran into Blue at some point, which he knew was very likely to happen since they operated in similar circles. Maybe by the time that happened, she would be completely out of his system.

"Come on. We need to get moving or we're going to be late," Lisa said, leading him to the bathroom by the hand. "It's a good thing I packed a bag last night. We can leave and head to Brooklyn straight from here."

Gavin just smiled again. He hadn't committed to the idea of letting her sleep over, but again, he didn't protest and it'd happened. Eventually, he knew he'd have to show up at the other end of their conversations or else he'd find himself in a one-sided situation that would be difficult to escape.

They managed to get dressed quickly. Wearing a tunic dress that ended mid-thigh but continued with another inch of fringe, Lisa looked like she was fit to grace the runways of Paris. Her strong legs robbed Gavin of his focus. He attempted to complement her look with a polished flair of his own. A crisp, butter-colored, button-down, French-cuffed shirt, monogrammed cufflinks, and brown slacks with his dress shoes did the trick for him. Lisa smiled her approval as they walked out the door.

On the ride over the bridge, Gavin found himself worrying about Blue spending her first Thanksgiving alone. His second concern was meeting Lisa's family, wondering if this would push him further along in the relationship as he continued to participate from the sidelines. He felt like a benched basketball player who had no control or impact on whether or not his team made it to the playoffs. If they played well, he'd reap some of the benefits, but if they didn't, he could safely say he hadn't actually contributed to the loss. The passive position wasn't something he vied for. It just seemed safe.

Gavin finally tuned in completely to Lisa's conversation as they exited Manhattan by crossing over the Brooklyn Bridge.

"My sister and I are worlds apart, and my mother…well…let's just say she speaks her mind. Their mouths may be a bit much, but they're harmless," Lisa said.

"Okay. I'll be fine. They can't be any worse than my family. You haven't met my cousins," he chimed in and laughed as if he'd been mentally present for the entire conversation.

Lisa laughed. "Oh, I'd beg to differ. They may give your cousins a run for their money. You only get one family, so I have to accept them. Got to love 'em."

Lisa directed Gavin to a bustling neighborhood in the Crown Heights section of Brooklyn which featured a blend of stylishly renovated brownstones juxtaposed against a few dilapidated eyesores. A colorful tapestry of ethnicities sprinkled the block. It was unseasonably cold for the end of November as cold air whipped through the streets. A few pedestrians had wrapped themselves in winter gear to protect themselves from the elements, while others hung out on stoops without coats, as if it were the dead of spring.

Lisa's mother's house offered a modest facade that didn't compete with the fancy finishing touches of the newly renovated homes, but it also didn't fall among the unkempt models that lacked attention and curb appeal. Lisa's mother greeted them at the door with her head cocked and one eye shut as the smoke from her Newport spiraled in the air. She took a deep pull, twisted her lips, and let the smoke out the side of her mouth while keeping her eyes on Gavin. Popping the cigarette out of her mouth, she held it low beside her thigh as she leaned in to give Lisa a one-armed embrace.

"Hey, baby!" she greeted. Her husky voice defied her petite presence. She was a darker version of her daughter, but slightly thicker around the edges.

Lisa wrapped both arms around her mom and kissed her on the cheek. Then she turned to Gavin. "Ma, this is Gavin Gray. Gavin, this is my mother, Sandra Langley, but you can call her, Sandra. She can't stand for a grown person to call her Mrs. Langley."

"You got that right," Sandra quipped. "Y'all come on in here," she said, stepping aside for them to pass. She sized Gavin up from head to toe as he passed. "Um! Nice," she commented while following behind him. "Lee's here," she announced as they made their way into the house.

The atmosphere held a warm and jovial existence. Family memories captured in varying frames gave life to the beige walls. Large cozy furniture filled the room, along with lively conversations from holiday guests and loud voices emanating from the flat-screen TV perched on a black stand near the front entrance. A savory medley of delicious aromas filled the space, causing Gavin's mouth to water. Immediately, he recognized the smell of collard greens, turkey, and the sweet scent of candied yams.

"Hey, Lee," sang a thick, short woman who also favored Lisa.

Two rambunctious look-a-likes zoomed around Lisa and latched onto her legs, giggling their greetings to their favorite auntie. Lisa lifted each boy one by one and snuggled her nose into their puffy cheeks.

"Hey, Angela," Lisa said, leaning over to kiss the slightly shorter woman. "Gavin, this is my sister Angie." Lisa paused as Gavin smiled and shook Angela's hand. "Everyone, this is my..." Lisa looked at Gavin "...friend Gavin. Gavin, this is my brother-in-law Rob, my uncle Hubert, my aunt Leslie, and my nephews Ethan and Evan. Everyone, say hello and be on your best behavior. I don't want you scaring my company away."

"Oh girl, hush!" teased a heavyset woman, who Lisa introduced as her aunt. After a few attempts, she finally pulled herself up off the couch and waddled toward Gavin for an embrace. "Hi, baby. Nice to meet you. You sure are handsome. Um," she said before turning her attention to her niece. "Chile, come here and give me some sugar!" Leslie squeezed her niece tight, then pulled her back at arm's length and took a good look. "You pretty, but is that all the dress you have? 'Cause your ass is out!" she said, attempting to look behind Lisa. "You bet not bend over or we gonna see all your goods," she added before waddling back to her spot on the couch.

Lisa rolled her eyes and shook her head.

"What's up, man?" Lisa's brother-in-law greeted Gavin with a firm handshake.

"It's good to meet you."

"Thanks, man. Good to meet you, too," Gavin said to Rob, but his mind was still stuck on Aunt Leslie's comment to Lisa about her dress. The woman was bold and he couldn't tell whether she was joking or not.

Uncle Hubert stood behind Rob, ready for his turn in the receiving line. "Don't pay my wife too much attention. She has never been able to control her mouth. Stuff hits the brain and out the mouth it comes. It's nice to meet you, young man. Lee must really like you if she's bringing you around the family. I wish y'all the best, and hope I don't ever have to hunt you down and shoot you," he said while shaking Gavin's hand. The smell of whiskey sailed past Gavin's nose.

Gavin chuckled at Hubert's wisecrack, until he looked up and realized Hubert wasn't smiling.

"Uh, it's great to meet you, too, sir," he replied and turned to Lisa, who didn't seem moved by her uncle's threat.

"Dinner's ready!" Sandra announced.

Everyone quickly filed into the narrow dining room and took their places at a large oak table set for ten. Lisa's nephews scrambled to sit on either side of her, until their father ordered them to sit near him.

"Auntie has company. You two sit here by me. You'll have

plenty of time to hang with auntie," Rob instructed.

"You need to come to Brooklyn more, Lee. The boys really miss
you," Angela said.

"I know. Maybe I'll come by, pick them up, and let them spend
the weekend with me. I've been so booked up lately that I've barely had
time for myself. I'll have to do it soon before all the Christmas parties
kick in. I'm scheduled for a lot of holiday events. But, my boys come
first. Right, boys!"

"Yeah!" they yelled together.

"Auntie, can you take us to the museum again? We want to see
the dinosaurs," one said.

"Yeah. The dinosaurs were fun! I told my teacher about them,"
the other said.

"You got it. I'll pick you guys up, and we'll go see the dinosaurs
and get something to eat."

"Yes!" one yelled and pumped his fist. The other squealed with
laughter along with the rest of the family.

"Alright, boys. Settle down and let Grandma bless the food so we
can eat! Let's bow our heads," Sandra said, then started rattling off one of
the longest Thanksgiving prayers Gavin had ever heard in his life.

Every time she paused, he'd lift his head thinking she was
finished. When he saw everyone else's eyes were still closed except
Uncle Hubert's, which were intently watching him, he'd quickly lower
his head and pretend to listen to Sandra's long-winded supplication.

When Sandra finally finished, Gavin made sure to be the last to
lift his head out of respect. He'd only hoped no one had heard his
stomach growling. He couldn't take the scent of all that great smelling

food a moment longer. Conversations were limited as the family indulged, but increased by the time everyone got to the end of the first serving. Then the questions came.

"So, how long have you two been dating?" Uncle Hubert asked.

Before either of them could respond, Aunt Leslie shot off a few questions of her own. "You're not one of the metro-down-low-sexuals, are you? A lot of them are real clean cut and dress sharp, just like you."

Lisa and Angie both yelled," Auntie!"

Uncle Hubert looked at Gavin's mouth like he was awaiting his answer.

"Les, you need to stop," Sandra said, snickering.

"No, ma'am. I'm not gay nor am I on the down-low."

"Well, that's good," she said while slathering her third serving of turkey with cranberry sauce. "It's hard to tell these days. I see you wearing some nice cufflinks. I know quality when I see it. What you do for a living?" she asked while chewing a wad of turkey.

"I own a sports agency," Gavin replied politely.

"Very nice! I hope you went to school for that, because we didn't invest all our time getting Lee through school to be messing around with just any kind of man. Lee always had dreams, and I'd hate to see her with someone who isn't worth her time. She's a great catch," Leslie stated without even looking at Gavin.

The consensus around the table confirmed the fact that trying to bridle Leslie's tongue was futile. Everyone except Hubert just rolled their eyes and chimed in every now and then, trying to change the subject. Somehow, Leslie always brought the conversation back to Gavin. Where was his family from? How long had he been in business? Had he ever been to jail? How many baby mamas did he have? Leslie was delighted that he wasn't gay and hadn't gotten any stray women pregnant. Gavin hung in there like a trooper, tickled by Leslie's honesty and curiosity. By the end of dinner, Lisa's eyes begged for his forgiveness. Gavin wasn't bothered at all. He appreciated her family's authenticity.

On the way home, Lisa and he joked about the evening as she continued to apologize.

"Do you want me to take you straight home?" Gavin asked as he sped through midtown on the FDR.

"It's up to you. I don't know about you, but I don't have to work tomorrow. I could stay another night if you don't have anything to do."

Gavin stayed quiet. His phone vibrated. In his heart, he felt like it was Blue. He let his silence do the talking once again and pulled off at his exit near the Upper East Side. If it was Blue calling and he went home alone, he'd surely call her back. Keeping Lisa around gave him an excuse to keep ignoring her.

When they reached his penthouse, Gavin poured them a drink, unbuttoned his shirt, and slopped lazily on the couch with Lisa in his arms. After only moments of sipping, Lisa fell into a light sleep. Gavin eased himself from under her, headed to the bathroom, and pulled out his phone, thumbing through his messages and missed calls. He paused when he saw Blue's one missed call and then checked his text messages. Among many Thanksgiving wishes, there was one from Blue stating, *I just wanted to say Happy Thanksgiving. I miss you, my friend.*

Instinctively, Gavin pressed the talk button, dialing Blue's number, and she answered on the first ring. When she said hello, a flutter surged through him. He disconnected the call without responding.

CHAPTER 54

Blue

Blue needed to see Gavin. He'd been on her mind for the past few days and she decided that there was no better time than the present. She pulled on a jacket to ward off the crisp, cool evening air and jumped in a taxi, anxious about her unplanned visit. She fought reservations about just showing up during the entire ride over and as she entered the building then called up to Gavin's penthouse from the lobby phone.

"Hello!" Gavin answered quickly and cheerfully.

"Hi," she said, hoping he wouldn't hang up.

"Blue?"

"Can I come up?"

After a long pause, he finally responded as she shifted impatiently on her feet. "I only have a few minutes to spare."

"This won't take long. I promise."

When she reached the penthouse, Gavin was out on the balcony. Weary footsteps carried her across the floor. Each one weighted with foreboding. Surely Gavin knew she was there, but he never turned to acknowledge her. Blue contemplated taking lighter steps back towards the elevator, but instead, she pressed on.

"Hi," she said to his back.

"Hi," he responded without turning. "What brings you here?" He finally turned around, stone-faced.

"Gavin…" Now that she was in front of him, she didn't know where to start, but then the words rushed out. "I need you." Blue wished she had better control on the reigns holding them in. "I know you've been avoiding me. I'm sorry…again. I admit it. I wanted to make Jay jealous. But, that's not the only reason I made love to you."

Gavin stood firm on his feet and dared Blue visually. The stern gaze felt like pine needles prickling her skin.

"I made love to you because I wanted to. I'd wanted to for so long. I needed that…from you." Blue quieted. "After this, I'll leave." She paused again. His rigidity taunted her nerves. She shifted her sight away from him. For a few moments, she stared at the floor. She could feel his impatience heightening. Finally, she lifted her eyes to meet his.

"I love you."

Blue started her long walk back to the elevator. She hated the fact that she'd failed Gavin. She felt his eyes on her back as she walked out of his life for good. Besides realizing she was in love with him, she recognized that he was also a true friend. His absence left a gaping hole in her life. If she couldn't move on with him in her life as a lover, she at least wanted her friend back. Either way, she needed to put it all on the line, let the chips fall where they may. One way or the other, she had to bring closure to the distance that had grown between them.

"You love me?" He sounded surprised.

She froze. "I do," she said without turning back to face him. She started walking again, hoping he'd say something else, yet knowing he probably wouldn't.

"How do you know?" he asked.

Blue's heart pounded in her chest. "I realized it that day. After that, I knew for sure when you refused to talk to me or answer my calls," she said, still afraid to look at him.

She wanted to say more, but her lips wouldn't cooperate with her mind. She couldn't bring herself to say that she found herself needing him more than she'd ever felt she needed Jay. She wished he could read her mind so she wouldn't have to search for the words to explain how his absence suffocated her. Surely she couldn't tell him that she'd come by so many times before but didn't have the courage to ask to be invited in. Though she had nothing against her personally, she could never mention how much she envied Lisa for simply being able to have a normal conversation with him. The destruction of their friendship and whatever else they could have had, had fallen on her.

"That's funny," Gavin said.

Blue sucked her teeth and picked up her pace.

"Because I love you, too…and I always have," he added, causing her to stop in her tracks.

Stunned by Gavin's admission, Blue played with the words in her head, second-guessing what she'd heard.

"But, you belonged to Jay," he continued. "When he hurt you, I wanted to rescue you from all the pain, but then you did what you did."

Blue faced him. They locked eyes. Neither of them heard the elevator chime. Then the doors opened, and Lisa stepped into the penthouse.

"I'm so sorry, Gavin," Blue said as hot tears fell from her eyes. "If you could ever forgive me, I promise…" Blue noticed the shift in Gavin's eyes and turned around.

Lisa stood with her hand on her hip and her lips tight. "Don't let me interrupt."

Her tone was polite, but Blue felt the bitterness behind the words. She didn't know how much Lisa knew about her, but she sensed she didn't like her. Women knew when other women had interests in their men. Blue detected that Lisa saw her as a threat by way of her demeanor and her scrutinizing eyes. Lisa's intent stare was confirmation. Some knowledge of Blue had obviously preceded this chance meeting. Why else would Lisa seem to cast such a callous vibe? Especially since this was the first time Blue had ever set eyes on this woman.

Blue looked to Gavin. He looked between the two women and took a deep breath. It seemed like everyone in the room waited for him to determine where the moment would go from there.

"Blue, I'll call you," he said dismissively, and then he turned his attention to Lisa. "I need to talk to you."

Feeling an odd mix of dejection and excitement, Blue dragged herself to the elevator to leave. She replayed the words that contributed to her state of flux over and over in her head.

Because I love you, too, but then you did what you did.

CHAPTER 55
Mia

Despite fatigue, sleep evaded Mia for most of the night, again.
For days, her nerves had been twisted in knots. She squeezed her eyes
shut, then gave up and huffed. Her night spent in jail, Jay's behavior since
their trip to New York, and the possibility of going to prison made her
weary. She threw the covers back and went to the bathroom. Once she
returned, she decided to check in on Jay. She found herself standing in the
doorway, watching him sleep in the other room. In her mind, she slipped
into the bed beside him. In reality, she knew he'd protest. The certainty of
rejection sent her dragging back to her room.

Mia slid back into bed alone and longed for sleep. Suddenly, her
eyes popped open from the surge of pain in her abdomen. The quick bolt
took her breath away and left her clutching her lower stomach. Ten
minutes later, it was back. This time, Mia sat straight up in bed spurting
labored breaths. She thought about what she'd eaten the night before, and
then blamed it on the anxiety from the turmoil infiltrating her life.
Another surge struck her, and she cried out, swung her legs over the side
of the bed, and panted.

When the pain subsided, Mia was able to catch her breath. She
suppressed her fears and stood on wobbly legs.

"Jay!" she yelled, and immediately felt pressure on her pelvis.
Afraid to move, she braced her belly. "Oh my God!" She screamed
louder, "Jay!"

Seconds passed, but they felt like minutes. Realizing she was in
labor, Mia held onto her stomach, anticipating the next contraction as she

cautiously trudged towards Jay's room. Moments later, another pain shot through her. She doubled over and cried out. Jay jerked out of his sleep.

"I'm…having the…baby!" Mia sputtered.

"Now?" Jay leapt from his bed.

"Yes, now!" Mia said breathlessly as she held firmly to her stomach.

"Oh shit!" he said, running circles. Then he walked her to the bathroom to shower and get ready for the hospital.

After Mia contacted the doctor, they jumped in the car. Jay sped through the streets without talking. Mia wanted to focus on the baby coming, but couldn't help wondering what was on Jay's mind, except when the contractions snuck in and snatched her focus every couple of minutes.

Jay screeched to a hard stop in the bay at the hospital's entrance, jumped out of the car, and raced inside to find help. He quickly returned with a portly orderly pushing a wheelchair. Mia was just catching her breath from the latest contraction when they stopped at her side of the car.

"Good morning…" he said. His pleasant baby face, small eyes, and calm voice contrasted his sturdy stature.

"Ms. Reynolds," she panted.

"Good morning, Ms. Reynolds. I'm Darren. Is this your first?" he asked while easily helping her into the wheelchair.

"Yes…yes, it is," she stammered. "Owww!" she cried.

"Don't worry. You're in good hands. Just take nice, easy breaths. This will all be over before you know it," he said. His lips spread into a wide comforting smile.

"It hurts…bad," she said, bending forward as much as she could in the wheelchair.

Jay still hadn't said much as he trailed behind them. The orderly's cool voice soothed Mia. It made her feel like someone was in her corner.

She cried out again. The loudest since the pain began. The guy picked up his speed as he rolled her through the bright sterile corridor, through a large set of double doors, and past rushing medical staff. As they entered the labor and delivery wing, Mia heard other mothers screaming in anguish. The melody of labor, doctors commanding patients to push, babies trying out their lungs, and the scurry of the medical staff made Mia's heart race. She second-guessed her condition and then held out her hand for Jay to hold, looking for his comfort. Jay missed the signal.

"Jay! Come…here…please."

"What's up?" he asked calmly.

His casual tone brought Mia's emotions to the surface. Her eyes watered, but she blinked back the tears as he came to her side. She reached for his hand, held it tight, and waited for him to match the intensity of her grip. He didn't. She wanted him to pacify her—rub her back and promise her that everything would be alright. She wanted him to share her anxiety and excitement. Jay didn't release her hand, but barely held her back. Eventually, Mia dropped his hand and wrapped her arms around herself, wincing when the contractions hit her.

A male nurse set Mia up in a small white room filled with machines she'd never seen before. He patted her hand and smiled. "You're doing fine. The doctor will be right in."

On cue, Dr. Lisbon entered the room. His erect posture made him appear almost as tall as Jay. His strong chin and cleanly shaven face gave him a young polished look. His hazel eyes were penetrating but soothing, which complemented his brunette crop. He looked more like an actor than a real doctor.

"How's my favorite patient?"

"This hurts!" she moaned.

He chuckled. "I know, but you're doing fine." He turned to Jay. "You must be the lucky father."

"Not sure. How soon can we do a DNA test?" Jay asked.

Mia's mouth dropped. She closed it before Dr. Lisbon turned back to her direction. She could tell by the awkward expression lurking just under the surface of his professional coolness that he was just as shocked as she was. The male nurse, Darren, busied himself checking her vital signs.

"Well, Mr…"

"Mack. Jaylin Mack." Jay shook the doctor's hand.

"I wouldn't necessarily be responsible for that kind of testing," he said, and then went to wash his hands in the small basin at the corner of the room.

Darren worked diligently, hooking Mia up to the noisy machinery. Mia felt like a robot connected to all the cords and beeping units. Several monitors checked her and the baby's heart rate, her blood pressure, and the contractions. The unit monitoring the baby sounded like horses stampeding inside her belly.

"I can offer you some information on how to order the tests," Dr. Lisbon continued.

"Okay, thanks," Jay said as he stepped out of the medical staff's way.

Besides the blips and beeps of the monitors, the room remained quiet as Dr. Lisbon and his crew of residents examined Mia.

"Okay. We have a little time. Your water hasn't broken, and you've only dilated about six centimeters. Your contractions are still several minutes apart. Just try to relax and remember your breathing techniques. I'll be back to check on you shortly." He pulled a cord from behind the hospital bed and handed it to Mia. "If you begin to feel really uncomfortable, just press this button." He showed Mia the small red button at the end of the wire.

"Thank you, Doctor."

Dr. Lisbon touched Mia's shoulder, then he and Darren both smiled as they exited the small room. When they left, Mia squinted at Jay, who sat in the chair beside the bed.

"Why did you have to ask the doctor that?" she scolded Jay.

"Ask what?" At first, Jay looked puzzled. Then the realization hit him. "About the DNA test?"

"Yes! What do you think?" she snapped.

"Because I want to know as soon as possible," he said.

"Can't you even give the baby a chance to come out?" Mia's voice wavered.

"Let's not pretend we're a happy couple anticipating our firstborn."

Mia turned away from Jay and bit down on her quivering lip. When she turned back to him, he was sitting with his head in his hands. The tightness she felt in her heart was almost as jarring as her contractions. She laid her head back on the pillow and stared at the ceiling. She wanted Jay to leave, but having him there was better than going through this completely alone. When he saw the baby, he'd warm up to the situation, or at least that's what she hoped.

Mia dozed off but was jolted awake by a strong contraction. She pushed the red button. When Dr. Lisbon came in, she asked for the anesthesiologist.

"Are you sure?" Dr. Lisbon asked. "You were doing so well."

Mia cringed from the pain. "I'm absolutely sure," she said, looking forward to being numb.

"Okay. Let me check you out, and then we'll get you all set up." Dr. Lisbon washed his hands once again and re-examined her. "I'm afraid it's a little too late for anesthesia. It's time."

Mia gasped. The next contraction caused beads of sweat to pop out across her forehead. She clutched the rails along the side of the bed, screamed, and pulled her torso forward. She lay back and squirmed about, trying to find comfort. Tears spilled from the sides of her eyes, and her breathing grew frantic. Dr. Lisbon called in his staff.

"I feel like I'm peeing on myself!"

"Your water broke," Dr. Lisbon informed her. "We're ready," he instructed his staff.

Everyone took their positions. Jay moved his chair out of their way, but remained seated.

"Okay. I need you to push with your next contraction, okay?"

Mia shook her head. Tears mixed with streams of sweat. Her damp crop laid slick against her head.

Dr. Lisbon set his eyes on the monitor. "Okay. Here we go. Now push!"

Mia pushed and bawled. She felt the baby move further down the birth canal.

"Great job, Mia. Now do it again just like that."

Mia pushed again and again before screaming, "I can't do this!"

"We're almost there. I can see the top of the baby's head," Dr. Lisbon encouraged.

"You can do it," Darren added.

Mia felt like passing out. She'd never imagined the pain she felt. An older stubby nurse took Mia's hand and allowed Mia to squeeze hers.

"One more, Mia. We're almost there."

Mia mustered all the strength she could and howled as she pushed once again. She felt a pop and instant relief. She wasn't sure what happened, until she heard the first cries of her newborn baby.

"Congratulations, Mia. You have a baby girl!"

Still panting, Mia covered her face and cried into her hands.

CHAPTER 56

Mia

Jay met the mailman halfway down the walkway as he had every day for the past few weeks. Mia watched him from the window upstairs as she gently rocked Myla in her arms. She'd begun to anticipate the mailman's arrival as much as he did. The confirmation would set her free. Only minimal conversation had passed between the two of them since they'd returned from New York. And even less since the baby came. She didn't know how much longer she could stand it. She laid the sleeping baby in her frilly pink bassinette and marveled at the sweetness of her pouted lips. It was too early to tell who she looked like, but so far, she had Mia's fair complexion and almond eyes. She leaned forward and kissed the baby's chubby cheek, then gently tousled the large black curls framing her angelic face.

Mia's resolve completely dissipated under the influence of her precious baby. Jay had been unmoved from the day she was born. Even Mia questioned his doggedness to maintain such distance.

Mia wandered down the steps and found Jay standing in the doorway with his face buried in a letter. When he looked up, the look of relief made Mia's heart fall into her stomach. She didn't want to ask.

Jay handed her the letter.

She refused it.

"Read it, Mia," he said.

She turned away and walked to the kitchen. Jay left the door open and followed her.

He extended the letter to her again, raised his brow, and repeated,

"Read it."

Mia snatched the letter from his hand. She tried to push back the lump in her throat and looked at the floor. After a while, she lifted her head to face Jay.

"So now what?"

"This is it!" he said.

"We can—" she started.

"No, we can't. This is over," he told her.

Mia folded her arms across her chest and looked away. "This doesn't have to be the end of us," she said.

"It's not just this," Jay admitted.

"Then what is it?" she asked.

Jay took a moment to respond. "I saw the DVDs."

Mia covered her face with her hands. "I can explain."

Jay held his hand up. "No need to. The baby isn't mine anyway. Just find yourself another place to stay. You have two weeks," Jay said and walked off.

None of her jumbled thoughts made it past her lips. She couldn't think clearly enough to focus on a way to get Jay to allow her to stay. Mia dropped her shoulders. This chapter was closed, and she knew it in her core. She'd wanted so badly for Jay and her to be together.

Mia tried to shake away her sadness as she trudged to her room. The next thought stopped her in her tracks. Based on the timing of her pregnancy, if the baby wasn't Jay's, then she knew who the other possible father was. He had a wife who was a force to be reckoned with. Mia knew she'd have to prepare for a battle. For the first time, she almost bemoaned her decision to have a baby, but it was far too late for regrets.

CHAPTER 57

Blue

Blue sat next to Victor in the Atlanta courtroom wringing her hands, much like she had a few months back. She refused to acknowledge Jay's or Mia's presence. From her peripheral, she could see both of them staring at her. She looked back at Gavin seated in the front row. His wink and supportive smile reassured her. The past few weeks with Gavin had been the best of her life. In the short time they'd been together, he'd showed her how a woman could be loved the right way. They'd agreed to take things slow, yet had already talked about getting engaged once the ink dried on the divorce papers.

Jay had finally relented and rescinded many of his outrageous demands. Once the rest of the paperwork was completed on the divorce, both of them could go their separate ways with no strings attached. They had already sold the Atlanta townhouse and split the proceeds. Jay had found a modest condo and was in negotiations with the local team. There was a strong possibility he would be playing again soon.

She smiled back at Gavin and felt the heat of Jay's glare. It was apparent Jay still wasn't used to the idea of Gavin and Blue being an official couple. Blue looked his way and read his pain. It was familiar. Mia fidgeted next to him. Blue turned back around, straightened her back, and took a deep breath.

"Don't worry, Blue. This will all be over today," Victor told her.

"I know, but I just don't understand why it had to take so long," she said and huffed.

"Scott managed to keep getting the dates postponed because of

Mia and her baby," Victor said.

Blue glanced back at a petite Latino woman, with tanned skin and narrow eyes, seated behind Mia and Jay, rocking the baby girl all wrapped in pink. She pouted her lips and cooed at the baby. A lump formed in Blue's throat, surprised the betrayal still stung—especially in person.

Judge Samuels finally lifted his head from the paperwork and scanned the wood-paneled courtroom over the rim of his glasses. As he opened his mouth, a hush swept over the room.

The only sounds Blue could hear were that of her own heart beating as if it were trying to break through her chest cavity. She sucked in two deep breaths to slow her racing pulse. The moment had come. Once again, reservations gnawed at her conscience. Maybe she didn't have to go this far. Then again, she did. Mia and Jay were like fire, and she had to fight fire with fire.

The judged ordered Mia and Jay to stand.

The pace of Blue's heart rate increased again. She took another glimpse at the people around her. Victor was cool and professional. Gavin had scooted to the edge of his seat. A single stream of sweat crept down the side of Jay's face. A clear view of Mia was blocked by Jay's overbearing stature, so Blue couldn't see what she was doing. She could imagine what was going on in Mia's head, though. With her desire for the finer things in life, surely she wasn't built for jail. Blue doubted the penitentiary housed celebrity hairstylists or uniforms in the hottest colors or latest styles.

Judge Samuels handed down their sentences. Mia gasped out loud when the judge told her that she'd have to pay five thousand dollars in restitution, serve two years of probation, and would not be allowed to leave the state of Georgia for the duration of her probationary period. Jay got off a little easier since the home was really his. The judge slapped him with one year of probation and ordered that he remain in the state of Georgia for the duration of his probation, as well. He also had to serve eight hundred hours of community service and pay one thousand dollars in restitution.

Blue opened her mouth and realized she'd been holding her breath. She'd accomplished her goal and sent a strong message. She doubted they'd take her for granted ever again. Jay didn't look totally happy, but she knew things could have been worse. Mia grabbed her baby from the nanny and held her tight with her eyes closed.

"We're all done here. Are you okay with the outcome?" Victor asked.

"Yes. These past few months have been a nightmare," Blue said.

When Gavin placed his hand on Blue's shoulder, she stood to embrace him.

"It's finally over," she said with her face buried in his chest.

"I know." Gavin rubbed her back.

When Blue pulled away, she saw Jay staring. He didn't look angry.

"Come on. Let's go and get something good to eat before we head for the airport. Now that the butterflies have left my stomach, it's empty."

Gavin smiled, took her by the hand, and turned to head out of the courtroom.

"Blue," Jay called out to her.

Several heads whipped in response to Jay calling her name. Gavin tightened his grip on her hand. Mia glared, and the attorneys simply stopped what they were doing and stood still.

"Can I talk to you for a moment...privately?" Jay looked at Gavin when he said 'privately'.

Blue gestured towards Gavin to gauge if he was comfortable with Jay's request, but Gavin gave no indication. She placed a reassuring hand over his. He raised his brows and released her hand, then walked toward the back of the courtroom. Mia walked up behind Jay.

"You wanted to speak to me in *private*," Blue said to Jay, then looked back at Mia.

Jay caught the signal and turned around. Mia stood behind him with pleading in her eyes. Then she walked back to the other side of the courtroom. She rocked Myla in her arms until the nanny gently took the baby.

Returning his attention to Blue, Jay leaned in and whispered, "I took a DNA test. The baby isn't mine."

"Good for you," Blue said sincerely and forced a reassuring smile.

His posture slumped when Blue walked past him. She paused briefly and looked at Mia, who owned a bitter but pitiful expression. When Mia caught her staring, she looked away.

Gavin reached for Blue, but she gestured for him to give her a moment. She started towards Mia but stopped midway. She decided there was nothing more she needed to say. Instead, she painted a smile on her face and held her gaze long enough for Mia to feel the heat of her glare. When Mia finally looked her way, Blue raised her head, admonished Mia by shaking her head in a way that exuded pity, and sauntered off holding Gavin's hand in hers.

~~~~

Renee Daniel Flagler is a teaching artist, award-winning freelance journalist, marketing professional, and the author of four novels, *Mountain High Valley Low*, *Miss-Guided*, *In Her Mind* and, *Raging Blue*. Renee resides in New York and is currently at work on her next novel, *Still Raging* and her first nonfiction work, *The Relationship Survival Guide*. Connect with Renee on Facebook, Twitter or www.ReneeDanielFlagler.com.

CPSIA information can be obtained at www.ICGtesting.com
Printed in the USA
LVOW07s0231190913

353041LV00024B/798/P